Margar and her earliest London Blitz. She began writing in her mid-thirties and had her first novel published in 1976. She is married to American aviation author, Philip Kaplan, and lives in Gloucestershire. Her previous novels, *Bluebirds*, *The Crew*, *The Little Ship*, *Our Yanks*, *The Pathfinder* and *Those in Peril*, are also published by Corgi.

www.**booksattransworld**.co.uk

Also by Margaret Mayhew

BLUEBIRDS
THE CREW
THE LITTLE SHIP
OUR YANKS
THE PATHFINDER
THOSE IN PERIL

and published by Corgi Books

I'LL BE SEEING YOU

Margaret Mayhew

CORGI BOOKS

I'LL BE SEEING YOU
A CORGI BOOK: 0 552 15086 X

First publication in Great Britain

PRINTING HISTORY
Corgi edition published 2004

3 5 7 9 10 8 6 4

Set in 11/13pt Baskerville by
Falcon Oast Graphic Art Ltd.

Corgi Books are published by Transworld Publishers,
61–63 Uxbridge Road, London W5 5SA,
a division of The Random House Group Ltd,
in Australia by Random House Australia (Pty) Ltd,
20 Alfred Street, Milsons Point, Sydney, NSW 2061, Australia,
in New Zealand by Random House New Zealand Ltd,
18 Poland Road, Glenfield, Auckland 10, New Zealand
and in South Africa by Random House (Pty) Ltd,
Endulini, 5a Jubilee Road, Parktown 2193, South Africa.

Printed and bound in Great Britain by
Clays Ltd, St Ives plc

Papers used by Transworld Publishers are natural, recyclable products made from wood grown in sustainable forests. The manufacturing processes conform to the environmental regulations of the country of origin.

For Debbie and Fergus

Acknowledgements

My very grateful thanks to Shirley McGlade who created and runs the organization *War Babes*, to Quentin Bland of Grafton Underwood, to John and Alice Pawsey of Lavenham, to Bob Cooper and Bill Harvey – American 8th Air Force veterans, to Jane Leycester Paige, artist, to my American husband, Philip Kaplan, and to my editor, Linda Evans.

PART I

One

My mother was buried on a bitterly cold day in mid-February, 1992. It had snowed on the day that she died and a hard frost had followed – so hard and so lasting that there was a problem about digging the grave. The funeral director was smoothly apologetic. Unfortunately, arrangements would take rather longer than usual. The cemetery was experiencing difficulties; the grave-diggers, faced with earth as hard as iron, were being unco-operative.

My brother and I sat in front of his desk while he explained this to us. While he talked, I noticed that the previously old-fashioned funeral parlour had undergone a complete makeover since my father's death eleven years before. On that occasion, I remembered sombre furniture, sober colour, sepia photos of horse-drawn hearses, black horses with black head-plumes, and pall-bearers with top hats swathed in black veils. Those photos had disappeared and in their place hung a large, framed declaration, a professional testimony in black, gilt-edged letters: *DIGNITY. PERSONAL, CARING SERVICE AT ALL TIMES. PRIVATE CHAPEL*

OF REST. FUNERALS COMPLETELY FURNISHED.

The Dickensian décor had been updated to silver-and-grey striped wallpaper, fitted carpeting, venetian blinds and modern office furniture, while the elderly undertaker had been superseded by this much younger funeral director, smartly dressed and seated behind an Ikea desk. He slid an open folder across its shiny surface towards us and revolved it deftly for our inspection. Inside there were coloured photographs of coffins made in different styles and woods. Solid oak, he informed us, was the best, the most durable and, naturally, the most expensive. For that reason, it was normally only chosen for burials, together with handles of solid brass – also rather expensive. But there were more reasonably priced options; he turned a page, indicating other photographs with a well-manicured forefinger. Oak veneer, he assured us, was considered a perfectly acceptable alternative for burials, as well as half the price – and the handles were often what was known in the trade as brassed.

'Brassed?'

'Plastic covered with brass, Mrs Porter. Particularly suitable for cremations, which are becoming increasingly the norm – what with the shortage of land and the change in people's lifestyles. Though, of course, here we're concerned with a burial.'

His manner was brisk now that we had got

down to business; quite matter-of-fact. He might have been selling refrigerators, or washing machines or any other consumer durable. He must have decided that this was the most effective way to deal with bereaved families and achieve the painful decisions necessary to dispose of the loved one decently, efficiently and quickly. And for the same reasons that any good salesman targets the woman rather than the man, he had twitched the folder slightly in my direction, away from my brother, and addressed his remarks to me. He turned another page and flicked at the only photo dismissively.

'This one is made of pine and the cheapest. It's really only used in cases where there are no known relatives and the local council bears the cost.'

'Paupers' funerals?'

'Exactly.' He went back to the beginning and the solid oak. I fumbled for my reading glasses and took a closer look before I shifted the book back in Drew's direction. 'Which do you think?'

He peered at the photos. 'Up to you, Ju.'

The funeral director said, 'The raised-lid design is *very* popular.'

'Is it possible to see one? I mean, do you have samples here?'

He hesitated. 'As it happens we *do* have one of that particular style on the premises – in our private chapel here – but I'm afraid there's a lady resting in it. Of course, you're quite welcome to view, if you have no objections.'

In my state of shock and grief, I had a ludicrous vision of some exhausted passer-by clambering into a spare coffin for a lie-down. And then I understood him. 'No, no . . . that won't be necessary.'

The decision was finally made. Anything other than solid oak was really unthinkable and I felt my mother would have preferred the simplest style without the fancy lid. And solid brass handles – the plainest design. The black folder was closed and returned immediately to a desk drawer; perhaps the funeral director had also learned that, if not, the woman in question might start changing her mind. Again, he looked at me, rather than my brother.

'Will you wish there to be floral tributes – other than from the close family? Many people prefer not. The trend these days is very much towards donations to some favourite cause instead. It can be specified in the newspaper announcement.'

There was a black urn containing white plastic lilies placed on the window sill behind him. For some reason, I found them even more distressing than the coffin photos or the lady resting close by.

'Our mother adored flowers. The more people send, the better.'

'Yes, of course, Mrs Porter. It's entirely as you prefer.' Another desk drawer was opened, another folder placed on the desk, turned round and slid towards us. I read the words on its cover: *The Flower Basket: Sympathy Guide*. 'We find

find this local florist very satisfactory. As you will see, they offer some most attractive and original arrangements – the old-style wreaths have rather gone out of fashion these days. I assume that you and Dr Byrne will wish your own personal tributes to be placed on the coffin?'

I looked at more colour photographs – this time of flowers contorted into a bewildering variety of shapes: cushions, crosses, hearts, teardrops, teddy bears, toy trains, anchors, harps, guitars, open books, gates of heaven . . . The blooms all looked perfect specimens of their kind – presumably real, but just as depressing as the plastic lilies.

The funeral director said encouragingly, 'The tributes would be delivered here on the morning of the funeral and we will take care of the rest for you. We offer a complete package, you know. The announcement in the press, limousines, service sheets, pall-bearers, even making the arrangements with a priest or minister, if necessary – not so in your case, of course, but the majority of people these days are not regular churchgoers. You'd be surprised at how many never go at all, but they still want a religious service of some kind. We arrange everything for them. It takes a lot of the stress out of the whole sad experience.'

'Is that such a good thing? Isn't stress rather a natural part of it?'

He said blandly, 'We find our clients appreciate the support, Mrs Porter.'

I closed the florist's *Sympathy Guide* and sent it back across the desk. We also declined the limousines, assistance with the announcement in the press and with the printing of the service sheets. I wondered if the completely furnished funeral package included choosing the hymns and the music too, as well as the readings? Almost certainly. Perhaps they could even supply someone to deliver an appropriate eulogy – about somebody they'd never met?

We must have been a disappointment to the man, but it was well hidden. More condolences were expressed, assurances given of every personal care and attention, and we were conducted smoothly to the door and out into the Oxford street. I shivered and took Drew's arm for moral support, as well as to avoid slipping on the icy pavement. 'I could do with a stiff drink.'

'Me too. Let's find a pub.'

It was close to lunchtime and the pub bar was filling up, but I found an empty table and staked a claim to it while Drew fetched the drinks. All around me, people were talking and laughing, drinking and smoking and eating. Brutally, life went on just the same without missing a beat.

Drew came back. 'I made it a double.'

'Thanks.'

The drink worked its magic and I pulled myself together. 'We're due at the vicarage at two. Have you any thoughts about hymns?'

He shook his head. 'Not really. You'd know

what she'd have liked. I can't remember the last time I went to church.'

'Flavia and I went with her at Christmas when we were staying there. She seemed perfectly all right then. A bit thinner, that's all – I do remember noticing that. I rang her regularly afterwards as usual, of course, but she always sounded fine. I'd no *idea* anything was the matter. Not a clue.'

'Perhaps she hadn't either.'

'But she *had*. The doctor told me that she was diagnosed early in October. She insisted on knowing exactly what the situation was and he gave it to her straight out. She knew from the very beginning that there wasn't really a hope and she refused point-blank to have chemotherapy. I was going to see her, you know, towards the end of January, but she put me off – told me she'd got some charity committee meeting that she'd forgotten about and had to go to. I just wish to heaven she'd told me that she was so ill, Drew. If only she had.'

'You know what she was like, Ju. Could never stand a fuss.'

'We wouldn't have fussed.'

'We probably would. Or *you* would have, almost certainly.'

'I still wish we'd known. We could have spent more time with her.'

'Would that have helped?'

'She wouldn't have had to face it alone. And it wouldn't have been such a ghastly shock for us. I suppose it's very selfish of me to think like that

– if that's the way she wanted it – but I hate the fact that we never had a chance to say goodbye. That's what saddens me most of all. Flavia too.'

'Mmm.' He picked up his beer again. 'Not really Ma's style to have us gathered round the bedside, was it? I can't see her going for that. And she always hated goodbyes of any kind.'

It was true, which helped – a bit. She had never been one for lingering over partings. No prolonged wavings or watery words or looking back. It had always been a smile, a hug and then she was gone.

'Will you stay on till the funeral, Drew?'

He took off his glasses and polished them carefully with his handkerchief. 'Well, I really ought to get back to Cambridge for a couple of days or so. I'm meant to be lecturing this week. I was thinking of going off first thing tomorrow and coming back the day before it – that's if you can manage the rest.'

'I should think so. Flavia will probably come up at the weekend and give me a hand. We'll need to get the house ready and organize the catering.'

'Catering?'

'For after the funeral. People will expect to be invited back. Sandwiches and tea, at least. And something stronger.'

'Oh, Lord. Can't we skip all that?'

'Not really. I expect there'll be quite a few turning up. She and Da had a lot of friends. Remember all the people at *his* funeral?'

Drew replaced the specs, frowning. 'Speaking of the house, what the hell are we going to do about it?'

Apart from a separate bequest to her granddaughter, Flavia, and donations to charities, my mother's will had left the remainder of her estate, including the house, equally to us.

'Sell it, I imagine. Unless you've any better ideas.'

'I didn't mean that. Selling the house itself shouldn't be too difficult, but what are we going to do about the *contents*? The furniture. All the rest of the books. Ma's stuff. There's an awful lot.'

'I know. We could try and go through some of it this evening. Decide what to keep.'

'The trouble is, Sonia and I just don't have any space left for anything else. I could maybe squeeze in a few more books and the odd picture, and Da's chess set – if you don't want it, Ju – but that's about it.'

I knew it was true. Drew's small house in Cambridge, as well as his rooms in college, were already crammed full.

I said, 'It seems an awful shame. I'll take as many books as I can and some pictures, but I couldn't get most of the furniture up the stairs – even if I had the room, which I haven't.'

'How about Flavia?'

I smiled. 'Flavia likes Conran. All very sleek and modern. But I'll ask her, of course.'

'Most of it will have to be sold with the house, then. Nothing for it.'

'Do you mind if I have Ma's writing bureau? The one in her bedroom.'

'No, of course I don't. Take anything you want, Ju. Anything. Now, what about a sandwich or something to eat? I think they do bar snacks and I could do with a bite.'

I watched him amble off in search of a menu: a tall and professional figure with slightly hunched shoulders, dressed in an old tweed overcoat that he had had for aeons, with a woollen scarf wrapped round his neck. He was a repeat version of our father – rather eccentric, rather vague, his mind seemingly operating on some other and more rarefied plane. This was indeed the case. My brother was a brilliant mathematician; my father's intellect had been even more outstanding. And mathematicians at that level inhabit a world of their own.

After the pub we called at the vicarage. There had been several changes of vicars since my childhood days and I hardly knew this one, who was quite new. Like the funeral director, he was a relatively young man, but I liked him a great deal more. The hymns were settled, readings chosen and the old form of service would be used – all the *Thees* and the *Thous* and the beautiful old words. I felt that, with him, Ma was in safe hands – a lot safer than with the funeral director's complete caring package.

The house referred to by Drew, where our parents had lived for so long and where we had grown up, was in Summertown, in the northern part of Oxford. Victorian red brick, slate-roofed, gabled, stone-mullioned, castellated and crenellated, laurels at the front and a large and rambling garden at the back with a magnificent beech tree. It had been built, of course, for a Victorian-sized family, complete with staff. The main rooms were lofty, the sash windows fitted with wooden shutters that folded back, clanking and thudding, into deep recesses, the fireplaces were black cast-iron monstrosities. The kitchen had been equipped with a coke-guzzling range which was supposed to heat the radiators as well as cook the food, but they rarely rose above lukewarm. In any case, the shortage of fuel in those early post-war days meant that they were seldom turned on at all.

I had been three years old when we had moved in during 1947, soon after my father had taken up a post at Oxford university, and my brother, Andrew, had been born three years later. The only staff had been Mrs Collins who came twice a week, on Mondays and Fridays, to help with the cleaning – excluding my father's study at the far end of the hall. With her penchant for chat and her noisily flailing brooms and flapping dusters Mrs Collins was forbidden access and the room remained undisturbed and uncleaned, except sporadically by my mother, for years and years.

My father was, as I have said, a brilliant mathematician, but we only understood quite how brilliant after his death. The obituaries referred to him as a genius, describing his work at the codebreaking centre, Bletchley Park, deciphering German codes during the Second World War. The Enigma machine codes had been broken, but the fiendishly complicated machine, Fish, used by the German Army High Command for top-level communications, had proved even more difficult. A twelve-wheel contraption with hundreds of metal lugs turned each character into a string of electrical impulses converted into code before transmission. Cracking the code had taken many months, involving highly abstruse mathematical calculations based on one lucky careless slip by a German radio operator. My father had been a vital part of the team which had finally unlocked Fish's secrets. Unlike the breaking of the Enigma codes, this had been accomplished without ever seeing the machine. The method of deduction alluded to in the newspaper was incomprehensible to me – I have trouble with basic arithmetic – though Drew, of course, had understood. But our father had never once spoken of his time at Bletchley Park, and even Ma had only the haziest idea of what he had been doing during the war. 'Something very dull to do with communications,' was all he would tell her – or us, whenever we asked him. He was not, apparently, the only one to clam up. While others were trumpeting aloud their wartime exploits, those at Bletchley Park remained silent. Churchill called them the geese that laid the golden eggs but never cackled.

The call on the vicar concluded, Drew and I went back to the house. The range had been replaced during the Seventies with an oil-fired Aga, but the Victorian radiators had stayed stubbornly lukewarm and the hallway, as we entered, felt damp and chill. We kept our coats on. Drew lit the gas fire in the study and I went to make some tea. The kitchen had always been the hub of the house. We ate there at the big scrubbed-wood table and the lodger students that my mother took in to fill up empty bedrooms always joined us in termtime. Something was always cooking on or in the range: soups, stews, potatoes, puddings, pies – simmering, baking, bubbling, sizzling, with the kettle hissing for the next cup of tea or coffee.

I filled the kettle, set it on the hotplate and fetched mugs, tea bags, milk, sugar. The two third-year St Hilda's students still living in the house had left their mugs and bowls and plates washed up and draining neatly on the rack and while I was waiting for the kettle to boil, one of them returned. Her bespectacled face appeared uncertainly round the edge of the door, framed in the nylon fur of her anorak hood. She was the one who had found Ma unconscious on the kitchen floor and sent for the ambulance.

'Is there anything we can do, Mrs Porter?'

There wasn't, I assured her. And they were welcome to stay on until the house was sold. I promised to keep them informed.

'We're so sorry,' she said. 'We liked your mother. Very much. Everybody did.'

I knew it was true. As far as I was aware she had had no enemies, only friends.

I carried the tea through to the study where the old gas fire was making its usual pop-popping noises. How many times over the years had I carried a mug of tea to my father at work in there, and how often had I returned later to find it scummily cold and untouched on his desk? As a very small child, I could remember stretching up on tiptoe to reach the brass handle, pushing open the door and wandering around the book-lined room, fingering this and touching that. The study door was never locked, admission never denied – except to Mrs Collins. The outsize chess set on the table by the fire was always an attraction: pawns, bishops, rooks, knights, queens and kings drawn up and poised for battle, black team against white. I would shunt them to and fro across the squares. The humble pawns could be made to scoot about, the bishops and rooks to slide, but the majestic kings and queens had to be lifted. Sometimes Da would look up from his desk to smile and make some kindly and indulgent remark; at other times, he was too absorbed in his work to notice me at all.

Drew was at the bookshelves, taking down a dusty volume and opening it up. When Da had died a lot of his books, as well as his papers, had been given to the university but there were still plenty left in the study and in the rest of the house – shelves of them in almost every room, including many of our books from childhood. I put Drew's mug on the desk, close to the silver-framed photograph of Ma in her WAAF uniform. She smiled at me from out of the past. Trim and slim, tie neatly tied, uniform cap stylishly worn, her dark hair rolled up behind the ears, Forties fashion. People had always said how alike we were: same build, same features, same colour hair – until hers had eventually gone pepper and salt in her late sixties. Throughout my life she had been there at all the stages, for the good times and the bad, the easy and the hard; suddenly, she wasn't. She had gone and she had denied me the comfort of some last words together. I felt, childishly and I knew unreasonably, that, at the end, she had deserted me.

'Tea's up.'

Drew grunted, already engrossed in the book. Like father, like son. I left him to it and took my own tea upstairs to the main bedroom, as glacially cold as the hall. I switched on the lights and stood for a moment in the silence, warming my hands round the mug. Ma's dressing gown was still hanging on the hook behind the door, her slippers placed beside the big double bed, her woollen cardigan draped across the back of a chair, her string of pearls lying on the dressing table, and there was a faint trace of the floral scent that she always wore. Her death seemed quite unreal: a horrible misunderstanding. I had never, after all, witnessed her dead. By the time I had reached the hospital she had been taken away to the mortuary and I had refused, in cowardly panic, to see her, afraid that the sight of her dead might erase the memory of her alive. Now, I could almost believe that she might come back at any moment. The front door would click open and shut, her footsteps would sound across the hall, her voice call out from the stairs:

'Juliet, darling, is that you? I'd no idea you were coming. What a lovely surprise!'

Instead, there was only silence.

For no particular reason, I went over to her desk – an Edwardian lady's kneehole writing bureau with drawers down each side and a fold-up lid. On the top was a photograph of Drew and myself as children, arms linked together, and, beside it, one of my daughter, Flavia, taken twenty years ago at four years old. Her only grandchild.

The desk lid was closed but the key had been left in the lock. I sat down where she had sat, put the tea mug aside on the floor and turned the key, lowering the lid gently onto its brass hinges. In front of the pigeonholes, propped up conspicuously so that it could not possibly be missed, was an envelope addressed to me in my mother's hand, in the royal blue ink she always used. *For Juliet.*

I picked it up and turned it over. More

writing, but smaller, on the back. I took my reading glasses out of my coat pocket. *To be opened by her, and her alone, after my death.*

I felt no premonition or apprehension. I simply thought that it was probably about some wish that she wanted carried out, not already mentioned specifically in her will. Something she felt she could rely on me to see to rather than Drew. She had known, after all, that she was dying and there had been plenty of time to think about such things, to make additions and amendments. I slit open the envelope with the ivory paperknife kept in one of the pigeonholes, and took out a folded sheet of writing paper and, tucked inside, an old black and white photograph. I glanced at the photo briefly. It showed a group of men – obviously an air crew dressed for flying – in front of a large plane. The men at the back were standing, the ones in the front crouched down on their haunches. I put it aside on the desk, wondering who on earth they were, and opened out the letter. It was dated three days before she died and the writing was shaky.

My darling Juliet,
I have known for several weeks that I am going to die soon and I hope that you and Drew will understand my reason for not telling you, or anyone. I truly believe that this way has made it easier for all of us, without spoiling the precious time left.

There has been time, too, for me to think about things past and to reach another decision, which I pray is also the right one. I believe that I should tell you something that I have always kept from you – again, for what I felt were also good reasons. But now things are different. Vernon has gone and I shall soon be gone. I think you should know the truth and there is no way to tell it except straight out.

Vernon was not your natural father. Your real father was an American pilot serving over here in England in the war with their Eighth Air Force. He was the captain of a bomber crew and I met him when I was in the WAAF. We fell in love. Deeply in love. We were going to be married as soon as his tour was over but he was shot down over France in 1944 and posted missing, presumed killed in action. I found out then that I was pregnant with you – his child. Vernon, whom I had already known for many years, offered to marry me and to accept you as his own. I agreed because I truly believed that it was the best thing for you. In those days, to be born out of wedlock was a terrible stigma. Later, I discovered that your real father was still alive and had been hidden by the French for months in Occupied France. When he got back to England, he found out that I had married someone else and he went home to the United States without knowing of your existence. I never told him, partly in fairness to Vernon, and partly because telling the whole truth could only bring unhappiness to everyone concerned. As you know, Vernon loved you very dearly. So far as he was concerned, you were his daughter and he was a wonderful father to you, just as he was a wonderful husband to me.

I had never intended to tell you, but lately I've

changed my mind. Your real father was a wonderful man, too, and I never forgot him or stopped loving him. Not for a single day. You are a part of him, Juliet – all I had left – and I treasured you twice over. Incidentally, you get your artistic talent from him.

Even though you may never meet, I want you to know the truth before I die. It seems only fair to him now, as it was fair to Vernon before – though perhaps it's not so fair to you? Right or wrong, I feel that you should know. Whether or not you choose to tell Flavia is your decision alone, but I think she would understand. I hope and pray that you will.

With my everlasting love, Mama.

The handwriting had deteriorated progressively so that the final lines were hard to read, the signature a clumsy scrawl.

I don't know how long I sat there, clutching the letter in my hand – staring at it, rereading it and then reading it all over again, and yet again, as though doing so might somehow change its content or meaning. But my mother had, as she had felt compelled to do, given it to me straight out. The gentle, kind, quiet man I had adored was not, apparently, my father. Instead, my true father was some unknown bomber pilot who had met my mother when she had been the beautiful young WAAF in the photograph downstairs. One of those overpaid, oversexed, over-here Yanks. I simply couldn't believe it. I refused to. In her last days Ma must have become confused.

She had been prescribed strong drugs to combat the cancer and the pain – the doctor had told me so – and she had imagined the whole thing. Old memories mixed with new drugs had played silly tricks on her mind.

At last, I put down the letter and picked up the photograph to look at it more closely. I could see now that the air crew was wartime American. These were unmistakably Yanks. The four standing had high-peaked caps sporting big brass badges, while the six men crouching in front of them wore baseball-type ones. It must have been winter because there was snow on the ground and they were all dressed in heavy sheepskin jackets, with life jackets on top and a cumbersome assortment of clips and buckles and attachments. The plane, partly visible behind and dwarfing them, was obviously some kind of bomber. I could see giant propellers, a canopied nose turret, part of the wings, the cockpit high above. I turned the photo over but there was nothing written on the back. No date, no names, no place – nothing. Presumably the pilot my mother had referred to was one of the men in the photo but there was no way of telling which one he was. All insignia was hidden by the heavy flying gear.

I put the photograph and the letter back in the envelope and went downstairs to the study. Drew was still deep in a book, his tea ignored. I went over to him and held out the envelope.

'Look what I've just found in Ma's desk.'

He looked up – reluctantly. 'What is it?'

'A letter from her to me. I'd like you to read it.'

'Now?'

'Yes, *now*. If you don't mind.'

He took the envelope from me. While he was reading the letter – held in one hand, photo in the other – I went to sit beside the gas fire, hunched in my coat. The black chessmen on the table had their backs turned, the white ones faced me impassively. The room was silent except for the popping gas flame. Eventually, my brother spoke.

'Christ! Bit of a bombshell.'

I said, 'It can't possibly be true, Drew. The drugs must have made her imagine things. It *can't* be true.'

'Well, it could be.'

It wasn't the answer I needed, or wanted. 'What do you mean – could be?'

'That sort of thing happened in the war, didn't it?'

Sometimes he could be infuriating. 'For God's sake, Drew, I know it did. All right, Ma had a passionate love affair with some Yank years and years ago and then while she was ill and taking all those drugs she got confused and started mixing things up in her mind. Maybe she was going through her desk and found that old photo and it started her off dreaming – inventing things that might have been, but never actually happened. Sort of wishful thinking. That's possible too, isn't it?'

He held the photo up higher, studying it for a moment in the light from the standard lamp beside him. 'Mmm. The plane's a B-17, you know. A Flying Fortress.'

'I don't care what the hell it is.' I was close to tears now – not the tears of a rational, mature woman, but childish, stamp-my-foot ones.

'Crew of ten,' he went on, still looking at the photo with heartless interest. 'Officers standing behind – the rest of them sergeants. I think that's right. Funnily enough, I was reading about those Allied bombing raids recently. The RAF went in single file at night, armed with pea-shooters, while the Americans did their daylight trips in big box formations and lots of gun-power. Hence the name Flying Fortress. This plane's bristling with them, see.' He pointed with his forefinger. 'Ma says he was a pilot so he'd be one of these chaps standing. Probably the one in the middle. The pilot would have been the captain, like she told you.'

'Just burn it, will you,' I said furiously. 'Stick it in the gas fire.'

Drew peered at me over his spectacles. 'Sorry, Ju. I can see you're really upset. I'm sorry.'

'Well, wouldn't *you* be? If it were you?'

'Yes, I suppose I would. But even if it's true – and I'm not saying it is – Ma says he was a wonderful guy.'

'Is that really meant to make me feel better? Actually, it doesn't. Not a bit. And it doesn't matter *which* one he is or *what* he was like because he's got absolutely nothing to do with me. As far as I'm concerned, Da was my father – *our* father – and that's an end to it.' I held out my hand. 'I'll burn those, if you won't.'

He shrugged again. 'OK. If that's what you want.'

Using the gas fire would make a mess in the grate, so I took the envelope with the letter and the photograph through to the kitchen. And then, of course, I remembered that the Aga was oil-fired now with no handy incinerating maw, like in the old days. Drew had already used the last match in the study to light the gas fire and while I was hunting through drawers for more of them, the other St Hilda's student came into the kitchen.

'I just wondered if I could make a cup of coffee?'

I made an effort to smile at her. 'Of course. Help yourself. I'm looking for matches. You don't happen to have any on you, do you?'

'Sorry, no. But I've got some up in my room. Shall I fetch them?'

'No, don't worry – thanks all the same.' I went on hunting while she filled the kettle.

The girl said quietly, over her shoulder, 'I was very fond of your mother. I felt I could tell her about things and she always listened. My own mother died two years ago.'

I stopped searching, sensing her need to talk. 'I'm so sorry. How awful for you.'

'Mother had cancer, too. It's so cruel, isn't it?

So unfair – the way it just picks on people who've done nothing whatever to deserve it.'

'I know. It's cruel and horrible. Our mother never told us, you know. My brother and I had no idea that she was ill.'

'Nor did Karen and I. We ought to have guessed, though. When we came back after Christmas we did notice that she was hardly eating anything and was losing a lot of weight, but we thought perhaps she was on a diet. And her handwriting was different. She used to leave notes for us on the kitchen table sometimes – about food in the oven and things like that – and towards the end we could hardly read them.'

Like her fellow student, she was a serious, earnest sort of girl. Probably extremely clever; certainly someone whose word could be relied upon. I said, 'I wondered if the drugs she was taking might have had some other odd effect.'

'What sort of effect?'

'On her mind. Did she seem to be getting confused? Imagining things? Rambling about the past, perhaps? About the war?'

The girl shook her head firmly. 'No, not at all. The symptoms were physical, not mental. She did talk to me once about the war but she didn't seem at all confused.'

'When did she do that?'

'About a week before she died. I was making a cup of coffee, like now, and she came into the kitchen. She said she'd just been looking at an old wartime photo and that it had brought back very happy memories.'

'Did she say anything else?'

'Not really.'

'She didn't show you the photo?'

'No.'

'Or speak of people she'd known in the war? The people in the photo, for instance?'

'No. She just said it was an unforgettable time. That was the word she used – unforgettable. She seemed rather sad – but not in a bad way, if you know what I mean. Sad, but happy as well. I'm sorry I can't be of more help.'

'It's not important.'

I eventually discovered an old box of matches at the very back of a drawer, but the girl was still waiting for the kettle to boil and so I went back to the study. Drew looked up from his book.

'Did you do the deed, then?'

'Not yet. I'll do it later.' I stuffed the envelope and its contents in my coat pocket and sat down again by the gas fire. 'Ma was stationed in Suffolk during the war, wasn't she? I can't remember where, though, can you?'

'Not a clue.'

'She must have said, surely.'

'She didn't talk much about it, did she? Not much more than Da and he never said a thing.'

'I've been thinking how little we know about her life then. I wish she'd told us more about it. I wish they both had.'

'Well, Da couldn't and wouldn't. And Ma

obviously had her reasons.' Drew closed his book. 'Look, Ju, I think you were quite right. She must have got a bit confused at the end – bound to have done. Let's leave it at that. She didn't tell you the chap's name and he's probably dead by now, anyway. Best to burn that stuff and forget all about it. Da was your father. End of story.'

I stared at the fire, without seeing it. 'You know, Drew, I've often wondered why I'm so hopeless at maths.'

Two

Drew left for Cambridge the next morning and I set about dealing with all the other arrangements for the funeral. Flavia phoned from London, offering to take time off work, but I told her not to come until the weekend.

'Are you sure, Mum?'

'Quite sure. I can manage perfectly well.'

'OK. We'll come up on Friday evening then and stay until the funeral.'

We meant that she would be bringing Callum, when I'd rather hoped that he might find funerals outside his range. Three years ago the actor had moved into Flavia's half of the house that we shared and I could see no hope of him either marrying her or moving out. I could well understand, though, why Flavia had fallen for him. He was Welsh with darkly romantic Celtic good looks and a beautiful speaking voice, and he could be very charming. So far there had been only bit parts in TV soaps and commercials but he was waiting for the big break just around the corner. Maybe it would come one day, but whether it did or not, I couldn't help feeling that Callum was bad news for Flavia. My mother had thought so too, but, as she had reminded me, it was no good saying anything to a daughter. Comment had been fruitless when I had insisted on marrying Mark. On that particular occasion, Ma had offered me the polite but frank opinion that we were ill-suited, which, naturally, I had ignored.

Mark phoned on the day that the death announcement appeared in *The Times*.

'Juliet? I've just tried to get you at home but Flavia told me you were in Oxford, sorting things out. I was very sorry to read about your mother's death. Are you coping all right?'

'Fine, thanks.'

'Flavia says she'll be with you on Friday. I'll come to the funeral – if that's all right. I'd like to pay my respects.'

She had, after all, been his mother-in-law and was his daughter's grandmother; he would see it as the right and proper thing to do.

'Yes, of course.' There had been no mention of Caroline, so presumably she wouldn't be accompanying him.

'I'll arrange for flowers to be sent. No objections?'

'None at all.' They would be very expensive and in excellent taste – nothing like the ones in the *Flower Basket* folder.

'How are things otherwise, Juliet? Keeping busy with the bunnies?'

'Yes, pretty busy.'

'I saw one of your books in Waterstones the

other day. About hedgehogs.' I knew the one he meant: *Harry Hedgehog Goes on Holiday*. 'Actually, I bought it for Wizzie.'

'Wizzie?'

'Isabelle. Our youngest. She's four now. You're probably much in demand these days.'

'I wouldn't put it quite like that, but luckily I've got a good agent.'

A few more of our customarily polite exchanges and he rang off. I stood for a moment by the phone in the chilly wastes of the hall, thinking how bizarre it was that we could converse like virtual strangers in spite of having lived together for more than ten years and known each other for even longer.

I had met Mark when I was a student at the Ruskin School of Art in Oxford and he was an undergraduate at Balliol. He was three years older and, in my eyes, the epitome of sophistication. He dressed expensively, used a cigarette holder, drank cocktails, knew all about good restaurants, food and wine. A snap of his fingers brought waiters hurrying to his side and when he paid the large bill he barely glanced at it. At eighteen I was deeply impressed by such things. Of course, he took out other girls as well and after he went down from Oxford I didn't see him for nearly three years. We met again, by chance, at a party in London where I was living a lonely and fairly miserable existence in an Earl's Court bedsit, touting my portfolio unsuccessfully round the publishers. By then, Mark was something rather important in a City merchant bank. The casual, sweater-over-the-shoulders look that he'd affected at Oxford had moved on. His suits were Savile Row, his shirts and ties Jermyn Street, his shoes Lobbs. After the party he took me out to dinner and impressed me all over again with the way he handled the waiters and paid the bill, as well as with his considerable charm. For some reason, I also made an impression on him. Perhaps it was the fact that I was very different from the other girls that he usually took out – the debs in twinsets and pearls – or perhaps because, charming as he was, I wasn't the customarily easy pushover. Maybe I presented an unusual challenge as well as an unusual appearance.

We were married eighteen months later and Flavia was born the following year. I began getting regular commissions to illustrate children's books, mostly ones about furry animals. The bunnies, as Mark called them, though they weren't always rabbits.

After only one of the years, I realized that the marriage had been a mistake and I'm sure that Mark realized it too. Ma had been quite right. We had almost nothing in common, no shared interests at all – except for our daughter. When he came home from his City desk, Mark expected me to be waiting, agog to hear about his day, not working away feverishly on some deadline, having got Flavia to bed and to sleep at last. I was exhausted from looking after a small child and trying to complete commissions in snatched moments, but I stubbornly refused Mark's offer to employ a full-time nanny because I wanted to take care of Flavia myself. And I hated the dinner parties and the long evenings at expensive restaurants with important clients, and the international conferences in soulless hotels. The world of high finance was as uninteresting to me as the bunnies were to Mark. It was equal boredom on both sides. Equal disillusion. And, looking back, a lot of the fault and failure was mine. However, we staggered on until Caroline arrived to work as his secretary at the merchant bank. Ultra-efficient and groomed to a whisker, she understood exactly what Mark needed and was eager and able to provide it.

The divorce was very amicable. I opted for a clean-break lump sum instead of maintenance and used two-thirds of it to buy a house in Putney. Mark paid for Flavia's schooling and university and gave her a very generous allowance. There was no bitterness, only relief. Our lives simply diverged. Flavia lived with me and I went on with the illustrations and taught watercolour painting at adult evening classes, while, with Caroline's support and encouragement, Mark rose to great heights in the City, and had four more children. But I remained a divorcee. A wretched, long-drawn-out affair, involving a married man and dragging on over several years, taught me a painful lesson and, thereafter, I kept out of trouble.

When Flavia had finished university and started work in London, we split the Putney house into two flats. She occupied the ground floor while I lived upstairs with my studio in the attic above, and we both looked after the small front and back gardens. It was a very successful arrangement.

I had promised to telephone Aunt Primrose about the funeral. She was the last remaining of five sisters, all named after flowers: Violet, Lily, Iris, Primrose and the youngest, Marguerite, my mother, who had been called Daisy all her life. Reggie, Primrose's husband, was almost stone deaf and she bellowed down the phone at me from sheer habit.

'I'll be there, of course. Reggie's not up to it, I'm afraid, so I'll leave him behind.'

I could see her standing four-square to the draughts in the dilapidated drawing room of their ancient house in Wales, Uncle Reggie slumped in an armchair by the fire, the smelly old spaniels – four of them – flopped insensible on the hearthrug at his slippers.

I said, 'I'm starting to try and clear out things here a bit. Is there anything of Ma's you'd like to have?'

'Sweet of you to ask, dear. Nothing I can think of at the moment. We've got far too much here, as it is. But if you happen to come across any old family photos, I'd love to see them. From before the Flood, when she and I were young. Don't throw them out.'

I promised not to. 'If I find any, I'll keep them safe for you. By the way, did Ma ever talk to you about what she got up to in the WAAF during the war?'

'Well, she always told me she had a jolly good time. We all did, you know. Lily and Vi in the WRNS, Iris a Land Girl and me a FANY driving ambulances all over the place. We'd none of us have missed it for the world. Not the done thing to say so these days, I know, but who cares?'

'Did she ever talk about having a love affair?'

There was a chuckle and the faint clink of ice against glass – an early evening pick-me-up to hand.

'We *all* had those. Especially Iris. All those haystacks, and the Italian POWs working on the farms. She was very keen on *them*.'

'But was there somebody special with Ma? Someone she told you about?'

'Well, I seem to remember that there was an American . . . she was mad about him, but I think he was killed in action. She never mentioned him after the war, and, of course, it would have been before she married your father. Dear Vernon, he was always there, you know – waiting hopefully in the wings. Always dotty about Daisy, ever since we were children. Very sweet.'

'Did you ever meet the American?'

'Oh, no. Daisy and I hardly saw each other during the war. Too busy doing our own thing. Our leaves hardly ever coincided, and you couldn't get around like now. Journeys took for ever. But we wrote to each other and she mentioned him in her letters.'

'Do you still have any of them, by any chance?'

'Lord knows . . . I doubt it, but I'll have a search, if you're interested. I can't promise anything, though.'

'Did she happen to tell you his name?'

Another soft clink. 'Can't remember, I'm afraid. It's too long ago.'

'Where she was stationed?'

'Somewhere in Suffolk. A bomber station. I've forgotten what it was called. Some funny country name like Little Hogwash or Nether Snoring.' Another clink and a gulp. 'Why all these questions, dear?'

'Nothing really. I found an old photo in her desk – of an American bomber crew. I was just curious.'

'Well, the Yanks came over here in force after Pearl Harbor. Thousands of 'em. And jolly good fun they were, too. One of them taught me to jitterbug.' Another rich chuckle. 'But that was a long, long time ago. Couldn't do it now, not with my knees.'

I smiled. It was hard to imagine Aunt Primrose ever jitterbugging but I didn't doubt that it was true. 'Well, we'll see you next week. Would you like to stay the night here?'

'Love to but I'll have to get back to old Reggie and the dogs.' There was a pause, a slight lowering of the voice. 'You know, Juliet, when your mother dies, you suddenly realize all the things you wish you'd asked her before. I felt just the same when your grandmother went – so did Daisy, too. We both wished we had. Only somehow when they're alive, there's never quite the time or chance, is there?' A sigh and another faint clink. 'And then, of course, it's too late.'

Following my aunt's example, I went in search of a drink and poured a large malt whisky. It felt physically warming and gave me the courage to go upstairs and begin the task of clearing out my mother's desk. I sat down at the desk once more and began on the pigeonholes. I went through everything, making a pile for things that could be discarded and others that should be kept, and, as I worked, I kept having the eerie sensation that she was standing behind me, watching. I turned my head several times, hairs prickling on the back of my neck, but, of course, there was nobody there.

The letters I found were mostly recent – from friends, from Drew and Sonia, from Flavia and myself, from Aunt Primrose – and family snaps taken not so long ago. Her last year's diary, kept in the central pigeonhole with her old and tattered address book, showed regular appointments with the doctor and hospital from early October onwards. Beneath the pigeonhole there was a small drawer and inside it I found my mother's fountain pen and her marriage certificate. Marguerite Anne Woods had married Vernon Henry Byrne on 16th April 1944, at a register office in Buckinghamshire. Somehow Drew and I had never thought about how long they had been married. Their wedding anniversaries had passed almost unmarked – I'm sure Da forgot most of them – and this was the first time I had ever laid eyes on their marriage certificate. I was poor at arithmetic but I could do the sum. I had been born on 14th September 1944 – five months later.

I closed the desk lid and moved on to the drawers below. In them, I found bundles of much older letters – some of them going back a long time. I came across several that I had written to her as a child, handmade birthday cards I had given her over the years and some old school reports. There were more photos: ones of Drew and me as small children in the Oxford garden, of Da reading in a deckchair under the beech tree, of long-since dead pets – dogs, cats, rabbits. And even older photos of Ma herself with her sisters as young girls – one of all of them together with arms linked in a smiling row at the seaside, dressed in funny, old-fashioned woollen swimming costumes and rubber bathing caps: Violet, Lily, Iris, Primrose and, the youngest and smallest at the end of the row, my mother, Daisy. I put those aside for Aunt Primrose and opened another drawer. Old diaries, old theatre programmes, a box of paper clips, luggage labels, a bottle of blue Quink ink, a grease-stained notebook of post-war recipes that Ma had written down: tips on cooking with dried egg, ways of stretching the meat ration, new ideas for fish dishes. There was nothing that related to the American pilot. No more crew photos, no letters from him, no mementoes of any kind.

Until I came to the last drawer – the bottom drawer on the left. There were only two things in it and I took out the first. It was a small sketch-book – I had one rather like it myself that I carried about in my bag. This one was full of pencil drawings – sketches done on an air force station in wartime – and the people, the planes, the vehicles were all American. American uniforms, American Jeeps and American bombers with big white stars. The single exception was a drawing of my English mother in her WAAF uniform, seated at a table with a telephone beside her, papers in front of her, a fountain pen in one hand. As I turned the pages I might have been looking at my own work – the pencil strokes, the shading, the style and execution were all mine. *Incidentally, you get your artistic talent from him*. There was no name in the book, no writing at all, but I knew that it must have belonged to him.

The second thing in the drawer was an old 78 rpm record kept in a cardboard sleeve – the breakable, scratchable, fast-turning kind in use before vinyl long-players. I carried it downstairs to the old radiogram that had stood in a corner of the drawing room for many years. It had knobs to turn and twiddle and a dial for tuning in the wireless. The record-playing part pulled out from underneath and could take a stack of six and drop them automatically, one after the other. In the Forties it had probably been state-of-the-art; now, of course, it was obsolete. A museum piece. In fact, I couldn't remember the last time it had played anything at all. I switched on, hauled out the turntable and put the record on to play. The arm with its needle-head moved across and descended.

The singer was as famous as the song. I sat there in the gathering gloom of a snowy winter's afternoon in the icy drawing room while a young Frank Sinatra crooned the words softly to me.

As the record came to an end and clicked itself off, Karen, one of the St Hilda's students peered, white-faced, round the half-open door.

'Oh, it's you, Mrs Porter . . . I'm so sorry. You gave me a bit of a fright . . . Mrs Byrne used to play that in here quite often. We could hear it. It's a lovely old song, isn't it?'

'Yes, it's lovely.'

'Perhaps it brought back memories for her.'

I still hadn't destroyed the photograph. Later, I looked at it again. I found a magnifying glass in the study and moved it slowly along the two rows of faces, examining each one – the smiling, fresh-faced young men who would, by now, be in their seventies – if they were still alive. I stopped at the officer in the middle of the back row – the one Drew had thought must be the pilot. He was looking directly at the camera with his cap tilted back slightly so that I could see his face clearly. It was a nice face – open and friendly and honest. It was quite possible, though still incredible to me, that I was looking at my own father.

Flavia and Callum arrived late on Friday evening. They had driven up from London, taking twice the normal time because of the snow and ice. Flavia had done the driving – Callum either wouldn't, or couldn't – and looked tired, but lovely. She had inherited Mark's fair colouring and she was tall and slim, like him, and with an elegance that she had definitely not got from me.

'Sorry we're so late, Mum. I got held up at the office and then it was a ghastly journey. Cars skidding all over the place.'

I hugged her and air-kissed Callum dutifully. He was dressed all in black – not out of any respect for the occasion but because he seldom wore any other colour. Black leather jacket, black roll-necked sweater, black jeans. It was his style and it certainly suited him.

We had supper in the kitchen – a beef stew I'd cooked slowly in the Aga, and a bottle of red wine.

Flavia said sadly, 'It's so weird without Grandma. I keep thinking she's going to come into the room.'

'I know. So do I.'

She made an effort at normality. 'By the way,

Dad said he'd call you. He's coming to the funeral, you know.'

'Yes, he told me.'

'Not Caroline though, thank heavens. How are the arrangements going?'

'Most of it's done. And I've found some good caterers to take care of things here for afterwards. They'll bring all the crockery and glasses, as well as the food.'

'Grim to have to think about things like that now.'

'Actually, it helps.' It was quite true. All kinds of practical things had to be attended to, decided and carried out at speed. It was when it was over that I dreaded.

We had coffee in the study in front of the gas fire. Callum, Flavia told me, touching his arm proudly, had just been offered a part in a new television detective series set in Liverpool. 'Everyone thinks it's going to be a huge success.'

I said enthusiastically, 'That sounds very exciting, Callum. What sort of part?'

He shrugged. 'Not the one I was after.'

It wasn't the big break, then. I wondered how long Callum would go on waiting before he gave up hope. At the moment time was on his side. He was still young. He lived rent-free, supported by the State, and I knew that Flavia paid all the domestic bills. I guessed that she gave him money too, but it was absolutely none of my business. There was an unwritten rule between us that we might share a house but not our lives. I had broken it once, by asking her questions about Callum. He never spoke of his family or his home or his past life. The beautiful speaking voice was no real clue; he could do all kinds of accents and did – both on and off-screen. He was a chameleon, taking on whatever camouflage suited him. A closed book. A mystery. Flavia, not unnaturally, had felt that I was prying and told me so. She'd been angry and resentful.

'You don't like him, do you, Mum?'

I wished I'd kept my stupid mouth shut. 'I honestly don't feel I know him well enough to like or dislike him.'

'Well, you don't have to worry about us. I'm blissfully happy.'

'That's all that matters to me, Flavia.' I meant it. I'd spent too much of my own life not being at all happy to wish that state on her.

I said to her now, 'What about you, darling? How are things at work?'

She was the features editor of *Country Stile*, a coyly titled magazine peddling dreams of the rustic life in idyllic houses in idyllic places. According to Flavia, its readership was almost entirely composed of people living in cities and suburbs.

'We're doing a new series about people who've given up the Rat Race and started Another Life in the Country.'

Callum rolled his eyes. 'You know – throwing wonky clay pots and spinning greasy wool.

Carving lumps of wood into butter pats. The usual sort of crap.'

Flavia said defensively, 'Actually, there's one woman who's producing some wonderful hand-made organic cheeses. She's quite a success.'

'Don't tell me.' A dramatic retch. 'Goat's milk Brie and sheep's roulade.'

He always mocked the magazine; it was an easy target. But it never seemed to occur to him that doing so might upset Flavia. I hated to see her looking hurt, as she did whenever he taunted her. Sometimes I wondered whether he did it partly to annoy me; I was an easy target too.

I changed the subject and talked about the house contents. As I'd known, the furniture wasn't Flavia's sort of style but she asked if she could take a few small things of sentimental value – ornaments and bits and pieces that had been part of her childhood and would remind her of the grandparents she'd loved. I decided then and there that those memories should stay unchanged and unspoiled. And I knew that I should follow Drew's advice for my own sake – destroy the letter and the photograph; erase them completely from my mind.

Over the weekend Flavia gave me a hand with going through the clothes. Of all the distressing tasks to be faced in life, this has to be one of the saddest. The familiar garments, once so much a part of the warm and living person, are left behind like empty shells. We kept a few special things in a suitcase; the rest we burned on a bonfire in the garden. The idea of taking them to a charity shop, to be pawed over and worn by others, was unbearable.

The funeral was to take place on the Wednesday after the weekend. On Tuesday evening Drew returned from Cambridge with his wife, Sonia. She was almost as tall as him and wore loose-fitting clothes swathed about her large frame like a desert sheikh. She travelled all over the world with a chamber orchestra, giving concerts, and to look at her, you would guess her instrument to be something substantial to match her size – the cello, say, or the double bass. In fact, she played the flute, and like a dream.

She drew me aside, a heavy hand on my shoulder. 'Andrew's very worried about you, Juliet.' She never shortened names. 'He won't tell me exactly why or what it is, but I can *tell*. You don't look at all yourself.'

There was something of the all-seeing spiritual medium about her – a touch of Madame Arcati.

'I'm upset about Ma's death, that's all.'

She squeezed my shoulder, plainly unconvinced. 'You'll let me know if there's anything I can do.'

There was a fresh fall of snow during the night but luckily not enough to cause serious problems. Flavia and I had decorated the church with as many flowers as we could handle, and the wreaths and bouquets from other mourners lined the pathway up to the church door. The hearse, when it arrived, was overflowing with still more, the coffin crowned with what the funeral director called our personal tributes. The church was packed, the singing loud. I'd chosen hymns that I knew Ma had loved and that were also well known and loved by others: 'Lift Up Your Hearts', 'O Worship the King', 'Now Thank We all Our God'. Nothing dirge-like that she would have hated. Drew did the first reading, Flavia the second. The nice young vicar climbed up to the pulpit and spoke words of praise and thanks for a life well spent, service given to others, for a loving wife, mother and grandmother – a gift from God now reclaimed by Him. He must have done it many times before. I stared at the oak coffin and found it so hard to accept that my mother lay inside, out of my reach for ever.

From the church we went to the cemetery, a bleak place on the edge of the town where she was to be buried in a plot beside Da. I should have so much preferred a churchyard for them both but, as the funeral director had rightly pointed out, space was a problem.

And it was cold – so cold: snow and ice and an arctic wind. We gathered, shivering, round the spot where a piece of emerald green fake grass had been artfully draped over the newly dug grave, masking the bare earth.

Forasmuch as it has pleased Almighty God of his great mercy to take unto himself the soul of our dear sister, Marguerite, here departed, we therefore commit her body to the ground; earth to earth, ashes to ashes, dust to dust.

There was comfort in the dignified words and in the ancient ritual, but no comfort in watching the coffin being lowered down into the ground. The only consolation was that she would be lying next to Da. She might not have loved him passionately, as she had loved the American, but she had certainly been deeply fond of him and they had been happy together. And he had loved her.

Afterwards, at the house, I circulated dutifully among the two hundred people or so who turned up. Most were from Oxford – town, as well as gown – Ma had by no means confined her friendships to the latter. Others had come from all over the country – people from out of her past, at different stages in her life, and some I had never met or heard of. One of these, a white-haired, bright-eyed woman from Yorkshire, told me that she had been in the WAAF with her during the war.

'We did our initial training together, at Morecambe, billeted at the same digs. Hell on earth, I can tell you. Square-bashing up and down the prom in pouring rain, outdoor PT in our blackout knickers, everyone yelling at us. And the food was diabolical. Still, your mother and I managed lots of good laughs in spite of it. She was a lovely person.'

'Were you posted to the same place afterwards?'

'Oh, no, different places, worse luck. I stayed up north and Daisy was sent off to Suffolk. But we still kept in touch, you know. When you've shared that sort of experience, there's always a bond.'

'Did she write to you during the war?'

'Once or twice. There wasn't much spare time, you know. We were kept very busy. We met up occasionally after it was all over, and we always sent Christmas cards.'

I said, 'I gather she got to know some of the American Air Force.'

The woman smiled. 'Well, she couldn't very well help it. The Americans took over her station and she had to stay on with the RAF liaison officer. They'd've made a bee-line for your mother, of course, with her looks. They were like that. Big flirts. It didn't do to take them too seriously.'

I said casually, 'Any of them, in particular?'

'There was one she was rather keen on, if I remember rightly.'

'Did she give his name?'

'I expect she did, but I can't remember. It was all so long ago.'

I was about to ask the name of the station in Suffolk when we were interrupted by a very old and very deaf friend of Ma's who claimed my full attention. When I was free again and looked round the room, the ex-WAAF had vanished.

The catering people were going round and round with tea and sandwiches and cakes and there was the harder stuff for those that wanted it. I could have done with some of it myself and then, right on cue, Mark came up with a glass in hand.

'I thought you might need this.'

'Thanks.'

As I said, there was no bitterness between us; we were very civilized. I hadn't seen him for more than a year and he looked prosperous and satisfied with life – a bit overweight, perhaps, and quite grey now, but he was still a handsome man. I sometimes tried to remember how it had once been with us when we had been in love, but I always failed. I'm sure he had forgotten too.

He said again how sorry he was about Ma. 'I always liked her, as you know. Much better, I have to say, than my second mother-in-law. I'm sure you'll miss her very much.'

'Yes, I will.'

'Flavia's pretty cut up too, isn't she?'

'Very. She adored her.'

'I wish she'd get rid of that useless chap she's living with. No hope of it, I suppose?'

'Not that I can see, I'm afraid.'

'No good saying anything, of course.'

'None at all. In fact, it would probably make her more determined, wouldn't it?'

'Well, she knows what *I* think of him. And Caroline agrees. We had them both to dinner once and it was a disaster. He turned up in a sweater and jeans and, of course, he didn't fit in at all – or even try to. Quite rude, in fact.

Caroline won't have him in the house again.'

I could imagine the scene, knowing it well: the black-tie dinner party, the long table set with silver and crystal and bowls of beautifully arranged flowers. Jewels sparkling, candles flickering, the conversational ball rolling adroitly to and fro. And Callum, probably putting on his best Michael Caine accent, and doing his absolute worst. He would have enjoyed baiting Caroline.

Mark went on, 'Wizzie loves your book, by the way.'

'Not *my* book. I only did the illustrations.'

'Well, that's the part small children look at, isn't it? The pictures. You were always rather good at animals. Especially the bunnies.'

I was used to the condescension, which was quite unintentional. 'You're looking very well, Mark.'

'So are you. You hardly seem to change with the years, Juliet. Still just the same.'

I smiled. 'The same old mess, you mean.' I knew that he had hated the way I dressed – the odd clothes thrown together, often vintage ones culled from flea markets and charity shops – and the casual way I did my hair, screwed up in a wispy knot at the back and held there with a big tortoiseshell clip.

'Well, it seems to suit you.'

It had never suited him; Caroline's faultless appearance was his ideal and I didn't blame him. Even when he'd paid for my clothes and I could have shopped at all the good stores, I'd refused to be conventional.

I moved on to listen to more recollections of Ma coming from kindly people with kindly faces and kindly hands that clutched at mine in sympathy. To my relief, they started, at last, to leave. I kept on looking for the ex-WAAF but she must have gone after speaking to me. She had introduced herself but I couldn't, for the life of me, remember her name.

Aunt Primrose, in firm possession of a large gin, stayed on while I showed her the old family photographs that I had found for her. She was delighted with them. 'Sweet of you, dear. Such good memories.'

'I didn't find any photos of Ma and Da on their wedding day. I don't think I've ever seen one, have you?'

'There weren't any, dear. They got married in secret, didn't you know? In a register office somewhere.'

'They never talked about it. When was that?' I wondered how much my aunt knew; she had been close to my mother, after all.

She shrugged, without a sign of guilt. 'I don't think I ever knew the exact date – sometime in January '44. I was busy doing the ambulances and the others were away, too. They didn't tell a single soul, not even the parents. That sort of thing happened in wartime, you know. People would decide to get married on the spur of the moment . . . everything was topsy-turvy. Daisy went back to the WAAF and Vernon went on doing his decoding, of course. Then she got very ill with pneumonia and came home and that's when they finally told everybody – they had to because you were on the way. It was a big surprise, I can tell you. I'm not sure Mother ever quite forgave her for doing her out of a proper wedding.'

They'd simply turned the clock back from April to January – to explain me. 'I don't suppose you found any of Ma's letters?'

'Just one, that's all, I'm afraid.' She delved into her handbag. 'Here you are. Keep it, if you like. It's something of your dear mother.'

She left as soon as she had finished the drink, hurrying to get back to Reggie and the spaniels.

The caterers began to clear things away, and the few people still lingering took the hint and went.

Drew came to find me.

'Sonia and I are going to head off fairly soon, Ju – if you don't mind. She's leaving on tour first thing tomorrow and I've got an early tutorial. I'll get back at the weekend, if you like.'

'Not necessary. The estate agents are coming round tomorrow to value the house and take all the details. I'll let you know what they say. Do you want us to go ahead and put it on the market straight away?'

'I should think so. Not much point hanging around, is there?'

'They may think it's better to wait until the spring.'

'It'd have to be looked after and we're both busy with other things. Best to get on with it. When will you go back to London?'

'Probably the day after – I need to do some work. The students have said they'll keep an eye on things for us and the agents can have a key.'

'That other business . . . Ma's letter. Much the best, Ju, if you forget all about it.'

'Easier said than done, as I'm discovering,' I said drily. 'And it's not your paternity that's in question, Drew. Is it?'

'I know, but there's no sense upsetting yourself when it's almost certainly not true.'

'Oh, I think it's true all right. I found their marriage certificate in the desk. I was a very premature baby indeed.'

'Still doesn't prove anything. Maybe they jumped the gun.'

'Unlikely, I'd say, wouldn't you? Not Da's style at all. By the way, Ma left a sketchbook too – I came across it in the bottom drawer of her desk.'

'Oh? I didn't know she could draw.'

'She couldn't. She was hopeless. Da couldn't either. Remember his matchstick people? It must have been the Yank's. They're sketches of life on an American wartime airfield. Good ones, as a matter of fact. Remember what Ma said in the letter – that I get my talent from him?'

'Not necessarily. It might have come from a

grandparent, or a great. Talent can skip generations.'

'Odd it skipped to me, not to you. And that I missed out completely on the maths. Don't you think?'

'Still no proof, Ju.'

'It's funny,' I said. 'We've swopped places, Drew. At the start, you were telling me it could be true while I was denying it. Now, it's the other way round.'

'Well, I was wrong before.'

I said, 'No you weren't. She left a record too.'

'A record? What sort of record?'

'The kind you play. An old 78. The St Hilda students say she played it quite often on the old radiogram.'

'I expect she liked it.'

'I'd say it was rather more than that. I think it meant something very special to her. Do you mind if I have the radiogram, by the way? It's rather a nice old thing.'

'God, no.' He frowned. 'Ju, none of this makes any difference to us, you know.'

'You mean that we might only be half a brother and half a sister? No, of course it doesn't, Drew. Not in the slightest. You didn't say anything to Sonia, did you?'

'Definitely not.'

'Because she asked me if something was wrong.'

'Well, she smelled a rat. You know what she's like. A sixth sense. She'd've been burned as a witch two hundred years ago.'

'I'm not telling Flavia, by the way. Not yet, anyway.'

'Wise decision.' He took off his glasses and polished them hard with his handkerchief. I could see that he was still worried. 'You really *ought* to forget all about it, Ju. It could destroy your peace of mind, if you're not careful.'

'I can't forget it. You see, I'm curious now. *Very* curious. If some Yank's my father, I want to find out more about him.'

'I don't see how you can. You've only got that old photograph and you don't even know for sure which one he is.'

'The one you pointed out. He's obviously the pilot.'

He put the glasses back on and looked at me. 'It would be almost impossible to trace him without a name. You realize that?'

'I know,' I said. 'But I'm going to try.'

Later on, when I was alone, I read the letter that Aunt Primrose had given to me. She'd been right about there being no mention of the station but there was a date: 14th February 1943.

Darling Primmy,
Sorry not to have written back sooner but there hasn't been much time lately. Bad news – the American Air Force have taken over this station. The RAF were booted out at a moment's notice to make room for them – now that they've finally condescended to join in the war. Worse luck, I had to stay behind with an RAF liaison officer. We're supposed to show them the

ropes and act as a sort of nursemaid and go-between with the RAF.

Of course, they think they already know it all, even though they've only just arrived and have never been in combat. It makes me furious when they start criticizing the way we do things. I keep remembering how our RAF boys have been fighting alone for three years and all the ones who've died. Flight Lieutenant Dimmock is always terribly polite, though. You can see the Yanks thinking what an old fuddy-duddy he is but he's done two ops tours himself, so he jolly well knows what he's talking about.

I'm the only WAAF left here and I've been billeted at the farmhouse by the airfield. The farmer had to give up a lot of his land but he can still work the fields outside the perimeter. The family are awfully nice but I really miss the other WAAFs and the RAF. It's like a foreign land, Primmy – as though the Yanks had brought a great big chunk of the USA over with them and plonked it down in the middle of Suffolk. They thought the old station amenities were a pathetic joke – which they were, though I'd never admit it.

I go off on my bike to get away from them, only they're everywhere. In the good old RAF days we all used to go down to the Mad Monk in the village, but the Yanks have discovered it now and spoiled everything. They think you're just there to be picked up.

I had a letter from Vi the other day. Did you know she's fallen for a sailor – a lieutenant serving on submarines. I do hope nothing happens to him. I haven't heard from Lily or Iris for ages. Hope they're both all right. How are you and the ambulances, Primmy? Write and tell me all your news whenever you get the chance. Love, Daisy.

I put the letter back in the envelope, disappointed. No mention of the pilot. No helpful clues at all in the letter, except, perhaps, one. A local pub called the Mad Monk. With such an unusual name, it should be possible to track down the Suffolk village and, therefore, the airfield, close by. It wasn't much to go on, but it was a start.

Three

I drove back to London two days later, having left the Oxford house in the hands of the estate agents and made removal arrangements for the bureau and the old radiogram and some boxes of books and pictures. The semi-detached house that I had bought with the divorce settlement was in Putney, not far from the river. When I had first moved in, the tree-lined street had been run-down and seedy, the house cheap, but since then the other houses had been bought up and done up and now cost several times the price I had paid.

I found a parking place, with difficulty – the street being car-lined now as well as tree-lined. As I let myself in, the drone of some afternoon TV programme downstairs told me that Callum was at home 'resting'. I collected my post from the hall table and went on to my flat upstairs: bedroom, sitting room, kitchen, bathroom and, in the attic above, my studio.

The attic had attracted me to the house originally and kept me there ever since. In the beginning it had been nothing more than a loft, accessed through a trapdoor in the ceiling by an expanding ladder. The cold-water tank had gurgled away in one corner and there had been a cobwebbed collection of rubbish – boxes and boxes of empty jam jars, leftover rolls of hideous linoleum and fruit-frieze wallpaper, moth- and mouse-eaten carpeting. But as soon as I saw it from the top of the ladder, probing with a torch beam into the blackness, I knew what it could become. The loft extended the whole length and breadth of the roof, the ceiling easily high enough for a person to stand upright and the floor sound.

The ladder was eventually replaced by a spiral staircase, the rubbish was cleared away, the water cistern boarded in, and a dormer window inserted into the north side of the roof, together with two Velux skylights. Electricity, central heating and a phone line were extended upwards, and running water to a nice old sink that I had rescued from the garden, while the spaces between the roof beams were filled in with plasterboard and painted white. I bought sisal matting for the floor, a big trestle table, a comfortable office chair that could be adjusted to different heights, a side table, bookshelves, cupboards, lamps . . . and, hey presto, the loft became my studio. I could work up there for hours, undisturbed, with the London sparrows and the pigeons for company and a wonderful view over chimney pots and tree tops all the way down to the river.

I had brought a bundle of unopened letters of

condolence with me from Oxford and there were several more among the post from the hall table. I took them all into the sitting room. The letters invariably made me weep: so many kind words, so much sympathy, so much affection expressed for my mother, and so many good memories told of her. They were intended to console and they did, but they also made hard reading. Among them was one from the ex-WAAF who had been at the funeral. There was an address in Leeds and a name at the bottom: Joyce Atkins.

I found her phone number through Directory Enquiries. She sounded surprised that I'd called her but I invented the excuse of trying to trace another old wartime friend of Ma's.

'She served on the same station in Suffolk as her, before the Americans arrived. I hoped you might be able to tell me the name of it.'

'I'm sorry . . . I just can't remember, you know. It was a nice sort of name – I do know that. The village name, I suppose.'

'Apparently, the local pub was called the Mad Monk.'

'Was it? What an odd name for a pub! I've never been to Suffolk myself – it's a bit too much off the beaten track.'

I persisted. 'You said my mother wrote to you occasionally. Perhaps the name of her station would have been on her letters.'

'Oh, I'm afraid those would have been thrown out years ago. My late husband was never keen on a lot of clutter. He used to insist on regular clear-outs of everything. He always said it was a fire risk.'

I went on doggedly. 'You mentioned that she met an American she was rather keen on.'

'Did I? Oh, yes. A pilot, I think he was. I don't think she ever told me his name. He was killed, though – I'm sure of that. A lot of the American air crew were, you know, especially when they first came over. The Luftwaffe fighters used to shoot them down like flies, before they got the Mustangs to escort them. Were you hoping to trace him, too?'

'I was just curious. I don't seem to know anything about my mother's service life. It's rather a pity.'

'Well, some people never stop going on about what they did in the war – half of it invented, of course – and others, like your mother, aren't the sort to say anything much. The WAAF did a wonderful job, you know, and *I* don't mind saying it. They made all the difference to the RAF. Well, so did the women in *all* the services, but it's never been properly acknowledged. No statues, or anything like that.' A deep sigh. 'You might be able to trace that WAAF through the MOD records, if you've got her name. They won't let you have her address but they'd let her know you'd like to get in touch, and leave it up to her. It's worth a try.'

'Thank you.'

'Lucky it's not the American you're after. One

WAAF I knew wanted to find a GI she'd got engaged to during the war, but she never did. Their service people wouldn't help her at all. Quite nasty to her about it. She gave up in the end – probably just as well. He can't have been very keen, can he?'

'Do you still keep in touch with other ex-WAAFs?'

'One or two. I used to go to the reunions, but I can't be bothered any more. There aren't many of the WAAFs I knew still attending. A lot of the others who go are post-war and don't know anything about those days, though they try to pretend they do.'

'If you should happen to come across anyone who knew my mother, would you let me know?'

'Of course I will. And if I ever remember the name of that place in Suffolk I'll be sure to tell you.'

I went up to the studio and tried to get down to the work waiting for me on the trestle table: watercolour illustrations for a children's book of nursery rhymes. I had been delighted with the commission – the first of its kind for me – and had settled down happily to put new pictures to old favourites from my own childhood. I had a collection of old toys that I often used as models. Some of them were my own, kept from my childhood, and others I had found abandoned in dusty corners of junk shops or charity shops or at jumble sales. Teddies, dolls, golliwogs, dogs, elephants . . . anything that tugged at my heartstrings. I was using a particularly fine old knitted frog dressed in a green tailcoat and yellow waistcoat as a model for 'A Frog he would A-wooing Go'. I had rescued him from the bottom of an Oxfam bin and now I reassembled water, brushes and paints to continue with the hopeful suitor and his encounters with Mr Rat, Mrs Mousey, a Cat and her Kittens, and the lily-white Duck.

The work absorbed me for a time. Mark had been right, of course, about small children focusing so intently on the pictures. Certain images, as we discover, can remain fixed somewhere in the mind's eye for ever, and seeing a favourite illustration again as an adult, years and years later, brings back our childhood like magic. Cosy cuteness is not necessarily a requirement. The bunnies have their place but children can take the rough with the smooth – witches being shoved into ovens, cats pouncing on mice, foxes devouring hens, and, in this particular case, poor Froggy being gobbled up by the lily-white Duck, one webbed foot left sticking forlornly out of the duck's yellow beak.

I worked on during the afternoon, mixing colours, rinsing and wiping brushes, putting paint to paper. As it grew darker, I switched on the daylight lamp beside the table. Normally, I would have continued until early evening, but I found myself starting to lose concentration, my mind wandering from the work in hand. I took a break, made a mug of coffee and drank it, standing at the dormer window. It was almost dark, street lamps lit, lights glowing at other windows, the river gleaming blackly through bare trees, here and there white patches of slushy London snow.

It could destroy your peace of mind. Drew was right; it was already being destroyed. Since finding the letter, I had gone through shock, disbelief, bewilderment, curiosity, and, right now, I was feeling a bitter resentment – something I had never, ever, felt towards my mother. Death, desertion, betrayal . . . they had all merged into one. She had kept the truth from me; she had gone without saying goodbye; she had deliberately chosen to unburden herself, to purge herself of whatever guilt or regret was involved, at my expense. Why, in God's name, had she told me? *I want you to know the truth before I die . . . It seems only fair to him now . . . though perhaps it's not so fair to you?* No, it damn well wasn't. She had been well aware of the shattering effect the letter would have on me, and yet she had still written it. That was hard to forgive – at least in my present state of mind.

Your real father was a wonderful man, too. Still no excuse; no justifiable reason. The Yank belonged to the past, not the present; his memory belonged to *her*, not to me. I might be his daughter, genetically speaking, but Da had been my actual father for all the years of my life. *Incidentally, you get your artistic talent from him*. For some reason, this was harder to dismiss. I think

I might have succeeded in following Drew's advice, if it hadn't been for that particular nugget of information which linked me inescapably to this man, like a chain. I could draw and paint and earn my living doing so, because of him – a man I had never met and was never likely to meet. *You're a part of him, Juliet.* I resented this almost more than anything else: to be a part of a complete stranger – bound to somebody I had never met, knew nothing about and certainly cared nothing about.

The telephone rang and I went to answer it. Flavia, home from work, wanted to know if I had got back safely and whether I would like to have supper with them downstairs.

'It's only pasta but I thought you might like a bit of company.'

It was typically thoughtful of her and I blessed her for it, but I knew she would be tired after work, and that the company would, inevitably, include Callum and I didn't feel up to him. I invented another invitation as an excuse and because company did seem like a good idea, I rang someone who I knew would provide it unhesitatingly, as well as wise counsel.

I had known Adrian Legget since my Ruskin days when I had taken part in university theatricals, painting scenery for several stage productions. Adrian, up at Magdalen and a leading light of the Oxford University Dramatic Society, had already begun what was to be a stellar career as a set designer. He was a homosexual, but discreetly so. Not for him the protest marches, the lobbying for rights, the hanging round the bars and the clubs. He had lived quietly and devotedly with his equally discreet partner, Eric, for more than twenty years until Eric's miserable and lingering death from cancer. He knew all about the indiscriminate cruelty of the disease, and all about bereavement.

'Come round at once, darling. I can offer some excellent scallops I bought today from Harrods, if you'd care to share them.'

I changed out of my jeans and shirt into something more respectable and went round to the flat in Chelsea – a place of understated elegance, all muted colours and spare lines and very expensive fabrics and, always, large vases of beautifully arranged, fresh white flowers. Always white. Vivaldi was playing softly in the background. Adrian greeted me fondly, kissing my hand and then putting an arm lightly round my shoulders. Silver-haired, Armani-clad, faultlessly groomed.

'A drink, darling. I've opened a rather nice bottle of wine in your honour – but would you prefer something a little stronger to start with?'

'Wine would be lovely, thank you.'

He handed me a glass and showed me sketches he was working on for a play in the West End. 'A drawing-room comedy revival, complete with French windows. Nothing I can really get my teeth into, unfortunately, but the money boys are too scared to do anything other than play safe with the tourists and coachloads these days. Still, I'm fairly pleased with it.'

He had won awards for his work and deservedly so; as with his living space and his lifestyle, it was deceptively simple, brilliantly effective and inimitable.

In the kitchen – another model of streamlining that made so many other kitchens look a complicated shambles – he busied himself with the plump and glistening scallops. A fish-eating vegetarian, he haunted the fish counter at Harrods. I watched him heating butter in a pan until it foamed and subsided, searing the scallops on each side, then adding crushed garlic to more melted butter with chopped parsley, and pouring the sauce over the scallops. The green salad was ready on the table, a dressing prepared, a loaf of granary bread waiting to be sliced.

We sat down and Adrian entertained me with theatre gossip and general chit-chat. He was thinking of selling his place in Provence, he told me, when we had moved on to the fruit stage – a bowl of luscious black grapes placed strategically between us. I had stayed there several times and loved the old farmhouse which he had restored from a ruin. It was hidden away up in the hills, unpretentious and sublimely peaceful.

'That seems an awful pity.'

He shrugged. 'Eric and I worked on the place together for years, as you know – the house, the terrace, the olive grove, everything. It's simply not the same without him. Life changes. One has to move on and not cling to the past.'

I said, 'Well, life's certainly changed for me.'

He poured more wine. 'Looking at you, darling, I'd say it was for the worst. Is that why you're here? To talk about it? I'm a wonderful sounding board, and the absolute soul of discretion, as you know. What has changed your life so dramatically?'

I knew that I could, indeed, trust him and I needed to talk to someone other than Drew – someone who could be utterly objective. 'My mother died recently.'

'I'm sorry, I didn't know. You have my sympathy, Juliet. Mine died many years ago but I still grieve for her.'

'She had cancer . . . well, you know what that's like. Thank God, her illness was fairly short.'

'But it's not just that which has affected you so badly, is it?'

'She left me a letter. She'd written it a few days before she died – I found it in her writing desk, sealed in an envelope addressed to me.'

'And what did it say?'

I told him briefly.

He raised an eyebrow. 'No wonder you're so upset, darling. It must have been a most ghastly shock. Have you said anything to anyone else?'

'Only my brother.'

'And what does *he* think?'

'That I should tear up the letter and forget all

about it. So did I – at first. I was convinced that my mother must have been affected by the drugs she was taking.'

'Very possible. Eric had the most extraordinary hallucinations towards the end. He imagined all kinds of strange things.'

'But I don't believe that any more. I'm sure the letter told the truth. For one thing, the students living in her house said she was perfectly rational, not a bit muddled. And then I found her marriage certificate and unearthed the interesting fact that I was born five months after the date, which fits exactly with what she said in the letter – that I was already on the way.'

'And she thought this American pilot – your natural father – was dead. Which left her in a very sad and frightening situation in those puritanical days.'

'There was a photo with the letter as well.'

'Of what?'

'An American bomber crew. No names, or any clues, but this man is obviously one of them. Whichever one is the pilot.'

'Do you have it with you?'

I took it from my bag and handed it over, pointing with my finger. 'My brother thinks he's probably the one in the middle at the back.'

He studied it in silence for a long moment before returning it. 'Well, he looks a very decent sort of chap. Clean-cut. A regular guy, as the Americans say. But I wonder why your mother decided to tell you about him at that late stage.'

'She said he was a wonderful man and that it was only fair to him to put the record straight.'

'Well, that should console you a little.'

'That she thought he was wonderful? So was my other father.'

'Of course, and you were extremely fond of him, as he was of you. More grapes? No?' He snipped at the bunch of grapes with elegant little silver shears. 'Does it bother you to think of yourself as half American?'

'I hadn't thought about it. I can't get used to the idea of having a different father, let alone an American one.'

'You'd be in quite exalted company. Winston Churchill's mother was.'

'So she was. Somehow I don't feel any better.'

'Well, it seems that you have a straight choice, Juliet darling. Either you try to find out more about this mysterious man, or you forget all about him. Put the whole thing right out of your mind. Personally, I'd definitely do the latter – that's my advice, if you want it. But then I never had a father – or not one that I can remember. Mine departed when I was a babe-in-arms and, from all accounts, he was very far from wonderful. And I have to admit that I've never missed having one. Not in the least. I'd never want to find mine again. God forbid!'

'I can't put it out of my mind. I've tried. It won't go away.'

'All right.' Another snip at the grapes. 'What else did she tell you about him?'

'That I'd inherited his artistic talent.'

'You were lucky. The only thing I inherited from my father was flat feet.'

'I found a sketchbook in the desk, as well as the letter. Pencil drawings done on an American bomber station. They're obviously his. And I draw in almost exactly the same way. It's uncanny. And there was something else – an old 78 record of Frank Sinatra singing "I'll be Seeing You". I've been listening to it . . . it's rather like hearing the past.'

'Those golden oldies are powerful stuff. I didn't know Sinatra had recorded it. I've only heard the Jo Stafford version.'

'The students told me that my mother kept playing it before she died.'

'Well, I expect it was *their* tune. It reminded her of him. Rather sad that she never *did* see him again.'

'She also said in the letter that she'd never stopped loving him. Never forgot him for a single day.'

'That's very touching.'

'Actually, I'd far sooner she'd kept it to herself.'

'Your mother paid you the compliment of thinking you'd understand, darling. But obviously you don't.'

'I know what it's like to be completely potty over a man.'

'You're surely not speaking of your ex? And if you mean that other one you were carrying on with for all those wasted years, then *potty* is exactly the right word. Thank God you came to your senses – eventually.'

I had wept many times on Adrian's exquisitely tailored shoulder. I said huffily, 'Anyway, I don't know what to do next.'

'I think you should take my advice. No need for shredders or histrionics. Simply put the letter and photo away at the back of a drawer and stop thinking about them.'

'I'd like to know, at least, if he's alive or dead. Whoever he is.'

'In short, you're determined to track him down like a bloodhound, whatever I say.'

I smiled faintly. 'The trail's rather old and cold, Adrian. I don't know his name or where he came from, or even the name of the bomber station where he served. Only that it's somewhere in Suffolk.'

'Well, you have a photo of him.'

'I don't see how it can help.'

'Nor do I, darling. But it's something. And you're not alone in your predicament, you know. I remember coming home once, several years ago, to find Eric blubbing away in front of the television. You remember what a great big softie he was. Heart of gold. He'd been watching some programme where a woman had found her long-lost GI father. The two of them had never actually met but she'd somehow managed to trace him. It took her years, apparently, but she never gave up. The BBC – I think it was – had got hold of the story and flown him over from America. They clapped eyes on each other for the very first time in the television studio in front of an audience, with everyone clapping. Not a dry eye in the house.'

'I'd absolutely hate that.'

'I agree. But it made very good entertainment. Eric was most moved.'

'Did he happen to say how the woman had managed to trace her father?'

'If he did, I can't remember.' He laid a hand on mine. 'Listen, darling, what you have to consider very carefully is that your father – *if* he's still alive – will have a family of his own: children – grandchildren, most probably. Is there really any point in stirring things up? What good would it do? What possible harm? Think about that. He doesn't know that you even exist. He's an elderly man now and you're a middle-aged woman – not Daddy's little girl to be bounced on his knee and spoilt rotten. That delightful relationship never happened between you, and it never can. And he won't look like he does in that photo any more. You've had one perfectly good and loving father and there's no guarantee that you'd care for this man. Lots of people don't actually like their parents at all – they're just stuck with them. Why run the terrible risk?'

'I've thought about all that, Adrian. I wouldn't necessarily want to meet him, or let him know anything about me, but I'd still like to find out something about *him*.'

'Don't delude yourself. If you trace him, you'll want to meet him. To talk to him, see what he's like, get to know him. And it could be such a *big* mistake.'

I said slowly, 'I wonder if *he* still remembers her in the same way.'

'Unlikely. Let's be realistic, darling. A wartime romance . . . young people thrown together in high-octane circumstances: alive today, dead tomorrow. And the Americans made hay while the sun shone. He probably can't even remember her name.'

'My mother was pretty special,' I said. 'I think he would have remembered her.'

'Oh dear,' he snipped at the grapes again. 'I can see you're quite determined.'

'So, where do I go next? What do I do?'

He chewed thoughtfully. 'The Americans call their ex-servicemen veterans, don't they? Vets. They must have associations, just like our service people do, and all associations have magazines for their members. Nostalgic articles, reunion photos, terrible poems, letters, *Where Are They Now?* appeals . . . all that sort of thing. If you contact the American Air Force lot who were over here in the Second World War, then you might be able to persuade them to print your photo in their magazine and see if it rings a bell with anyone.'

'How on earth would I find them?'

He nibbled at another grape. 'If I were you, darling, I'd start by ringing up the American Embassy.'

Four

It was several weeks before I rang the American Embassy. Now that I had taken the big decision, the need to act on it somehow seemed less pressing, as well as more daunting. Besides, there were other things that demanded my attention – the illustrations for the nursery-rhyme book, for example. I finished the Frog a-Wooing and was pleased with it, but not so happy with Sing a Song of Sixpence which took several attempts before I felt satisfied. I strove, as always, to create images that would endure in a child's mind – not only instantly appealing but lastingly memorable. At the same time, as the publishers reminded me, the person who buys the book, handing over the hard cash, is a grown-up with different perceptions. Commercial nursery designs, of all kinds, must aim primarily to please the parents, godparents, grandparents, aunts and uncles. Why else embroider babies' bibs with cute words which the wearer cannot read?

And then there were the evening classes. On Tuesday and Thursday evenings I taught watercolour painting to adult students in the art room of a nearby comprehensive school. Tuesdays was beginners, Thursdays intermediate. The standard in both varied wildly from hopeless to not bad at all and one woman in the Thursday class was a natural. I enjoyed both evenings. The students were there for pleasure as much as anything else; they took it seriously, but not too seriously.

I gave the beginners exercises in colour-mixing, making a wheel of many different shades from only three colours – say, Indian Yellow, Cobalt Blue and Scarlet Lake. They soon learned the magic that was at their fingertips. I explained to them that learning to paint took time and practice, that their mind, eye and hand would gradually begin to work in unison, and I encouraged them to draw with the brush, instead of pencil, to experiment with different strokes, to make hard and soft edges, to understand the value of a colour – how it relates to white or black – to simplify complicated forms and not to overwork a subject. I brought along things for both classes to paint – flowers in vases, plants in pots, wooden spoons in jugs, strings of onions, bowls of fruit . . . whatever I could find that would make a good subject. At the end of the class I gave them an idea to work on during the week and at the beginning of the next we all discussed the results. Much as I appreciated my attic studio, it was a welcome change to come out of solitary confinement for a while, added to which I greatly enjoyed teaching. The students were a thoroughly nice bunch. We were on first-name terms and several had become real friends.

After the Thursday class, I had fallen into the habit of going to a coffee bar round the corner with Monica, the star of the class. She was about my own age, the widow of a naval officer who had died suddenly in his late forties and with a grown-up architect son who had gone to live in Vancouver. As an antidote to loneliness and boredom, she had taken up painting. I thought that she was good enough to get professional work, perhaps as an illustrator like myself, and had said so, while feeling obliged to warn her of the fearsome competition and the grim reality of hard-to-please, flint-hearted art editors. But with money no problem, Monica had – probably sensibly – chosen to stay amateur and simply enjoy her painting.

On one of our coffee-bar visits, I asked her whether her husband had belonged to any service association. She shook her head.

'John died before he got to that stage. In any case, I don't think he'd have enjoyed reunions much. It wasn't his sort of thing. Not like his father. He was a navigator in the war and he likes nothing better than meeting up with all his old cronies and chinwagging about the good old days.'

'Does he belong to a naval association?'

'Not naval – air force. The Bomber Command Association. He was in the RAF, navigating

Lancasters in the dark to Occupied Europe and back. Heaven knows how they managed it. He says practically all they had was a stopwatch, a pencil and a ruler – nothing like today when it's all done for them by computers.'

'Do they have a regular magazine?'

'Indeed they do. Quarterly. He reads it from cover to cover and saves them all in a great big dust-collecting pile – much to my mother-in-law's annoyance.'

I said, 'Do you think he'd know anything about the American Air Force in England during the war? What associations they have for their ex-servicemen?'

'He might. I'll ask him, if you like.' She looked at me, mildly curious. 'Why the interest?'

'I'd like to try and trace an old American friend of my mother's – a bomber pilot. He was based somewhere in Suffolk.'

'Well, I'm seeing my parents-in-law this week. John was their only son and I try to visit fairly regularly. I'll find out what I can.'

There was a certain amount of nerve involved in ringing the American Embassy. I had no idea which department to ask for or what to say, but eventually I summoned up my courage. I was passed from extension to extension and, finally, yet another American voice came on the line.

'How can I help you, ma'am?'

He sounded quite uninterested in doing anything of the kind. I explained that I was trying to find out the names and addresses of associations belonging to the American Eighth Air Force stationed in England during the Second World War.

'We're not able to help you in this department.'

'Can you suggest who could?'

'You could try writing to the Pentagon in Washington, DC. I'll give you the address.'

I wrote it down. 'Thank you.'

'May I ask what this is all about, ma'am?'

The tone was bordering on offensive and I should have answered, no, you may not. Instead I repeated the half-truth that I had given Monica – that I was trying to trace an old friend of my late mother's.

'The National Personnel Records Centre in the US usually deals with enquiries of that nature, ma'am. They send you a form requesting certain data: full name, date of birth, rank, serial number and branch of service, matrimonial status.'

'Well, I'm afraid I don't have any of those.'

'Then they couldn't proceed.'

'But I do have a photograph. That's why I thought an association might be able to help. Some of their members might recognize this particular officer.'

'You should be aware that in the United States we have a Privacy Act. Nobody's going to hand out the home address of any ex-service personnel to you, or anybody else. They're not releasable to the public. No information regarding a veteran can be given without the veteran's written permission.'

'So, it's virtually impossible to trace them?'

'All I can say, ma'am, is that all enquiries are referred to the official government departments in the US. If the authorities are given sufficient information and can locate the relevant records, they'll sometimes forward a letter to the last known address. That way there's no invasion of privacy.'

He made it sound as though all decent, law-abiding, upstanding American citizens needed shielding from importunate foreigners like myself. I rang off, feeling upset and with the suspicion that it was embassy policy, in such cases, to be as unhelpful and discouraging as possible. It was obviously pointless to write to the National Personnel Records without having any of the red-tape answers.

After the next Thursday evening class, Monica reported on her visit to her father-in-law.

'He said he didn't really have anything to do with the American Air Force – they were mainly in East Anglia and the Midlands, while he was stationed up in Yorkshire. But they certainly have ex-service associations – just the same as the RAF. He met an American navigator who was a guest at a Bomber Command Association dinner and belonged to one of their Bomb Group Associations – a group based in Suffolk, like you were after. They still correspond from time to time so he's going to write and ask if he could let him have some information. Oh, and he gave me this magazine to lend to you, but he'd like it back.'

I thanked her and later, at home, I sat down to read the quarterly magazine of the Bomber Command Association. There was a rather nice painting on the cover of a Lancaster coming in to land over a hedge and I was impressed by the contents. Notices of events and reunions being held all over the country, well-written articles, photographs, wreath-layings, book reviews, poems, obituaries . . . there was clearly a huge amount of interest and activity. Towards the end I found a page of letters and one had included a wartime photograph of an RAF bomber crew, with the request for the men in it to get in touch with the writer. If the magazine was prepared to carry such appeals, then, as Adrian had suggested, the Americans might too. There was really nothing to be done now but wait for Monica's father-in-law's letter to wing its way across the Atlantic and for the reply.

The Oxford estate agents phoned a week later to say that there had been a firm offer of the asking price on the house and would we wish to accept? Drew and I both agreed that we did and I went back to Oxford to tell the two students and to arrange the sale of the remaining contents. Most of it went to an auction house, except a few large pieces that our purchasers wanted to buy.

I was still hard at work on the nursery-rhyme book, with the deadline looming, and so I put everything firmly out of my mind except for the likes of 'Old Mother Hubbard', 'The Three Little Kittens', 'Jack and Jill', 'The Grand Old Duke of York' and the others still waiting patiently to be brought to life on paper.

It was mid-May before Monica handed me the reply her father-in-law had received from his American friend. She brought it round to the flat one evening, instead of waiting for the Thursday class.

'I thought you'd want to see it as soon as possible, considering how long it's taken. The chap's been away – that's why.'

'Thanks, Monica, and thanks to your kind father-in-law. Have a glass of wine?'

'Willingly.' She settled herself comfortably on the sofa – a large, big-boned, grey-haired woman dressed in a plain skirt and sweater and sensible court shoes. As with Drew's wife, Sonia, appearances were deceptive. You would have taken her for a magistrate or a chairman of the local Women's Institute, possibly a head teacher; certainly not for a very talented artist with a magically light touch. 'You know, I can't help being a wee bit curious about your search, Juliet. Do you mind?'

I didn't mind, but I wasn't going to tell her the whole truth – much as I liked her. I had felt the need to talk to Adrian but that need had passed. I said, 'There's not much to tell. My mother met this American when she was serving in the WAAF during the war.'

'A romance?'

'I imagine so. But then they lost touch – as happened. She told me about him before she died. I think she'd been thinking a lot about the past. Isn't that what people tend to do at the end of the road? Go back over their lives . . . remember things they haven't thought about for years.'

'John died so suddenly he didn't have time to think of anything, and my parents are both still very much alive and kicking, but I expect you're right. This particular American must have made a big impression, don't you think?'

'It would seem so.'

She put her head on one side, considering me. She was nobody's fool, Monica. 'And you're still going to try and find him – even after your mother's death? Is there any point now?'

'Not really, I suppose. But I thought it would be nice to pass on a message – if I do happen to come across him.'

I could see that she was far from convinced but she was tactful enough not to pursue that line of enquiry. 'When you read his letter, you'll see that Father-in-law's American buddy has come up with a suggestion or two. Apparently, a photograph would come in handy, as well as a name.'

'Well, I don't have a name, but I do have a photo. Of his bomber crew.'

She sat up straight. 'How fascinating! May I see it?'

I handed it over and, like Drew and Adrian, she studied it closely. What was its particular appeal, I wondered? Everyone seemed transfixed by it.

Monica said at last, 'They all look so strong and full of life, don't they? They'd be getting on for old men now, of course. But when this was taken, they were golden youths engaged in the greatest adventure of their lives. Taking part in history. Making it, actually. Which is yours?'

I pointed. 'That one, I think.'

'You think?'

'Well, he was the pilot, and captain, so he's the most likely – the officer in the middle.'

She took another long look, tilting the photo towards the lamplight. 'Well, he looks very nice. An honest sort of face, don't you think? A decent, straightforward sort of chap. Looks like he would have been jolly good at football or baseball, or whatever they play at American schools.' She passed the photo back. 'Well, I hope you're lucky finding him. Father-in-law says the American veterans are awfully keen on their associations and keeping up with each other – they take it all very seriously. So, there's a chance.'

I turned the conversation away into other channels and after another glass of wine, Monica left. I opened the envelope she had brought and took out the letter from America, skipping over the friendly greetings, the apologies for the late reply and the general news, down to the part that answered my question.

Tell your friend in England that our magazine does sometimes feature appeals for renewing old wartime contacts. They usually print a letter with a photo plus the name and any other details – place, dates, etc, asking the guy, or guys, to get in touch with the writer via the magazine which then forwards any replies. That way there's no harm done, privacy-wise. If she writes me with some details, I'll be glad to ask the magazine to run it.

I'm giving some of the contact names and addresses of other Bomb Group Associations who were based in Suffolk, so she could try these too. And maybe she should write to the 8th Air Force Historical Society. If she's got enough information, they might be able to come up with something. They wouldn't put her in direct touch, but they'd probably pass on a letter.

Tell your friend it'll be a pretty long shot. I wouldn't want to raise her hopes too much. There were a lot of us guys over there in England and it was a long time ago.

The letter was signed Ray White and he lived in Wichita, Kansas. He had attached details of a dozen or more American Bomb Group Associations.

I went round to the local chemist and ordered copies of the photo. The middle-aged woman behind the counter looked at it with interest.

'They're American Air Force, aren't they? I remember them during the war – when I was a little girl. My eldest sister used to go to the dances up at the base near our home.'

'Where was that?'
'Suffolk. It was crawling with Yanks.'
'You don't by any chance know of a pub called the Mad Monk, do you?'
She shook her head. 'No. Our village had four pubs but none of them was called that. Funny sort of name for one.' She pulled a pad of forms towards her and felt for a biro in the top pocket of her white coat. 'They'll have to make a negative first to do the copies, so it'll be a bit expensive and it'll take longer. About a week. That all right?'
I called in at a bookshop and looked in *The Good Pub Guide* under Suffolk but there was no Mad Monk recommended. Directory Enquiries, similarly, drew a blank.
'I'm sorry but we have no number listed anywhere in Suffolk for a pub of that name.'
'Are you absolutely *sure*?'
'I'm afraid so. We can find them easily.' The operator sounded sympathetic, rather than impatient, as though he had understood that it was important to me.
Obviously, the Mad Monk no longer existed. Where it had once been common to have four or five pubs in a village, many were now reduced to one. Like village stores and post offices and bakers and butchers all over England, they were a vanishing species – metamorphosed into more profitable private properties. The only chance of tracing the Mad Monk lay in my going to Suffolk and driving all round the county, asking anyone

who looked old enough to remember if they had known such a pub in their village. But first I had to finish the illustrations for the nursery-rhyme book.

As soon as the copies of the crew photograph were ready I wrote to Ray White and all the American bomb group associations on his list, enclosing the photo and my appeal. *If any of your readers recognize any member of this B-17 bomber crew, stationed somewhere in Suffolk, England, during the Second World War, and have news of them, would they please get in touch with me. I am trying to trace the pilot, who was a family friend at that time.* I had spread the net to catch not only the one man, but anyone who might be able to help find him.

That done and the letters posted, I settled down to finish the illustrations. By the end of June I had completed them all except for one – 'Wynken, Blynken and Nod'. In summer the studio was invariably hot and stuffy, even with the dormer window and both skylights wide open. An electric fan helped, but had to be kept at a distance or it dried paint too fast and blew things about on the trestle table. Outside, my attic view had changed now that the trees were in all their glory, camouflaging houses and gardens and reducing the river to an occasional flashing glint between leaves.

'Wynken, Blynken and Nod' was a pleasure to do. I enjoyed creating pictures for the magical words – the fishermen three sailing off in their wooden shoe on their river of crystal light into a sea of dew, trailing their nets of silver and gold for the herring fish. I was absorbed in it all when Flavia came up into the studio.

'Still working, Mum? Sorry to interrupt, I thought you'd have knocked off by now.'

I rinsed out my brush in the water jar beside me and wiped the tip. 'I was just going to. Stay and have a glass of wine with me.'

'Actually, that's what I was going to ask *you* to do, and if you'd like some supper as well. Callum's away doing the detective series, so I'm on my own.'

'I'd love to.'

'Lamb chops, if that's OK.'

'Sounds lovely.'

She came closer and admired the illustration. 'It's "Wynken, Blynken and Nod", isn't it? One of my favourites.

All night long their nets they threw
To the stars in the twinkling foam –
Then down from the skies came the wooden shoe,
Bringing the fishermen home.'

'Those are wonderful pictures.'

'Thank you. I only hope the art editor agrees with you.'

I started clearing up at the sink while she wandered about the room, looking at some of the paintings I'd had framed and hung. 'I don't remember this one, Mum? Where is it?'

'Somewhere in the depths of Kent. I drove out there last autumn. Would you like to have it?' Landscapes made a change from the bunnies.

Sometimes I painted outdoors, other times I made sketches and then did the painting back in the studio. In fact, I never went anywhere without a sketchbook. Daily life is wonderful fodder – the park, a bus queue, a doctor's waiting room . . . ordinary people and ordinary places can inspire just as much as extraordinary ones. I thought of that other sketchbook in the desk drawer; its owner had known that too.

'Very much – if you're sure.'

'Quite sure.'

She prowled on. 'Who are these men?'

I turned from the sink to see that she had picked up the bomber-crew photo that I had left on the side table. 'I don't know,' I said truthfully. 'It was just an old photo I came across in Grandma's desk when I was clearing it out.'

She took it over to the window to see better. Once again, I wondered at its magnetic effect. 'It's from the wartime isn't it? When Grandma was in the air force. But they don't look like RAF.'

'They're not. They're Americans.'

'What was she doing with a lot of Yanks?'

'Apparently, her station was taken over by the American Air Force.'

'Hey, maybe she fell for one of these. I wouldn't blame her – they look pretty hunky to me. Specially this one at the back. And she kept the photo all these years. Grandma's secret past!'

She was smiling and joking and so close to the truth, and I was so close to telling her. After all, she was no longer a child who needed to be shielded from anything that might upset her. The moment passed.

I said, 'She already knew Granda then, so it's not very likely.'

'So she did. They were a wonderful couple, weren't they? A perfect marriage. And now they're together again.'

I turned off the sink tap. 'I'm ready for that drink now.'

She put the photo back on the table. 'OK. Let's go down, then.'

On the Underground, one day, I saw my married man – the one I'd been potty about. He was strap-hanging further along the crowded carriage, his back turned to me, reading a newspaper. I thought of Adrian's acid comment about the wasted years and my coming to my senses at last. I found that I could look at him dispassionately without any stomach-churning or racing hearts. Nothing much at all. The cure, it seemed, was complete. He folded his newspaper and got off at the next station and I watched him walk away out of my life.

Five

The evening classes stopped for the summer holidays in mid-July. After the final session, Monica and I adjourned for our usual coffee round the corner and she produced a newspaper cutting from nowhere and laid it like a conjuror's trick card on the table before me.

'I happened to see this in the *Standard* the other day. I thought it might interest you.'

I picked it up. The headline said: *War baby meets American GI father fifty years on*. There was an unflattering photograph of a plump, bespectacled, middle-aged woman with her arm linked firmly through the arm of an elderly, bald man; the woman was beaming happily, the man, I thought, looked rather confused and not quite so ecstatically happy.

Monica said, 'I know it's not the same as your case, but there's some useful stuff about how she found him. Somebody helped her and it gives their name.'

I folded the cutting and put it in my bag. 'Thanks, I'll read it later.'

'Any progress?'

'No. It seems rather a hopeless cause.'

'She thought so too – the woman in that article. The American authorities didn't want to know . . . wouldn't help her at all. Apparently, their servicemen over here were actively discouraged from continuing relationships with British girls. She says her mother was offered a hundred pounds if she signed an agreement not to try and get in touch again with her father or make any demands on him.'

'I hope she refused.'

'Yes, but she didn't try very hard and, eventually, she married someone else. It wasn't until five years ago that the daughter – the one in the photo – thought she'd have a go and see if she could find her father. She knew his name and service number.'

'*Five years!* It took her *that* long to find him, even with that information?'

'She said she came up against a brick wall at every turn. The American Embassy gave her the addresses of some government departments to write to and they sent back forms with a long list of questions she couldn't answer. She found out later that even if she'd been able to answer every single one, they still wouldn't have released any information on a veteran. They have something called a Privacy Act.'

'Yes, I've discovered that. None of which gives me much hope.'

'Ah, but this woman persevered. She hung on like a bull terrier, in spite of everything, and her luck turned in the end. Apparently, she heard an interview on her local radio with another woman who *had* managed to find her GI father and knew all about the problems and how to get round them. So she got in touch with her and she helped. It can be done.' Monica put down her coffee cup. 'Of course, you probably wouldn't want to go to all that bother for an old friend of your mother's.' She looked at me with no particular expression, but, as I said, she was nobody's fool. 'Have you had any replies from the Bomb Group Associations?'

'Yes, several.' After the Embassy experience, their warmth and friendliness had restored my shaken faith in Americans. One of them had even sent their Group magazine – shorter than the RAF one I had seen, but otherwise very similar. Articles, photos of reunions and wreath-layings at memorials, old wartime photos, personal memories, poems, and, at the end, letters which included three appeals from researchers for information and, encouragingly, one asking for names to be put to faces in an old group photo. 'They all said they'd try to find space to print the photo and my letter in their magazine. No promises because they get so many, and it wouldn't be for months. It's a long shot, of course.'

'But worth a try. Don't you have any other clues at all about your chap? Did your mother ever say where he came from in the US?'

'No, I'm afraid not.'

'Well, if she met him during the war, she

would probably have been stationed somewhere near him, wouldn't she?'

'As a matter of fact, she was on the *same* station. The Americans took it over from the RAF. But I don't remember the name of it, and nor does anybody else. She didn't talk much about the war to us – more's the pity.'

'So unlike John's dear father who never stops talking about it, bless him.'

'There is one thing, though . . .'

'Oh? What one thing?'

'There was a pub called the Mad Monk near the bomber station – or there was once. My mother mentioned it in a letter to her sister. Only it doesn't seem to exist any longer – I've tried looking it up.'

'Weren't the Mad Monks the Hellfire Club lot?'

'They were in Bucks. This is Suffolk.'

'Well, it's not your common Red Lion or your White Horse. You ought to be able to trace it.'

'I thought perhaps I'd go and do a trawl round Suffolk – see if I can. Next week, probably. I'd like to do some sketching there anyway.'

She said regretfully, 'I'd come with you like a shot if I could, Juliet, but my son's coming over from Vancouver with his family. I'm booked to be mum and grandma for a month.'

It was good of her, but I knew that this was something I wanted to do on my own.

I read the news cutting Monica had given me later and contacted the woman who had helped to find the GI father. The paper had given her name as Stella Morrison and mentioned the town where she lived; Directory Enquiries provided the rest. I told my story to her briefly and related my complete lack of progress. She was understanding and sympathetic.

'I'm afraid that even if you knew his name, rank and service number, the American government departments wouldn't do a thing except send you forms that are impossible to fill in. They ask questions you wouldn't have a clue about and, even if you *did* know all the answers, they'll only offer to forward a letter which you have to leave unsealed so they can read it first before they put it in the rubbish bin. One of their excuses is that there was a big fire in the Seventies which destroyed lots of records, but what they *don't* ever tell you is that they have other records that could give the same information.'

'But you did trace your father, in the end?'

'Oh yes. It took a long time, but I did it – no thanks to the American authorities. I knew his name, you see, and my mother suddenly remembered him saying he'd been born in the same town as John Wayne – Winterset, Iowa. It's a small town, so I got in touch with the postmaster there and then with the local school. In the end it was easy. I was lucky, though. Not quite so easy if he'd been born in somewhere like New York or Chicago. I've been helping others in the same situation ever since and nagging the American government to change things.'

'Have you been getting anywhere?'

'Slowly. They have something called the Freedom of Information Act which gives individuals the right of access to documents held by federal agencies – and you don't have to be a US citizen.'

'What about their Privacy Act?'

'It doesn't overrule the Freedom of Information one. A legal firm over there has offered to take on our case for free. They're going to take out a lawsuit to try and make the Government release information to war children of American servicemen, but, of course, it could mean years and the fathers aren't getting any younger. Still, I'm going to keep on making a nuisance of myself. By the way, most of the ordinary American people I've come across are happy to help if they can, so long as they think you're genuine.'

'That's a comfort.'

'And it was a good idea of yours to ask the Bomb Group Associations' help in their magazines. It only takes one person to recognize someone in the photo and you've got a start.'

'I'm keeping my fingers crossed.'

'You said you're going to try and find the pub that was near the airfield. Take your photo with you and keep showing it to anyone who would have been around at that time. That's how one of my war children found her father. Some old man recognized him from a photo and remembered his name. Luck's got a lot to do with it. And keep in touch with me. I may be able to help you later on, a bit further down the road.' She paused. 'I hope you don't mind my asking this, Juliet, but how much do you want to find your father? How much does it mean to you?'

'I don't think I'll be able to come to terms with the situation until I do.'

'That's what most of us feel. I only ask because the reality can be a big let-down. I've helped one or two whose fathers have turned out to be a great disappointment or who wanted nothing whatever to do with them. And sometimes the wives and families kick up a big fuss. It can cause a lot of heartache if it goes wrong. My advice is, unless you're prepared to risk that sort of thing happening, don't go on. Sometimes dreams are best left as dreams.'

Adrian came round the evening before I left for Suffolk, bringing a bottle of extremely good wine. I cooked mushroom omelettes and concocted a passable salad and we ate at the table by the open window. London was stifling in the July heat and I was glad to be getting away from it. Adrian was leaving, too, but for a villa in the South of France.

'Belonging to some dear old friends of mine, darling. No effort required, thank heavens. I'm not up to it any more.' He poured another glass of wine for me. 'I must say I had hoped you might have given up your bloodhound activities by now, but here you are still doggedly sniffing out the trail. Does Flavia know anything about it?'

'No. Nothing whatever. I've told her I'm going off to do some sketching and painting in Suffolk – which is perfectly true.'

'Well, it'll do you good to get away for a while. I'm rather intrigued, though, darling – never having met your mother and hearing this romantic story. Tell me, what was she like?'

I fetched the photograph of her in her WAAF uniform that I had brought back from Oxford and he considered it in his quiet, contemplative way. 'Very like you – or you like her, I should say, since it was that way round. But I really meant, what was she like as a person? Not the usual platitudes, please – give me the essence of her distilled into one word.'

I understood him, but it was a hard question to answer about anyone. I thought for a moment about the way that Ma had been: the unwavering quality and style that had set her apart; the refusal to bow to fads or fashions or outside pressures. 'True to herself.'

'That's three words and it's a terrible cliché, but it will do. An excellent thing to be. *This above all: to thine own self be true, and it must follow, as the night the day, thou canst not then be false to any man.*'

'She was pretty false to me.'

'No, she wasn't, darling. She was marble-constant, as Shakespeare also said. An illegitimate baby was a huge black mark in those days, remember. She could easily have had you adopted, but she didn't. She hung onto you and she married another man because she thought it was the best thing for you. Presumably he knew all about you being on the way, and about your real father?'

'So she said in her letter. He wanted to marry her, just the same.'

'I'm sure he did. And the marriage worked – except, of course, that she never quite forgot her lover. She kept that photo and she played that record.'

'Why on earth didn't she tell me his name, Adrian? Or give me some clues? That's what I can't understand. What was the point of it? How could the record possibly be set straight?'

'Oh, I think *I* understand, darling. She didn't tell you his name because it made it easier for you to deal with. You'd only look for him – and maybe find him – if you *really* wanted to. Otherwise, you could just leave it alone.'

'That sounds like one of the Mad Hatter's riddles. Why is a raven like a writing desk?'

'I mean what I say, darling,' Adrian said blandly. 'And I say what I mean.'

Later, I played the Sinatra record on the old gramophone. Adrian listened in silence until the song had finished. Then he sighed.

'Ah, the potency of cheap music. Very Second World War. Very poignant. I wish you luck, Juliet, darling, but I fear for you. Don't get your hopes up too high. As you said yourself, the trail's old and cold and who knows what could lie at the end of it.'

Six

I had few hopes of any kind as I set off in my car for Suffolk. The week before I had bought a book in W.H. Smith about the airfields of the American Eighth Air Force in England and had spent some hours studying it. The map showing the airfields in the Midlands and East Anglia was a mass of black dots. I drew in the Suffolk borders and sorted the bomber stations from the fighter ones, ringing those dots in red. There were at least fifteen, most of which had probably long since fallen into decay, or perhaps vanished completely. And reading the chapters devoted to each one and its exact location, I soon discovered that the airfields themselves were by no means necessarily situated close to the village they were named after; some were as much as several miles away, nearer another village altogether. My only real clue remained the Mad Monk and my only plan of action to drive around the area of each airfield in turn, hoping to find out where the pub had once been.

I began in the north of the county, close to the border of Norfolk where there was the densest concentration of dots. The harvest had just begun and juggernaut combines were at work in the fields, tractors hogging the narrow lanes. It had been many years since I had last been there, on some stilted weekend visit to friends of Mark's who had owned a manor house near Bury St Edmunds, and I had almost forgotten how beautiful Suffolk was. Every county, of course, has its own look and feel, distinct from the rest. Suffolk has its switchback landscape, its open skies and, most of all, its wondrous light. I drove through villages, past crooked timber houses with plaster walls painted in colours that would have looked wrong anywhere else in England: crushed-strawberry pink, mustard yellow, olive green, deep terracotta. And everywhere, there were hollyhocks of all colours, standing tall against walls and fences, lining pathways, grouped outside front doors. In wartime, with no paint available, the houses would have looked woefully shabby, but, even so, the Americans must have been rather impressed by the antiquity, if not by the plumbing.

I stopped in any village that was within ten miles of a red-ringed dot, working my way steadily across the county. There were Crowns, Angels, White Horses, Black Horses, Red Lions, Four Horseshoes, Six Bells, Brewer's Arms, Foxes, White Harts, Green Dragons . . . and I asked in every village if there had ever been a Mad Monk in the vicinity. When the pubs were shut, I asked in the post office or the village shop, or stopped a local to enquire. I spent the night at a B & B and continued the search the next day, breaking off sometimes to sketch the scenery for relief. Out of curiosity and with some difficulty, I hunted down one of the old airfields a mile or two outside a village and found it had become an industrial estate. Rusty Nissen huts served as workshops alongside modern Portakabins and an old aircraft hangar was being used for storage, but there was little else to show what the place had once been.

A mechanic in overalls emerged from one of the huts, wiping his hands on an oily rag, and told me that the runways had been taken up the year before and sold for motorway hardcore and that only a short length of the perimeter track was left. The control tower had apparently collapsed several winters ago. They got American veterans coming back all the time, he said, and the poor blokes could never make out where everything had been because it had changed so much. He thought it was a shame really because they looked so disappointed, as though they'd somehow expected to see it all still there, just the same as when they'd been young. He'd found an old baseball once, buried in the long grass on the edge of the airfield, and kept it on a shelf in the Nissen hut for years. Eventually he'd given it to one of the Yanks. The old man had held it in his hand, staring at it without a word, and then started to weep.

I progressed slowly southwards but still with no success. For three days I sketched and painted – cornfields, woods, farmhouses, barns, stone bridges, whatever took my fancy – convinced now that it was a hopeless waste of time and energy to carry on looking for the pub. For all I knew I had passed it already, prettied up as somebody's private home – the smoke-filled, nicotine-ceilinged, rowdy bar where the RAF and the Yanks had drunk warm weak wartime beer transformed into a genteel sitting room. Only three airfields remained now and when they were crossed off, I planned to give up.

I did the same tour of the next two, driving round all the villages in the area and asking the same question. In the lounge bar of the Six Bells in one of them, I came across an American and his wife who were over from Phoenix in Arizona to revisit his old bomber airfield. He had thinning grey hair and sun-mottled skin. It was hard to imagine him as one of the fresh-faced young boys who had descended on a war-weary England.

'My first visit back. Never had the time before, or seen much reason, but when you get to my age you start to go backwards in time, to think about what's been important in your life – about what good you've ever done. I reckon what I did over here was just about the best thing I've ever managed.' He nodded towards his wife, dressed in a lilac tracksuit and white trainers, who was absorbed in going through her shoulder bag. 'Joan didn't want us to come. The past is past, she says. No point in looking back. But I wanted to do it once. To remember those times . . . and the boys I knew who didn't make it home.'

I asked him if he had been out to the old airfield yet. He nodded.

'Yep. Went there yesterday and had the darnedest time even finding the place. It's all different. Trees grown where there weren't any, half the buildings gone, the rest all grown over. I couldn't recognize a thing except the briefing room and that was in a real mess. Had to fight my way through the brambles to get to the door.' He held out scratched hands for me to see. 'Joan stayed outside while I went in and took a look at where we'd sat in rows while they told us what we were in for. The platform was still there, up one end, and some of the old wiring, and the holes where the stovepipes went, but the ceiling was coming down and the brambles and stuff were coming right in through the windows. I stood there, remembering how it was . . . all us guys sitting there listening real hard, that big map on the wall with the red ribbon pinned across it, that long stick pointing everything out like we were kids in class, the CO giving us his pep talk at the end . . . and, hell, I got *exactly* the same knot in the guts I used to get back then, like they were all screwed up in a vice. Just the same.' He shook his head. 'Spooky. Joan said she yelled at me to come out a couple of times, but I guess I never heard her. After that, we drove out onto the main runway and it was all weeds and potholes with a whole lot of turkey sheds and muck in the middle. I couldn't believe I'd ever taken off from there.'

'You were a pilot?'

'Co-pilot. On B-24s. Liberators you called them.'

'So, there were two pilots on a bomber? On B-17s as well?'

'Sure. Captain and co-pilot. We needed them. It was a tough job flying those heavy suckers and keeping formation with the others for hours on end. I'd take over from the captain for some of it – give him a break. We never understood how the RAF made do with only the one guy, but then your bombers were lighter to handle and they went on their own, not in formation.'

'Did you ever come across a pub called the Mad Monk?'

'Can't say I did. Crazy name! We always used to come in here or the Cross Keys down the road. There were two or three other pubs as well, but none of them was called that. I'd've remembered a name like that.'

I showed him the photo. 'Do you recognize any of these men, by any chance?'

He took his spectacles out of the breast pocket of his shirt to look at it. 'This is a B-17 crew. We were on 24s, like I said, so I wouldn't have come across these guys.' He handed the photo back, smiling, 'Say, you're too young to have known any of them.'

'My mother did.'

'That so?' He glanced at his wife, still busy poking around in her shoulder bag, and lowered his voice. 'I met an English girl when I was over here. Her name was Betty and she was in your Land Army. Matter of fact, I wanted to marry her and she said yes, at first, but then she didn't want to leave England and her family didn't want her to go either. I kept on writing when I got home but in the end I stopped because it wasn't doing any good.' He shrugged. 'She married someone else, finally.'

'But you didn't forget her?'

'I guess you always remember your first girl.'

He took me through to another part of the bar and showed me some old black and white wartime photos from the airfield, framed and hung on the wall. Bombers lined up on the tarmac, another crashed in a buckled heap, a baseball game being played out on the airfield grass, jitterbugging at a hangar dance, local village children gorging themselves at a Christmas party, and several crew groups. He pointed one out. 'That's me right there – back row on the left.' The man standing beside me was completely unrecognizable as the grinning young man in the photo. 'And that's Larry, our captain, Bill, our bombardier, Lloyd, our navigator. Down here's Gus, our radio operator, and these four guys are all gunners. Great guys.' He was using the present tense, I noticed. 'We'd just got back safe from a mission, that's why we look so happy. Jeez . . . I remember it like yesterday.' He went on looking at the photo for a moment in silence. Then he said heavily, 'I guess we've all changed a bit.'

The next day I moved on to investigate the last American airfield on the list. My reference book told me that, for once, this was within a mile of the village of its name and I was hoping for an easy one. Instead, I got lost in a maze of lanes that seemed to lead nowhere. They twisted and turned between high hedges and through long tree tunnels and I could see almost nothing of what lay beyond. After several miles, just as I was giving up hope of getting anywhere, the lane gave a final twist and emerged onto the wide open, sunlit space of a village green.

I stopped the car to admire it – the green, green grass, the shaven cricket pitch, the pavilion, the duck pond, complete with ducks, the Norman church, the mature trees and the old Suffolk houses ringing the perimeter, some roofs thatched, some tiled, some walls white-washed, others in soft pink or yellow – gentler versions of the bold colours I had been seeing before. A perfect English village, the stuff of picture postcards and British Tourist Board brochures.

There was a pub – naturally – on the other side of the green and I drove round and parked outside. The thatch-roofed Cricketers had clearly left its spit-and-sawdust days far behind, judging by the brand new thatch, the gleaming paintwork and the profusion of gaudy annuals spilling from hanging baskets and tubs. I went inside and found that the interior had been ruthlessly updated – in the same sort of way as the Oxford funeral parlour. Fitted carpeting, imitation flowers, chintz curtains, polished dining tables, and an impressive menu chalked up on a big blackboard with London prices to match. Only the inglenook had been spared. The place was still empty, except for a young man wiping drinking glasses behind the bar.

'I got a bit lost,' I told him. 'Could you tell me where I am?'

He smiled. 'You're not the only one to do that. You're in Halfpenny Green.'

'That's rather what I was hoping you'd say.'

I ordered a lager and as soon as he had set the glass down on the bar, I trotted out the usual questions. No, he said, there was no pub called the Mad Monk in the village. The Cricketers was the only one. But he couldn't say for certain if there'd ever been one or not. He actually lived in Sudbury and was a student at Cambridge doing summer vacation work. His aunt was a friend of the owners and she'd got him the job. And there wasn't a village shop or post office any longer. Sainsbury's wasn't far if you took the good road out – not the back lanes like I had done.

'I believe there's an old wartime airfield somewhere near here.'

'It's just outside the village. I've been up there myself a couple of times. It's beyond the woods on the opposite side of the green – up on the farm land.'

'Is there much left to see?'

He nodded. 'The runways are still there, so's the control tower and a couple of hangars, and they've kept the old huts. It's quite a place, really. There are some wartime photos of it on the wall over there by the inglenook, if you're interested. The owners left them there because the Americans still come back here and like to see them. And there's a board with names carved on it. One of the Yanks told me there used to be a whole lot more names on the ceiling but they must have got painted over. He was quite upset about that.'

I ordered a prawn salad and went to look at the photos. They were similar to the ones in the Six Bells – bombers lined up, nose to tail; life on the base; groups of air crews. I looked at those especially closely but none bore any resemblance to the men in my photo. The names were carved on a board screwed to the wall – an old score-board perhaps – and looked as though they'd been done with penknives, or kitchen knives, or keys, or whatever was to hand. Some of them were RAF but most were American: Lieutenant Willard Clark, Maine; Lieutenant Don Murtrie, Wisconsin; Lieutenant Herman Patzel, Kansas; Captain Floyd Schooler, Texas . . .

I carried my lager outside to sit at a table in the garden, overlooking the village green. A couple arrived in a shiny new Jaguar and went into the pub, and then another in an open Porsche drew up with a spurt of gravel – a girl with long blond hair and a man in a brass-buttoned blazer and cravat. There was no sign of any genuine locals – no rheumy-eyed old men in cloth caps sitting with their pipes over pints. Nobody to ask about times past. And the waitress who brought my elaborately adorned salad was even younger than the bartender.

When I had finished, I drove slowly round the green. As I did so, I passed a thatched cottage with the name on the gate, Elm Cottage, and a discreet B & B sign. A woman was working in the front garden and I stopped and got out and called to her. She came over, trowel in hand, wearing old gardening clothes and a floppy straw hat. Somewhere in her late fifties, I judged – old enough to have remembered something of the war. She only had the one room, she said, and it was free at the moment. I was very welcome to take a look at it.

As I followed her up the garden path between beds overflowing with cottage flowers, into the house and up a creaking staircase, she chattered away non-stop. Wasn't it hot? A real heatwave. The weather people said it was going to last for another week but, of course, they often got it wrong – look at how they missed the hurricane. At least the farmers didn't have anything to grumble about with the harvest, though they'd probably find something else to complain about soon enough. It'd be too dry instead of too wet, and they'd be saying they needed rain. They were never satisfied.

We reached the landing. A pause for breath, and the chatter continued. There was no en suite, or whatever they called it these days, but, so long as I didn't mind that, the room *was* rather nice, if she said so herself. She lifted up a latch and opened a door with a flourish, standing back. I saw that it was, indeed, rather nice: beams the colour of pale honey, white walls, plain blue linen curtains at the open window which gave onto the village green, fresh flowers in a vase on the chest of drawers, and a very comfortable-looking large double bed. No fussy frills, no cute ornaments, no awful pictures. I told her how lovely I thought it was and asked if I could stay two or three nights, which would give me time to do some more painting and sketching. She looked pleased.

'Most people seem to like staying here. They say it's very restful. Peaceful. Even the Americans don't mind not having an en suite, or a shower.'

'Do you get a lot of Americans?'

'A steady stream in summer. We should be very grateful to them for coming over here and spending their dollars. They all seem to love England – heaven knows why. Of course, most of the ones I get have come to revisit the old airfield.'

'You mean, they served there during the war?'

'Oh, yes. And you'd be surprised how many

come back to see it again – usually with their wives, during the summer. Private visits. They've got a big official reunion coming up this weekend, but they're all staying at a hotel in Ipswich so I haven't got any of them with me this time, else I'd have been full. They'll be having a dinner and speeches, I expect, and all that sort of thing. And there's some sort of do for them up at the airfield. The Laytons are organizing it in their barn.'

'The family that own the land?'

'That's right. It's the grandson now, of course, but Richard Layton, his grandfather, was the one during the war and he was very keen on keeping up the contact with the Americans afterwards. He died in the Seventies and the only son soon after him, so it passed to William and he's carried on the tradition – fortunately. Most young people today wouldn't care a row of beans about such things.'

'Have you lived in the village long?'

'Twenty-two years. My husband died five years ago and I started the B & B to keep myself occupied. I love it, I must say. You meet all sorts of interesting people from all over. Dutch, French, Germans, and the Americans, of course. They're the easiest, really. Something to do with speaking the same language, I suppose – more or less. Though the Dutch are very nice and always speak good English. I suppose they have to because nobody knows a word of Dutch, do they?'

'I expect the village has changed a bit since you first came here.'

'More's the pity. It used to be a real village with real villagers but now it's mostly commuters. You can get to London by train in less than an hour since the line's been electrified so commuters have snapped up nearly all the houses – priced the old locals right out of the market. It's a shame. And we had the Dutch elm disease, of course, and lost all the elms, including ours by the cottage – that's one thing I do hold against them, though I never say anything.'

'I had lunch just now at the Cricketers. I expect that's changed too.'

She sighed. 'New people bought it last year and spent a fortune on wrecking it. They cater to the commuters, of course – fancy food and fancy prices, but that's what they all seem to want. We've still got a cricket team but it's not the same as it was in the old days. But then nothing is, is it?'

I agreed with her, though it was fuddy-duddy of us both. 'Were there ever any other pubs in the village?'

'There used to be two more – the Plough and the Barley Sheaf – but they closed down a good while back, before the commuters arrived with the spending money. We had a post office-cum-general stores, too, but that's gone as well. Everyone's got cars now, so I suppose it doesn't matter but it was handy to be able to pop over for a pound of sugar, or whatever.'

I almost didn't bother to ask the question, but all stones needed to be thoroughly overturned.

'There was never a pub called the Mad Monk, then?'

'Well, yes, there was.'

I stared at her, hardly believing my ears. 'There was?'

'The Cricketers used to be called that. But the people who bought it changed the name. They didn't like the old one for some reason. I suppose they thought it didn't fit the new image. It *was* rather an odd name, I must admit, although you can have Jolly Friars as pubs, can't you, so why not Mad Monks? I don't know why it was ever called that – something to do with the old abbey near here, I imagine, though of course that's been in ruins for hundreds of years so there wouldn't have been any monks about, sane or otherwise, for a very long time.'

She talked on – about the price of the room, the tricky ways of the hot-water tap on the bath, the double tug necessary to work the lavatory (one short, one long), the need to keep the bedroom door shut so that the cat didn't get in . . . I wasn't really listening. I'd found the right pub, the right village and the right airfield: Halfpenny Green. *It was a nice sort of name. Some funny country name*. Between them, Joyce Atkins and Aunt Primrose had actually given me a big clue and I should have twigged long before. I had just been standing in the very bar where Ma had stood and where the Yanks had chatted her up. Perhaps where she had met my father.

'What time would you like breakfast?'

I came back to earth and we sorted out a time and whether I wanted the full works or the Continental. 'I thought I'd go up and see the old airfield. The young man in the pub told me there's still quite a lot of it left.'

'Thanks to the Laytons. I haven't been up there myself for a while but my American visitors are always thrilled to bits with it.'

'I gather it's quite easy to find.'

'Oh, yes. Just drive on about fifty yards from my gate and you'll come to Nightingale Lane. Go up there and you'll see a turning on the left by the old water tower. It takes you straight up onto the old perimeter track and you can drive all round the airfield. The Laytons don't mind so long as you steer clear of the crops.'

I thanked her. 'Are there really nightingales?'

She smiled. 'There used to be, but I haven't heard one singing for a long time. The commuters and their flash cars have probably frightened them all away.'

I found Nightingale Lane and the turning below the water tower. The car bumped and jolted up a rutted track and, at the top, the land levelled out onto a plateau of wheatfields. I could hear the clatter of a combine at work somewhere. I turned the car onto the old concrete perimeter track and drove round, scaring up some little brown and black birds – quail, I thought – that whirred into panicky flight before vanishing into the cover of the wheat.

The track continued for at least a mile and I passed several concrete bays overgrown with weeds and moss. Parking places for the bombers? The bombers would have used the perimeter track to get round the airfield, though it must have been much wider originally. I had only to keep going and sooner or later I would be bound to reach the runway. I rounded another corner and there it was – a hundred feet or more wide and extending far into the distance. A colossal pathway to the skies. Grasses and weeds and thistles sprouted from big cracks and concrete had crumbled into potholes, but it was still there. Eerie. Spine-tingling.

I switched off the engine and got out of the car. The combine had stopped. There was a soft little breeze and no sound except for the trill of the skylarks overhead and the rustle, like heavy skirts, of the Common Market wheat – short, dense and high-yielding. In wartime farmers would have grown the old-fashioned kind with long stalks and feathery ears that whispered in the wind.

I stood there, picturing the American bombers queuing up for their take-off run, roaring hell-for-leather down the runway, climbing away on some hideously dangerous mission. Men aged nineteen, twenty, twenty-one, twenty-two . . . Ten in each plane; ten lives in the balance. My father one of them.

Then the combine harvester started up again and broke the spell. I got back into the car and drove slowly down the runway, weaving a way between the potholes and the clumps of grass and the weeds. A hare accompanied me for part of the way, zigzagging ahead like a demented outrider, and then veered across the concrete to flatten itself, ears down, in a ditch. At the far end, I rejoined the perimeter track, turning left in the direction of a flat-roofed building with metal-framed windows, an ironwork balcony projecting at the front and round two sides and more railings on the roof: obviously the control tower that the barman had spoken of. And, soon after, there were more wartime buildings – brick-built and tin-built, and two curved hangars like giant Nissen huts.

Further on, I could see the tiled roof and cream walls of an old farmhouse and I took a gravelled driveway that led towards it, passing outbuildings and sheds, a barn and a pond surrounded by willow trees. A black Labrador lay panting in the shade outside a side door and struggled up as I approached, wagging its tail. There was a bell hanging outside the open door with a rope attached to the clapper and I rang it and waited. After a moment a girl appeared, carrying a child on her hip, another larger child in tow. She was dressed in jeans and a man's shirt, her long hair worn in a thick plait down her back, no make-up, very striking.

I said, 'I'm so sorry – I should have gone to the front.'

She smiled. 'Nobody ever does. Everyone comes and goes this way. It's easier. Can I help? Are you lost, or have you come to see the airfield?'

'To see the airfield, actually. I came up the Nightingale Lane way and I've been driving round a bit. I hope you don't mind.'

'Of course not. Anyone who's interested is welcome – unless they're yobs from the towns. We've had some of those riding up and down the runway on their motorbikes and they're a real nuisance.' She shifted the child more comfortably on her hip. 'I'm Jessica Layton.' She ruffled the child's blond mop. 'And this is Lottie and this one hiding behind me is Jack. He's a bit shy with strangers. Would you like a cold drink, or something? It's awfully hot, isn't it?'

I thanked her and she led the way through a scullery and into a proper farmhouse kitchen, the Labrador padding after us. The painted dresser and cupboards must have been at least eighty years old, likewise the pine table in the centre, the monster cooking range and the porcelain sink with a draining rack above. The only modern concession seemed to be a large fridge.

She saw me looking around. 'We haven't changed anything much since William took over from his father. We rather like it this way.'

'So do I.'

She fetched a jug of real lemonade from the fridge, and poured a glass for me and some for the children. 'You're not American, are you? You don't sound it. We get a lot of them wandering about, especially in the summer. They were stationed here during the war and they want to see it again. In fact, we've got a whole crowd of them coming this weekend. It's a big reunion and we're doing a lunch for them in the barn.'

I said, 'Actually, my mother served as a WAAF here.'

'When it was RAF, you mean? Before the Americans?'

'Yes, then. But she stayed on when it was taken over. As a matter of fact, she came to live here with your husband's family when the Americans moved in.'

Jessica smiled. 'I expect they thought she'd be a lot safer.'

I wondered if the Yanks had really deserved their reputation – in either sense of the meaning of the word. From all accounts, they'd had it pretty easy with the girls. Looks, glamour, money to burn. No great effort required on their part. 'She must have known this room very well.'

'Yes, she would have done. It's hardly altered. Has she been back at all?'

I had no idea. Perhaps she had come and had driven around, like I had just done. 'I'm not sure. It's possible. She died at the beginning of this year.'

'I'm so sorry. Well, if she *did* come we didn't

meet her. We'd have remembered it. There's a visitors' book in the old control tower, though. She might have gone in there and signed it. That's what some of them do. I suppose they don't like to bother us at the house, so they just write nice things in it and go away. Only William's always pleased to meet them. I'm sorry he's not here at the moment. He's terribly busy with the harvest but he'll be in to grab something to eat later, if you'd like to stay. He's got all sorts of stuff on the airfield – maps and photos and things. His grandfather lived here at the time, and his mother was born here a year or two before the war started. He could tell you a lot more than I can.'

The last thing I wanted was to be a nuisance, but it seemed stupid to resist the kind offer. I stayed to sit with the children for their supper and, by that time, Jack had come out of his shell enough to allow me to cut up toast soldiers for his egg. I helped clear away afterwards and Jessica took me on a tour of the house. The non-alteration applied to most of the other rooms, and I realized, as we progressed from one to another, that it was almost exactly as my mother would have known it – the same furniture, wall-papers, paintings and ornaments. I noticed an old gramophone of similar vintage to Ma's radio-gram in the drawing room and commented on it. It had belonged to the grandparents, Jessica said, like almost everything else in the house. I thought it was highly commendable that the young couple hadn't – as they might well have – modernized the lot.

'Do you still have any of the old 78 records?'

'Yes, we do. They're kept in that black case in the corner. The Yanks used to bring them to the house and play them and they got left here after the end of the war.'

'Would you mind very much if I took a look?'

'Of course not. Help yourself.'

She sat down, bouncing Lottie up and down on her knee, while I snapped open the clasps of the case and flicked through them. 'Paper Doll', 'In the Mood', 'How High the Moon', 'Green Eyes', 'Deep Purple' . . . I soon found what I was after: same song, same singer.

'Fantastic old tunes, aren't they?' Jessica said. 'We still play them sometimes.'

I shut the case and we went out through the French doors onto a lawn shaded by trees and splashed with sunlight.

We watched Jack race across the grass and Lottie toddle unsteadily, the Labrador ambling after them.

'William's grandparents used to invite the Americans over from the base all the time during the war. They thought it was the least they could do. And then, after the war, they kept in touch with them and preserved the buildings.'

'Did you ever meet them?'

'Not the grandfather. He died before I met William, but I knew his grandmother for a year or two before she died. William's father had inherited the farm by then, and she was living in a house in the village, but William took me to see her several times. She was lovely. Very kind, very sympathetic. I'm sure the Americans must have liked her a lot. His father, Peter, was nice too, but not so keen on the idea of preserving the airfield. He was all for selling off the runways and knocking down most of the buildings. The concrete's worth a fortune as hardcore, you see – they use it under motorways – so he had a point. Anyway, he died before anything like that happened and then William took over. His mother went on living here with us but she died, too, last year.'

We progressed upstairs with the children to look at gloriously old-fashioned bedrooms and a nursery with a rocking horse, a Victorian dolls' house, toys made out of wood, and an army of lead soldiers. The bathroom had a claw-footed tub and a lavatory with mahogany seat and a cistern chain with a china handle that said *Pull*. Jessica opened another door at the end of the house.

'This is the single spare room. Your mother most probably had this one. It's nice and quiet and it has one of the best views.'

The faded wallpaper was roses entwined with honeysuckle. There was a fireplace, a chest of drawers, a wardrobe with a mirror door, a bed with a green silk eiderdown. Jessica opened the window and pointed. 'You can't see it now, but the old runway's right there – going straight through the middle of the wheatfields. When you came up from Nightingale Lane onto the peri track which way did you turn?'

'Left. Then I went round until I found a runway and drove down it.'

'That would have been the main one – this one. There are two short ones that cross it but you probably didn't notice them because they intersect at an angle and the wheat hides them. Of course, during the war there wouldn't have been any crops growing on the airfield – William's grandfather was only allowed to farm outside the perimeter. So it would have been easy to see most of the main runway from this room and the bombers coming and going.'

I helped with the children's bathtime, pushing rubber ducks and boats up and down and blowing soap bubbles and getting wet. It seemed a very long time since I'd done that with Flavia. Jack graciously invited me to read the bedtime story and I was even allowed to choose from among the old books on the nursery shelves. It was a hard decision but, in the end, I went for an old favourite.

'*Once upon a time there was a poor miller who had one beautiful daughter . . .*'

William Layton returned soon after the children had gone to sleep. He was a tall, sunburned and clear-eyed young man; I could see at once why the tradition started by his grandfather had been carried on and why the old airfield was in such good hands. He must have been tired after a long day's harvesting but he didn't show it.

'Did Jess tell you there's a reunion lunch here this weekend? I hope you'll come to it. There'll be more than two hundred Americans who served at Halfpenny Green. And my aunt will be coming, too. She was here in this house all during the war, as a child, so she'll almost certainly remember your mother. You must talk to her. You'll stay to supper now, won't you?'

While Jessica was cooking, he fetched a big aerial photograph of the old airfield and smoothed it out on the kitchen table. 'Look, you can see the runways very clearly – the main one runs west to east, the cross ones go south-west to north-east and south-east to north-west. Then you've got the peri track going all the way round. Of course, when this photo was taken in 1944, the track was twice the width it is now but my grandfather narrowed it after the war – it took up too much crop space. When the RAF were here they were flying Blenheims and Bostons, then the Americans brought B-17s and put up a whole lot more buildings. There were nearly three thousand Americans serving on the base.'

The sites were marked in ink on the photograph: control tower, technical site, admin, mess, barracks, fuel stores, sick quarters, ammunition dump, bomb dump. He pointed them all out. 'Some of these were on land requisitioned from other farms. They dispersed everything quite a bit, so it didn't make an easy target. Our farmhouse is here – more or less in the middle of it. Grandfather lost fifty acres but he got it all back after the war.' He smiled at me. 'After supper, I'll take you on a quick tour, if you like.'

The tour was in an old Jeep that had been given by the appreciative invaders to William's grandfather. The grandson drove it like a Yank and we roared round the airfield on that summer's evening, top down and in great style with the black Labrador in the back, his ears flying. The family had always had black Labradors, William told me. This one, Smut, was six generations down from his grandfather's, called Susie, in a direct line. All given names beginning with S. He showed me inside one or two of the huts, including the old radio shack where there were pin-up paintings on the walls – improbably perfect naked girls in tottering heels, stepping into, or out of, frilly panties.

'We've done our best to preserve them,' William said. 'But the winters don't do them much good. Some people think they ought to be moved to a museum, but I think they should stay. This is where they belong, for better or worse.'

We zoomed round the peri track. There were more buildings scattered further afield but they had been left to their fate, overgrown with brambles and nettles and ivy, windows broken – like the Liberator co-pilot's briefing room. It was impossible, William said, to preserve them all. We finished at the control tower and he led the way up the concrete stairway into the flying control room above. It ran the width of the building, windows and balcony overlooking the airfield. The cream and green wall paint had flaked down to the brick in places and all the furniture and equipment had gone, except for a blackboard on the back wall, white lines dividing it into sections. On a small table lay the visitors' book.

'Perhaps your mother came back here and wrote in it. Would you like to take a look?'

Perhaps my father had too? I turned the pages, searching for Ma's name but without any real expectation of finding it. The visitors hailed from all over the United States; some had added comments.

Sure is great to see Halfpenny Green again. Seems like it was the best time of my life. Something I'll never forget. That one was from Idaho.

Glad I came back for one last look. North Dakota.

Gave me goosebumps to see the old place – and looking a lot better than I do. Thanks to all you good folks who've kept Halfpenny Green that way. Texas.

So many ghosts. So many memories. Maryland.

I went on turning pages, reading snatches here and there. And then, when I had almost reached the end of the entries, I saw her writing. Her signature, still strong: *Daisy Byrne* and the date, 15th October 1991, sandwiched in between Nebraska and Illinois. She must have come back soon after she had been diagnosed and had known that she was dying.

I said, 'She did come – last October. Her signature's here.'

'I'm sorry we didn't meet her.' He was looking at me sympathetically. 'A lot of them don't like to talk about it – I've found that out. I expect some memories can be too painful.'

I wondered if she had looked for *his* signature, and whether she had found it.

I said, 'I have an old photo too. Taken here of a B-17 crew. It belonged to my mother. If it's not a nuisance, I'd like to see if any of the Americans at the reunion recognize them.'

'We'll pass it around,' he said. 'See what happens.'

He drove me back to the farmhouse. The sun was setting, turning the skies to pale pink and bathing thc land in warm, golden light. William saw me to my car. 'My aunt has an old album that belonged to my grandmother – all wartime photos taken on the farm. I'll ask her to bring it to the reunion.'

With his permission, I spent the next day on the airfield, sketching and painting with my book, my pencils, my paintbox and a bottle of water, as well as some sandwiches provided by my kind B & B hostess. The old huts and hangers, the deserted control tower, the overgrown runways all made wonderful subjects.

On the day after, on an impulse, I drove over to the American war cemetery at Madingley outside Cambridge and looked at the rows and rows of white crosses, with here and there a Star of

David, and I walked along the long wall that bore the names of thousands more Americans with no known grave. There were several other visitors, one of them a man alone who was standing, hands in pockets, staring out over the graves. I guessed that he was an American – something about his build and his clothes and his hair, though it's not so easy to tell these days. He turned and walked towards me, passing with a nod and a smile – a man probably in his seventies and almost certainly ex-service. I smiled back and we started a casual conversation about the peacefulness of the cemetery, the lovely view over the Cambridgeshire countryside, how well it was kept, how beautiful the roses and the water-lily pools, and how impressive the chapel. How sad it all was.

He nodded towards the graves. 'I knew some of those guys. We were over here together – only I got to go home and they didn't. Still, this is a good place for them if it had to be that way.'

I said, 'Where were you stationed?'

'Rattlesden. 447th Bomb Group. I came over in mid '44.'

'As a pilot?'

'No, I was a bombardier.' He smiled. 'I only got to fly the plane when we dropped the bombs.'

I clutched at a straw. 'I don't suppose you ever came across any of the crews stationed at Halfpenny Green?'

'No, can't say I did. Only the guys at our own

base. We stayed around there, or Cambridge. Mostly we went to London if we could.' He looked at me uncertainly. 'Any connection here?'

'Not exactly. My mother was in the WAAF and stationed at Halfpenny Green.'

'You don't say? I came across a few of your WAAFs – they were pretty special. And your RAF – well, we thought a lot of those guys. We had our losses, but, oh boy, so did they.'

We chatted a bit more before he left to rejoin his wife, who was shopping in Cambridge. I stayed, sitting on a bench in the sunshine for a while, in company with the thousands of young Americans who had never gone back home.

At thc weekend, I returned to the farmhouse, as invited, just before midday. The weather was kind – a warm, sunny day with a bit of a breeze, blue skies and a few puffy white clouds to provide a perfect backdrop to the scene. The veterans were due to arrive with their wives by coach at half past and everything was ready, including a Scots piper in full Highland rig. They were right on time. I stood with William and Jessica and the two children, beside the perimeter track, and watched the tops of the coaches moving along between the fields of wheat. My heart was thudding away. It was quite possible that my father was one of them – that he might recognize himself in the photo when it was passed round. What then? What would I say? What story could I tell? I hadn't quite covered that.

The coaches came round the corner and drew to a halt. I could see faces at the windows – men and women, well past middle age – many of them wearing baseball caps. Some were smiling and waving, others simply staring out. The doors opened and the piper stepped forward with his bagpipes and, as the first of the Americans appeared, he began to play.

They came down the steps rather hesitantly and, after they had been greeted by William and Jessica, the piper led them in a long, straggling line towards the house. I had hung back, standing apart from the scene, and I searched the faces of the men as they passed by me. Not one looked anything like the pilot in the photo, but I did notice that one or two of them had tears in their eyes.

Thanks to the weather, the pre-lunch drinks were served outside on the lawn. A well-dressed woman came up to me, smiling.

'I'm Madeleine Lucas, William's aunt, and you must be Daisy's daughter,' she said. 'William told me you'd be here and I can see the likeness.'

'You remember her?'

'Certainly I do. I was seven when she came to live with us. Peter, my brother, was five. We called her Daisy right from the first and we adored her. She was one of the family. She'd play games with us and read bedtime stories, whenever she was off duty. I always remember how well she did the voices – she made the characters come alive for us. We were all very sorry when she went.'

'When did she leave exactly?'

'It would have been quite soon after my eighth birthday in early February 1944 – I remember that she made the cake for it. She was an awfully good cook – but of course you'd know that perfectly well – she used to help Mother quite a lot. Then she got ill – with very bad flu, I think – and was taken off to the base hospital. After that, they sent her home to convalesce. She never came back to Halfpenny Green, so I suppose they must have eventually posted her somewhere else.'

'Actually, she got married.'

'Did she? I'm not surprised. I've brought the old photo album, by the way. It's got a picture of your mother in it. I'll show you after lunch.'

There was no time for prevarication. 'Do you happen to remember if any of the Americans was . . . special to her?'

'One she was in love with, you mean? I'm not sure if we'd have noticed, at that age. But there must have been lots of them after her. I do remember them always coming into the kitchen whenever she was there.'

I brought out my photo. 'I found this after she'd died . . . do you recognize any of them?'

She looked at it carefully, but shook her head. 'I'm sorry, I can't say I do. My parents used to invite the crews to the house, but it was usually in the evenings when we'd have been in bed. They were coming and going the whole time so they didn't make a very lasting impression, and, of course, so many of them were killed.' She gave me back the photo. 'Are you hoping that one of these will be here today?'

'It's rather a vain hope.'

She shaded her eyes and looked around the not-so-young gathering. 'I'm afraid he wouldn't look quite the same.'

The barn had been hung with Stars and Stripes and Union Jacks, the long trestle tables decorated with flowers and more flags, caterers hired to serve the lunch. I found myself sitting next to a former weather officer. He'd been at the mission briefings, he told me, warning the crews what to expect weather-wise, and, mostly, it had been bad news. They'd sometimes had to fly in conditions that would have grounded the birds. The weather in Europe had been much worse in those days, he thought – colder, wetter, foggier. And if it was OK in England, it was clamped-in over Germany – or the other way around. There was no easy pattern, the weather changed constantly, so that forecasting wasn't much better than guesswork half the time. They might as well have used a crystal ball.

Towards the end of the lunch there were speeches – first one of thanks from the President of the Bomb Group Association, then a warm reply from William. There were toasts – to the Queen, to America and one, soberly, to absent friends. And then William was on his feet again, holding up my photo, ready to be passed round the tables. If anyone recognized themselves, or any of the crew, would they let him know. I watched it being handed from one man to the next and heads being shaken. The weather man was talking about the food on the base now and how he'd hated the Brussels sprouts and the dried eggs and the boiled mutton. And then his wife, sitting beyond him, leaned across and started to tell me about rationing in the US during the war and what *they'd* had to do without. They were a nice couple, but I hardly listened. The next man to look at the photo was taking his time over it and I held my breath until he, too, shook his head and passed it on.

The caterers were clearing away plates and some of the visitors were starting to get up from the table, blocking my view of the photo's progress. Eventually, it came down our side. The weather officer's wife, still talking, handed it on to her husband. He glanced at it briefly. He could never remember individual crews, he said. All he could remember was seeing rows and rows of faces at the briefings, and the faces changed all the time.

William was announcing that the coach would leave for a tour of the airfield in fifteen minutes and people were drifting away, out of the barn. I drifted with them.

And then I heard my name being called and William came up with a small man wearing a baseball cap and a zip-fronted nylon jacket over plaid trousers.

'This is Joe Deerfield from Arizona, Juliet. He was a ground crew chief at Halfpenny Green from 1943 onwards.'

I looked at him without much hope. 'Oh?'

The American held up the snapshot and tapped it with his forefinger. 'Yeah, one of our armourers was a camera freak and used to take pictures of the crews. Early '44 this'd've been. You can see the snow on the ground.'

'You recognize them?'

'Sure. I remember these guys – they were a great crew. One of the best I ever came across, specially the captain. Some of the pilots could be bastards and chew you out for things that weren't your fault. You know – make out you hadn't fixed somethin' good when *they'd* screwed up, or got the jitters. Some of 'em swore things weren't workin' just so's they had an excuse for turnin' back. Not too many of those, but it happened. Don't blame them now for it – they were just kids with a rotten job to do and some of them were real scared – but I sure as hell blamed them then.' The finger tapped again. 'Not this guy, though. Never him. No, sir. I remember he got his plane back when it was all shot to hell and the co-pilot hurt bad. He was killed later on, though. Matter of fact, I think it was just after this picture was taken – if I remember right. Tough, but it happened all the time.'

I said, 'He wasn't killed. He survived. He was

on the run in France for months and then repatriated.'

'Hey, is that so? Well, I'm sure glad to hear it. He was a great guy.'

I said, 'Do you also remember his name?'

'Hell, no . . . sorry. I'm good at faces, but names're somethin' else. And there were so many.' He tapped some more, frowning. 'Maybe it'll come to me, if I think real hard about it.'

I looked over his shoulder at the photo. He was tapping the wrong man. 'But *this* one's the pilot, isn't he? The one in the middle?'

He shook his head. 'Nope, that's the co-pilot. He'd only been with them two or three missions – took over from the one got hurt bad. *This* one here's the captain – the one I was talking about. This guy on the right.'

I'd been wrong all the time. It wasn't the one in the middle, cap tilted back, with the open, friendly and honest face. The regular-looking guy. It was the man standing at the end, a little apart, with hands balled into fists on hips, his sheepskin collar turned up round his ears, his cap brim pulled down at an angle so that I could only see part of his face – just the eyes, the nose and the corners of the mouth lifted in a sort of half-smile.

'Do you remember anything else about him? Where he came from, for instance?'

'Yeah, I do remember that. He and me used to joke about the English weather – us both coming from warmer climes, as you might say. Hell, we'd forgotten what the sun looked like. He was from California.'

'Do you know where in California?'

'Can't remember that. But it was California all right. I can see him now – standin' there just like in this photo – makin' some crack about the goddam Limey weather. Hey, I'll be darned, his name's just come back to me. They used to call him Ham.'

'Ham? Was that short for something?'

He shrugged. 'Must've been. I can only remember him as Ham.'

He gave me back my photo and moved off to board the coach. William followed, to give the conducted tour of the airfield, and I went into the house in search of his aunt. I found her sitting alone in the drawing room, an old photo album open on her knees. She looked up with a smile. 'I've been taking a trip down memory lane. And I've found the photo of Daisy. Do you know, I can even remember my mother snapping it with her box Brownie.' She patted the sofa seat beside her. 'Come and take a look.'

Ma wasn't in WAAF uniform; instead, she was wearing bibbed dungarees and a blouse and she was standing beside a cornstook. The dungarees looked much too big and she'd tied them round her waist with string. She was wearing a spotted scarf round her hair. I knew the scarf: it was red and white and she had had it for years. Flavia and I had found it when we were going through her clothes and had kept it in the suitcase, to remember her by.

'It was exactly this time of year – harvest time. She was helping with it, so I suppose she must have had some leave then. And I remember that the Americans used to come over and help too. Father must have been glad of all the extra hands he could get in those days. Here, you have it.'

She detached the photo carefully from its corners and gave it to me. We went through the album, looking at snaps of herself and her brother as children, of the house and the garden, of dogs and cats, the ducks on the pond, the farmworkers in the yard, the grandfather driving a tractor – still only a young man, then. And, further on, pictures of Americans in uniform standing around on the sunlit lawn, talking and drinking. I studied those closely but most had their backs turned, or were too far away to see clearly. There were a few shots of the airfield, too, taken at a distance – of the control tower and hangars, Jeeps and trucks and men, and of bombers – one of them taking off.

'Photography was strictly forbidden, of course,' Madeleine Lucas said. 'But Mother did it just the same. I've still got her box Brownie somewhere.' She closed the album. 'Did you have any luck with your crew photograph?'

'Some.' I told her what had happened and she asked to see it again. I pointed out the pilot.

She looked at it more closely than before. 'Of

course, you can't see him properly but, you know, I think I *do* remember him. It's that smile . . . One of them came upstairs once when Daisy was reading us a bedtime story. He stayed in the doorway, listening, and I'm sure it was this one. I might be wrong, though. The Americans were always smiling at us. Always laughing and joking and playing games. I suppose we must have reminded them of their brothers and sisters back home – the families they'd left behind. But I remember *his* smile particularly. I'm not quite sure why. You know how you remember certain things very vividly from childhood – for no particular reason.'

'He looks tall in the photo.'

'I expect he was – most of them were. Tall, strong young men. Or so they seemed to us, at our age. They used to pick Peter up and carry him around on their shoulders. I was a bit too big for that.' She looked at me. 'I won't ask why you want to find him so much – it's none of my business. But I do hope you do.'

I had part of a name and part of a face, and an American state. And two people remembered him. It was progress – of a kind.

Later, I drove back across the old airfield – past the huts and the hangers. I stopped at the control tower and went through the visitors' book again. There was only one entry of any possible significance – a Sven L. Hammerskeld, but he was from Minnesota which I knew was way up in the far north of the United States, almost in Canada. It seemed extremely unlikely that a warm-weather-loving Californian would ever have moved there.

I carried on slowly down the length of the main runway with its rustling skirts of wheat. And I thought of Maryland's heartfelt entry in the visitors' book. *So many ghosts. So many memories.*

PART II

Seven

When the war started on 3rd September 1939, Daisy Woods was sixteen years old, still at school and living with her family in Ealing, west London. Her older sisters, Violet and Lily, both secretaries, volunteered immediately for the WRNS. Iris, the next in age, escaped from a bank to join the Women's Land Army, while Primrose, who had just finished her schooling, went off to drive ambulances for the FANYs. It took Daisy a year to persuade her parents to let her leave school. By then the Battle of Britain was being fought and the country on the brink of invasion by the Germans. Then the Blitz began. She was still too young to join any of the services and so she spent the waiting time learning shorthand and typing. As soon as she had passed her diploma, she presented herself at a recruiting office for the Women's Auxiliary Royal Air Force and three months later she received a letter instructing her to report for initial training.

Morecambe in October was cold and wet, the billet uncomfortable and the food revolting, but she enjoyed the rest of it – the marching around, the PT, the lectures, even wearing the uniform, and she made friends easily with the other girls. When the training was over she was given seven days' leave which she spent at home in Ealing, during which time the Japanese bombed the American fleet at Pearl Harbor and the United States entered the war. Vernon from next door happened to be home too. In past years, when they were children, he would have climbed over the garden fence; now that they were grown-up he rang politely at the front door.

'I heard you were back, Daisy. How did it go?'

'Not so bad. I'm being posted to Suffolk – to an RAF bomber station. Aircraftwoman Woods, clerk, general duties – but I think I'm going to be chained to a typewriter.'

'Will you mind?'

'I'd sooner have done something a bit more exciting, but they latched onto my shorthand and typing. How about you, Vernon? How's Cambridge?'

He adjusted his spectacles. 'Actually, I'm not at Cambridge any more – not since last January. I've been given a wartime job. Sort of commandeered. Cambridge will have to wait until after it's all over.'

'What sort of job?'

'Oh, nothing very special. Just government communications. But it makes up for being turned down by the services.'

They'd rejected him because of his poor eyesight and she knew it had hurt. While other young men were marching off to war, he'd been left behind to explain why he hadn't gone with them. She said, 'I'm really glad for you. It's bound to be something important, if they've sought you out. Is it to do with the maths?'

'Sort of.'

'So we're both doing our bit.'

He smiled at her. 'Yes, we are.'

He'd grown up, but he had scarcely changed from the shy boy with wire-framed spectacles and sticking-up hair who had peered over the fence one day years ago when his family had moved in next door – the only child of old-fashioned parents who had seemed more like grandparents. Violet and Lily and Iris had alarmed him and Primrose had teased him, though not unkindly, but Daisy had understood his shyness and his loneliness. He was exceptionally clever, especially at maths which was her worst subject, and he had often helped her with her school homework. The A plus marks and 'Excellent's that she had received had been entirely due to Vernon, until finally the teacher had rumbled why her classwork was so poor by comparison. After that, she went back to the B minuses and Cs.

She said, 'I think the war's going to go on for ages, Vernon, don't you?'

'I'm afraid so. We haven't been doing too well in North Africa. Or in the Atlantic. And the Japanese seem to be going full steam ahead in the Far East. Still, we're getting one or two breaks, at last, and the Americans will make a big difference, now they're with us. It gives us a chance.'

'Why on earth didn't they come and help us before?'

'I suppose a lot of them didn't see why they should get involved, since it wasn't their war. They needed a good enough reason.'

'Well, they've got one now – thanks to the Japanese. I hope they're going to help us fight the Germans as well.'

He said, 'I think it's going to be a long, hard struggle, but we'll win through in the end. For one thing, Hitler never managed to invade England, so the Americans will have an ideal base for their troops to get at Germany.'

He didn't stay much longer. He had to get back, he said. They'd only given him the one day off to come home and see his father, who wasn't at all well.

'Yes, we know. I'm very sorry. I hope he gets better.' The man who had always seemed old as God to her, had had a stroke and was, apparently, in a bad way.

'Which RAF station in Suffolk are they posting you to?' he asked. 'I'll write to you there – if that's all right. And will you let me know how you're getting on?'

She promised she would and waved to him from the front door as he went. His clothes had never seemed to fit him in the past – the grey shorts always too long, the school caps too big or too small, the blazers looking as though they belonged to some other boy. Now, his tweed overcoat flapped about him as he walked, the brown trilby looked a size too small and the long woollen scarf trailed, unwound, from his neck.

'He's sweet on you – you know that, don't you?' Primrose had once told her. 'Dotty about you, poor old thing.'

He'd never said so in words, but she knew that it was true. And she knew that *he* knew that she was awfully fond of him – but that that was all. The difficulty was not to hurt him.

Halfpenny Green, the RAF station in Suffolk, turned out to be both good and bad. The good part was that it was in beautiful countryside near a lovely village; the bad that the station itself was cold, damp, muddy, and uncomfortable. It had been built – recently and hurriedly – on land requisitioned from a farmer and the buildings were prefabricated huts and sheds of corrugated iron, bolted together and laid on concrete foundations, heated, if at all, by temperamental stoves with a measly ration of coke. Draughty, cheerless and bleak. The squadron flew twin-engined bombers – Blenheims and Bostons – and shortly after she arrived, there was a raid on Bremen with no aircraft lost. Most ops, she soon discovered, were not anything like as successful. There had been steady losses of men and planes, repeated failures even to find targets, let alone hit them, and bombers constantly turning back. The winter weather hadn't exactly helped – the fogs, the dense cloud, the ice and snow, were all as much their enemy as the Germans.

She had no difficulty settling in with the other WAAFs, who were a decent, friendly lot. As she had expected, she found herself chained to a typewriter, bashing away at routine letters and memos and long lists, and envying the WAAFs who were doing far more interesting things – plotting in the ops room, enciphering and deciphering secret messages, operating radios, interpreting raid and reconnaissance photos. Her application to transfer trades was turned down flat; she had learned shorthand and typing too well to be spared.

She watched the crews come and go. Thirty ops to a tour and then they were done – if they survived. Some did, some didn't. The unlucky ones simply vanished. One moment they were there walking around, living and breathing, talking, laughing, the next they weren't. Lockers and drawers were instantly cleared, beds stripped, no traces left to discourage their replacements or upset station morale. Early on, she learned that it was better to avoid getting to know any of them too well: much less heartbreaking. But sometimes it happened.

She met Bill in the Mad Monk, the most popular of the three pubs in Halfpenny Green. There was a well-trodden footpath leading from the airfield perimeter down through a wood to the village – a wood where nightingales were supposed to sing in the spring and early summer. As usual, the bar was crowded with RAF and WAAF and with Land Army girls from the hostel nearby. Bill was standing at the bar, pint mug in his fist, talking to another officer, and turned his head and smiled at her across the room. From the wings on his chest, she saw that he was a pilot and therefore one of those who could so easily do the vanishing act at any time; it seemed only kind to smile back. After a while, he elbowed his way through the crush to where she was standing and smiled at her again.

'How do you do? I'm Bill Hudson. What're you drinking?'

He was from Yorkshire with a Yorkshireman's blunt speech and ways. She liked him a lot and went on liking him until he was killed three months later on a raid over Cologne. After that, she avoided the crews completely.

Spring arrived and the weather improved, making more bombing raids possible and more aircraft and their men liable to vanish. Bremen, Hamburg, Berlin, Wilhelmshaven, Düsseldorf, Hanover, Kiel . . . raid after raid throughout the spring and summer of 1941. During the summer and autumn more prefabricated buildings were erected on the station and there were rumours – rumours that the squadron might be switching to four-engined bombers, rumours of heavier and still heavier raids being planned, rumours of all kinds, including that the American Air Force was coming.

* * *

On the day when the Japanese had attacked the American fleet at Pearl Harbor, Howard Hamilton had been in his fourth and final year at Berkeley university in northern California. As soon as he had heard the news, he had slung his belongings together, got into his hot rod and driven very fast down the Pacific Coast highway to his home in Pasadena, east of Los Angeles. On arrival, he had told his parents that he was volunteering at once for the US Army Air Corps. They had made no attempt to dissuade him, knowing it would be a waste of breath. He was twenty-one, had held a private pilot's licence at seventeen and flown their Aeronca Chief all around California and the neighbouring states. His current girlfriend, Lola, the latest in a long line, had wept on his shoulder, but to no avail.

'What's the rush, Howard? Why not wait and see what happens?'

'It's already happened. We've finally got off our asses and I'm sure as hell not going to be left behind.'

'But why the Air Force? Wouldn't you be safer on the ground?'

'Not necessarily. And I like it better in the air.' He handed her his handkerchief. 'Come on, Lola, you'll soon find some other guy.'

She dabbed gingerly at her mascara. 'Not like you.'

He spent Christmas at home and, soon afterwards, received his Active Duty Orders and reported to a classification centre in San

Antonio, Texas. After the physical exam and the clothing and dog-tag issue, he was assigned to a cadet squadron and given a serial number. Then came Pre-Flight: classes, lectures, study, physical training, drill, parades. The senior medical officer gave them a talk on sex and VD which he didn't need – the guy had got it all wrong when he assumed only the married men knew about women. He graduated without trouble and went on to Primary Training at Sikeston, Missouri. His previous flying experience gave him a big advantage over most of the other cadets, some of whom got washed out, but he still had to go through the mill. Aerobatics were the fun part – snap rolls, slow rolls, loops and spins, practised again and again. He figured the better he could show he could do them, the more likely they'd assign him to fighters. For Basic Training he was sent to Independence, Kansas, and, after he'd got through that, he went to Eagle Pass, Texas, to fly AT-6s. It was at that point that he was told, to his bitter disappointment, that he'd been assigned to fly bombers. They gave him some good reasons: he was on the tall side for a fighter cockpit, he had a strong enough physique to handle the heavy controls of a bomber, and, just then, they needed bomber pilots more than they needed fighter guys.

At Pampa, Texas, he learned to fly twin-engined planes. He learned some formation flying, night flying, instrument flying, how to shoot landings, how to fly on one engine, how to compensate drag, all kinds of things. Most of it he found pretty easy, except for night flying in formation, trying to stay in position when all he could see was the white light on the tail of the lead plane. That was tough.

At graduation, he was given his commission – Second Lieutenant, Army of the United States – and his wings. After two weeks' leave, he went off to learn to fly B-17 four-engined bombers.

At Alexandria, Louisiana, he met his crew – three other officers and six enlisted men – and went with them to Moody Field, Georgia, for combat training. Much of the time was spent practising box-formation flying – socked in so tight his waist gunner swore he could have leaned out and shaken the next door tail gunner's hand. He saw planes collide and men die. By the end of the training, Hamilton had made First Lieutenant. He and his crew collected a brand spanking new B-17 Flying Fortress from Grand Island, Nebraska and took it over to Bangor, Maine. From there they flew to Goose Bay, Labrador, where they were holed up for over a week because of lousy weather. They took off across the North Atlantic in company with another forty-five bombers and headed for Iceland, and an overnight stop there. They landed at Prestwick in Scotland, minus two of the other B-17s, on a cold and drizzly morning in late April, 1943, sixteen months after he had left his home in Pasadena.

* * *

Daisy had been unchained from the typewriter and sent on an Admin course from which she emerged as Corporal Woods. After several more months had passed, the WAAF flight officer interviewed her again. She was considered, she was told, to have certain qualities that could make a good officer, and good officers were needed. What precisely those qualities were was left unsaid and she didn't ask. Another course – longer this time – turned her into an assistant section officer. The promotion brought her into closer contact with the bomber crews on the station. She saw them daily in the Mess, and around the station, chatted to them, learned their names, attended briefings, and, when she could, went down to the start of the runway with the faithful little band of station personnel to wave them off on ops. She knew which men were in which plane: Bob, Harry, John, Steve, Don, Ken . . . there was no escape from the horrible reality. And when they failed to return – which happened more and more – their faces stayed fixed in her mind's eye for a very long time afterwards. Faces belonging to boys not quite men – adolescent spots, peach-fuzz beards, eager grins. She had fended off the hopeful and clumsy advances as gently as possible, kept what distance she could, but it broke her heart when they went missing.

The rumour about the Americans was true. The RAF were moving out and handing the station over. The WAAF flight officer sent for

Daisy once more and told her that she had been assigned to stay on with an RAF liaison officer.

'Do I have to, ma'am? I'd prefer not to.'

'Of course you do. It's an order. We all have to make sacrifices in wartime. And I doubt if any of the other WAAFs on this station would have minded making this particular one.' The flight officer, an older woman, stared at her. 'You're not anti-American, are you?'

'I've never met any of them, ma'am. But they've taken an awful long time getting over here.'

'Don't hold it against them. They'll make up for it. You must put any personal prejudices behind you, Assistant Section Officer. It's your duty. The Americans are coming here to help us. We have to work together now to win the war, stand shoulder to shoulder. We're comrades-in-arms. That's going to be part of your job.'

'Yes, ma'am.'

'See that you remember it.'

'Yes, ma'am.'

She was given leave and went home to Ealing. Vernon's father had died while she had been away and she went next door to see his mother and sat dutifully in the gloomy and silent house, listening to Mrs Byrne talking of her late husband, and of her son.

'I hardly ever see Vernon these days . . . the last time was when he came home for the funeral and he looked exhausted. So pale and thin. They're working him much too hard.'

'I'm sure it's important work, Mrs Byrne.'

'He won't tell me anything about it. Not a word. Has he said anything to you?'

'Only that it's to do with government communications, or something like that.'

'I thought he might have told you more, seeing how much he cares for you. You *do* realize that, don't you? Not that he's admitted it to me, but I can tell. But you don't feel the same about him, do you?'

'Not quite the same. I'm sorry.'

'It's not something one can help. All I ask is that you don't hurt him.'

'I'll try not to, Mrs Byrne. I promise.'

At the end of her leave she returned to Halfpenny Green to find that the first Americans had already arrived and a huge Stars and Stripes was flapping from the station flagpole.

'We're in a foreign country now,' Flight Lieutenant Dimmock, the RAF liaison officer, remarked drily when she reported for duty. 'And we don't speak the language.'

She soon saw what he meant. The Yanks looked different, dressed differently, spoke differently, behaved differently. They even saluted differently – a casual, sloppy sort of flick of the hand, nothing like a smart RAF salute. She encountered them loping along like wolves, hands in pockets, chewing gum, leering at her and whistling after her as she passed them on her bike. And she heard them complaining loudly about the conditions – the mud and the draughty tin huts, the trickling cold showers and the useless stoves, and the uneatable food. What had they expected to find in a country that had been fighting for its life for more than three years? Steaks and fresh eggs? Five-star, luxury accommodation?

The Waafery had also been taken over – by American nurses and American Red Cross girls in fancy uniforms and nylon stockings. Instead, she had been billeted with the Layton family whose land had been requisitioned for the airfield. She hauled her kit on her bike over there, wondering if they had been obliged to have her, just as they'd been obliged to give up their acres. There was a black Labrador lying outside the side door of the farmhouse and it got to its feet and wagged its tail. She worked the clapper of the old bell hanging from the wall and patted the dog. The women who came to the door smiled at her in a friendly way, too. 'That's Susie; she's very gentle. And you must be Assistant Section Officer Woods who's going to live with us.'

She followed her through a scullery into an old-fashioned kitchen where she was introduced to the two children who were sitting at the table, having tea. The girl had long fair plaits tied with ribbons; the boy was smaller and darker and rather solemn.

'I'm Madeleine and I'm seven,' the girl told her. 'This is Peter and he's only five.'

'I'm Daisy,' she said. 'And I'm twenty.'

Mrs Layton took her upstairs. She was shown

a bathroom with the biggest bath she'd ever seen and a lavatory with a box-shaped wooden seat and a china handle that said *Pull* dangling from an overhead cistern. Her bedroom was at the end of the house. Its walls were papered with a pattern of roses entwined with honeysuckle, and the bed had a green silk eiderdown.

'I hope you'll be comfortable, Daisy.'

'It's lovely,' she said, thinking of the Nissen huts in the Waafery. 'Thank you.'

Left alone, she put her belongings away in the wardrobe and chest of drawers. Then she went and stood at the open window, looking out at the view across the airfield – to the woods and fields beyond, and then more woods and more fields beyond those, rolling away into the far distance. She could see the main runway quite clearly – a long dark gash across the farmland – and, as she stood there, a four-engined bomber began its take-off run. She watched it go roaring past, a big white star painted on its flank. It climbed effortlessly into the skies: powerful, pushy, American.

No sooner had Hamilton and his crew landed at Prestwick than the brand new B-17 Fort was taken away from them. They continued, ignominiously, by truck to Glasgow and by train from there on to their assigned combat station in Suffolk, in the east of England. Its name was Halfpenny Green.

His co-pilot, Gene, who had never been out

of the US, was bemused. 'What the hell sort of a name is that?'

'An English one. A half penny is one of their coins. Only they pronounce it hay penny. I guess the green part is a village green.'

The final stage of the journey was made in a toy train that fussed and puffed its way along. The countryside was beautiful and it was good to see a piece of England apparently untouched by war, unlike other places they'd seen since they'd arrived. The bomb damage had shocked them, so had the dreary shabbiness of it all – people, buildings, shops, streets . . . everything. Grey, grey, grey.

He smoked a cigarette and stared through the compartment window. This was *so* goddam green, the fields *so* small – hedgerows dividing them up into a patchwork quilt. Thatched cottages, little creeks spanned by hump-backed stone bridges, church spires and towers, ancient woods. Straight out of a kid's picture book. Maybe he'd get the chance to do some sketching while he was over. He'd been to England before in 1938, on a vacation trip to Europe on his own, but he'd spent all the time in London before he'd headed off for Paris and Florence and Rome and Berlin, drawing the sights by day, and painting the towns red by night. The German girls had been the best, he'd reckoned; he'd always preferred blondes.

The train stopped at a hundred little toy stations. They had no names and hardly anybody was about. Each time there was a lot of hissing from the engine and clouds of steam, maybe a couple of doors clunking open and shut, some old guy in uniform blowing a whistle and flapping a green flag, and they were off again, huffing and puffing along to the next one.

When they finally got where they were going, it was a different story. The platform was jam-packed with servicemen – mostly British army and RAF, but he spotted some American uniforms among them. From the way they were spruced up and looking so cheery, he figured they must be going on leave to London. The truck that picked up his crew took them on another picture-book ride through English lanes made by English yokels staggering home from the pub. As he had guessed, the Green after the Haypenny was a village green and, boy, what a green and what a village! Not even the rain bucketing down by then could spoil it. They were all impressed – Milo, the little ball-turret gunner from Brooklyn whose life had been spent in pool halls, had his mouth hanging wide open as they went by.

The base was a lot less impressive. During training, they'd all gotten pretty used to a lot of shitty deals, but this one took the cake. Nothing wrong with the surroundings – more gorgeous countryside – but the place had been built from tin on top of mud, the plumbing was a joke and, even in May, it was cold and damp as hell. He stood with Gene, his co-pilot, his bombardier,

Lee, and navigator, Don, grimly surveying their new home – corrugated metal, concrete floor, bare-bulb lighting, some kind of stove in the middle with a flue pipe that went up through a leaky roof, eight army issue cots – four on each side and each with a mattress and two blankets. His radio man, Carl, engineer, Cliff and the gunners, Ken, Milo, Merle and Alvin were in another building a couple of hundred yards or so away. They soon found out that there was no coal for the stove and that, even if there had been, the thing wasn't worth a damn, anyway.

The day after they were at the quartermaster, checking out their combat gear and finding their way round – mess halls, officers' and enlisted men's clubs, movie hall . . . all in the same sort of prefabricated metal huts and all within easy walking distance. The admin and flight buildings were a lot further away, out on the southern edge of the airfield, and they were trucked over there. As soon as they could, they bought bikes from some shark in the village who was making a killing selling old wrecks to Yanks. Unlike American bikes, the Limey ones had handlebar brakes and the first time he used them, he went clean over the top. Most of the other guys' brakes didn't work at all and they kept crashing into things.

For the first couple of weeks they'd learned the routine and collected yet more bruises in the blackout, walking into walls, tripping over kerbs and falling down steps before they'd finally gotten used to it. When they started flying they did practice missions, pretending to bomb places all over England. On one of them another rookie crew got careless and flew their Fort into a hill. Its officers had slept in the other four beds in Hamilton's hut; pretty soon four more had taken their place and nobody said a thing.

And it went on raining.

Flight Lieutenant Dimmock stuck his head round the door of Daisy's office, pipe in mouth. 'How about a drink down at the pub? I think we could both do with one.'

'Last time I went it was full of Yanks.'

'You'll be safe enough with me. I'll defend your honour.'

'To the death?'

'Absolutely.'

'All right, then.'

It had stopped raining and the sun had come out – a rather watery sun but it felt quite warm. Rather than bike down, they walked to the village by the short-cut path that led from the peri track through the nightingale woods. She had yet to hear one singing, but maybe this year?

Sandy Dimmock said, 'The Yanks'll be starting proper ops soon. That'll give them something else to think about.'

'It certainly will.'

She'd sat in on the practice-briefing sessions and she could tell that the sprog American crews, lolling about so airily, had no idea what they were in for. Crews never did. She'd seen the stunned look on the RAF faces when they came back from their first op. Nothing, it seemed, could prepare a man for the reality of facing a whole lot of other men doing their level best to kill him. For all their cockiness, she felt quite sorry for the Americans.

'How do you think they'll cope, Sandy?'

He shrugged. 'They can fly OK and they've got the guns and the guts, but, personally, I think it's lunatic to go in daylight. They've been having bloody big losses ever since they first got started last August, but it doesn't seem to put them off. The Germans have been making mincemeat of them. Of course, they can afford to lose chaps and planes – there's plenty more where they came from.'

He didn't like his job any more than she did. Put out to grass, was how he'd seen it. He'd done two tours of ops as a Blenheim pilot, got pretty badly wounded at the end and they'd grounded him ever since. Now he'd been made a messenger boy for the Yanks. His DFC wasn't much consolation.

As she'd predicted, the Mad Monk was full of Americans. In the RAF days, when she'd gone there with the other WAAFs, there had never been a problem. After they'd all been posted away, she'd made the mistake of going on her own. The landlord had served her her usual drink and she'd sat on a stool at the bar and chatted to him and his wife for a while, glad to be off the base. And then a whole lot of Yanks had arrived, disturbing the peace. They'd swaggered in like cowboys elbowing their way into a Western saloon bar – only lacking six-shooters at their hips. She'd soon been surrounded, pinned to the bar, unable to escape the relentless chatting-up, the repeated offers of another drink, the refusal to take no for an answer. In the end, she'd slid off the stool, ducked under their drinking arms and fled.

Sandy Dimmock said, 'What'll you have, Daisy?'

'Half a pint, please.'

He left her to go to the bar and, no sooner had he done so, the first Yank came over.

'Hi, there. What can I buy you?'

He was tall, handsome, smiling, full of confidence. And it had to be admitted that their uniform looked very good: smooth dark olive material worn with beige-coloured trousers. Well cut, well fitting. The shirts and ties were a mystery, though. Sometimes they wore a dark olive shirt with a light olive tie and sometimes the other way round, and sometimes dark with dark or light with light, and they tucked the end of the tie inside their shirt, between the buttons, instead of fixing it with a pin. She said politely, 'Nothing, thanks. Someone's getting it for me.'

'The RAF guy? Hey, he can't keep you all to himself – that's not fair.' He held out his hand. 'The name's Frank Daniels. You're Assistant

Section Officer Woods – have I got that right? We've been noticing you around the base.'

Sandy came back and did his best but the American refused to budge and, before long, three more joined him. They were all pilots and therefore all officers: no sergeant pilots, as in the RAF. Their enlisted men, presumably, went to the Barley Sheaf or the Plough. The RAF crews had always drunk together, regardless of rank; not so the Americans, for all their much-toted equality. She listened to their twanging speech, to the alien words and phrases. Sandy had been right about the foreign land. She felt suddenly very homesick for the sound of RAF voices and for self-deprecating RAF ways – for quiet, ironic humour.

'Seen you at the practice briefings,' one of them told her. 'I guess you'd've noticed me there.'

'I'm afraid not.' She never looked at individual faces for fear of encouraging them. At briefings, they were just rows of Yanks in brown leather jackets, smoking and chewing gum. This one was grinning at her persistently, unconvinced that she hadn't remembered him. She turned away and, oh God, there was another one of them over by the bar – not grinning though, just staring. She stared back coldly and, after a moment, he stopped and went on talking to the blond American Red Cross girl beside him.

'I think you guys are just great,' the girl was saying. 'You've got so much guts. All of you.'

She meant well. Saw it as her role to make them feel real fine fellas; a sort of Red Cross cheerleader. 'We haven't done anything yet,' Hamilton reminded her. 'Let's just wait and see how great we are.'

She said brightly, 'The Luftwaffe don't know what's going to hit them.'

'As a matter of fact, they do. They've got our number pretty well. They learned it fast when our guys first came over.'

'But there's a whole lot more of you now. You'll soon finish them off. The war'll be over before we know it.'

She wasn't bad-looking with an OK figure and he liked the blond hair – but the naivety and the brightness was irritating him. He said, 'Somehow I don't think it's going to be that easy. The RAF have been trying pretty hard for three years.'

'Oh,' she made a face. 'The RAF! They're not very much good, are they? Not compared with us.'

He swallowed some more of the Limey beer and, with it, the answer he might have given her – about the RAF hanging on by their fingernails and dying in their thousands but still fighting on. No point. She was too busy rooting for the USAAF.

The girl he'd noticed across the bar room was still there – the one in the British women's air force uniform; WAAFs they called them. He'd seen her with the RAF liaison officer around the base and sitting behind a table at the briefings, and he'd taken note. Very British, both of them. Reserved, correct, hiding their feelings. And they must have some interesting feelings towards the invasion of johnny-come-lately greenhorns who had finally arrived to win the war for them. She was small and dark-haired – just about the opposite of the kind he usually went for – but she was kind of interesting. He watched her some more. She'd been swatting Yanks away like troublesome flies, and he could tell she was fed up with having to do it. He didn't blame her; some of those guys weren't too subtle. She wasn't hiding her feelings that well now and when she'd seen him staring at her, she'd given him a black look. She'd be a tough nut to crack and there were plenty of other girls around who, he figured, would be a whole lot easier.

The Red Cross girl went on talking more crap but he didn't bother to listen. He lit a cigarette, smoked it slowly, and glanced across at the WAAF from time to time. Yeah, she was kind of interesting.

She left soon after with the RAF liaison officer shepherding her by the elbow through the slavering pack of wolves. He had a much better look when she passed quite close to him on the way out, and he gave her a hard stare. She gave him another big glare in return. No question about it, she was lovely.

It was almost dark when Daisy and the flight lieutenant left the pub, and in the woods it was darker still. They had one torch between them, but with its paper shield and failing battery it was next to useless. The half-moon was more help. They followed the pathway, the lieutenant leading the way. He stopped suddenly, a hand on her arm.

'Listen!'

He'd heard the sound before she did – perhaps because his ears were better attuned to such things. In the distance she heard the rumbling drone of bombers – RAF bombers.

'Heading for somewhere in the Ruhr, I'd guess,' he said, 'Essen, or maybe Düsseldorf. I wish to God I were going with them.'

'Why, Sandy? Weren't you terrified?'

'Lord, yes. We all were – those chaps up there will be, too. But I still wish I was going with them. I feel so damn useless down here.'

They stood in silence, listening to the bombers. And then a nightingale began singing somewhere in the wood – a piping, flute-like song rising above the drone of the engines. The duet went on and on, the wartime rumble of the bombers and the sweet peacetime song of the nightingale.

The Americans carried out their first bombing mission from Halfpenny Green in early June. The target was Bremen. Daisy had attended the briefing and the atmosphere had been electric. No lolling about this time, no grinning across at her. All eyes had been on the map on the wall, all ears attuned to the briefing officers and the CO with his gung-ho speech at the end: the Jerries who'd been dishing it out for years, he said, were now going to see what it was like to take it. There was no mention of the RAF having already shown them anything of the kind.

They had passed by her desk on the way out of the hut and she had smiled at those who looked her way – which most of them did – just as she had done with the RAF crews when they went off on an op. You smiled at them because you knew they could be going to die. Following RAF custom, Daisy and the flight lieutenant went out onto the airfield and watched twenty-one Flying Fortresses take off and fly away to assemble in their box formation before they headed for Germany.

He'd seen her standing with the RAF officer at the side of the runway and waving hard as they roared by and it had amused him. Considering what they probably felt about the cocky Yanks, he thought it had been jolly decent of them to do that. She'd even smiled at him as he'd passed her table when he was leaving the briefing, but then she was smiling at all the guys and he knew why. She'd done it all before with the RAF, and she knew the score.

Seven hours later, the bombers returned in a straggling group. There was a crowd out on the control tower balcony, binoculars raised, watching them go around and come in to land. The ground crews, who had been playing softball out on the apron, were pedalling furiously on their bikes towards the hardstands. Fire and ambulance emergency trucks were tearing towards the runway. Some of the bombers had feathered engines, some trailed smoke, and some hadn't come back at all.

Eight

The four other beds in the hut were empty once again. After a couple of days or so, four more new guys turned up to fill them. Nobody mentioned the previous occupants who'd gone down in a ball of fire over Germany. Not a goddam word. Hamilton had seen it happen and he wished he hadn't. Ten men hurtling to earth in a burning, spinning spiral with no hope of bailing out. It had sickened him to watch.

They'd notched up four more missions since that first one over Bremen and every time some didn't make it back. Twenty Forts had been lost from the base in one week. He'd started thinking real hard about it. Twenty-five missions to a duty tour and the average life of an Eighth Air Force bomber crew was fifteen missions. The odds against finishing were impressive. His navigator, Don, who'd trained as an insurance actuary before the war, put it bluntly: 'Mathematically, Ham, there's no way we're gonna live through this.'

He cursed the fact that he'd been assigned to bombers. In fighters, you stood much more of a chance; in a bomber you were a sitting duck with a lot of other sitting ducks, just waiting to get shot at. The only real defence was to stay in tight formation so the Luftwaffe guys couldn't get at you so easily without getting shot down themselves. God help a straggler or a wounded one – the German fighters picked those off in no time. They went for any ducks that went lame and for rookie crews who couldn't keep close up in proper formation. The Luftwaffe had learned pretty much every trick in the book by now, he reckoned; they'd had years of practice. As for the flak, there wasn't a damn thing you could do about that but pray.

The sane way out would be to request a transfer from flying status to some other kind of duty but then, he figured, somebody had to do the rotten, lousy job and it might as well be him. He didn't think he'd feel too good about chickening out. The rest of his crew apparently agreed, though nobody said it aloud. Pride was a part of it – no question. Pride got them into the airplane every time and made them stay there and keep on going – that and the pathetic belief that it was always going to happen to the other guys, never to them. Whenever he saw a kite go down, he never let himself think that the next one might be his. And, after the fifth mission, he'd decided to quit worrying about tomorrow. There was no tomorrow, or next week, or next month; only today. Today you were alive and you damn well enjoyed it. Forget tomorrow. That was the golden rule from now on.

He went down to London for a couple of days with Gene, took in a show, picked up some girls, spent a load of money and came back hung-over. The train had been packed with other servicemen, similarly making the most of still being alive and drowning their fears – British and Yanks cooped up tight together for several hours in an explosive mix. There'd been one hell of a fist fight that had ignited on the train and raged out of control on the platform when they'd finally arrived. The military police had stood by until it had burned itself out and then arrested any guy left standing. He and Gene had taken off before that happened.

'My husband thinks we should invite some of the crews over one evening, Daisy – that it's the very least we can do. Could you ask Flight Lieutenant Dimmock about it? See what he thinks?'

'How many would you want, Mrs Layton?'

'We've got room for thirty people or so at a time, perhaps even more. I was thinking of sandwiches and beer, if we can cope. You'd help, wouldn't you, Daisy?'

'Yes, of course.'

'Poor things, it's been going so badly for them. I've been counting the planes when they go off and when they come back and there's always some missing.'

At briefings, the leather-jacketed rows listened hard to every word, every instruction given, every warning that might help save their lives:

flak concentrations, enemy fighters, coastal defences, bad weather. At Interrogation, after the missions, Daisy sat at a desk beside the flight lieutenant ready to pass on any useful information gleaned from the American bomber crews to the RAF, or to Air Sea Rescue if co-ordinates were known for a ditched bomber. A B-17 could float for quite a while and give its crew time to get out and into the dinghy – if they were lucky. Some were, but an awful lot of them weren't.

Sandy Dimmock thought the Laytons' invitation was a good idea, so did the base commanding officer. A notice went up in the Officers' Club.

The Americans arrived early in the evening. They seemed unusually subdued and rather ill at ease, as though they weren't sure what was expected of them. The Laytons did their best. There was no talk of the war at all and Daisy could hear Mrs Layton telling a group of them about the annual flower show in the village. They were listening politely as if it was the most interesting thing they'd ever heard.

'We have vegetables as well as flowers,' Mrs Layton was explaining brightly. 'Different classes for different kinds, you see. The judge chooses the best potatoes, or onions, or carrots . . . and there's a small prize for the winner. And there's a Homecraft Section for the best cake, or jam, or chutney – though, of course, that's not quite so easy with the rationing, but it's wonderful what people can manage these days, isn't it?'

The Americans, whose business was death and destruction, all nodded their heads. One, whom she remembered from the Mad Monk, detached himself from the group and came up to her. He seemed to have aged ten years since she'd last seen him.

'Hi, there, Daisy. How're you doing?'

'All right, thanks.'

'Say, this is real nice to be asked into an English home. First time ever for me. Are we behaving OK?'

'Impeccably.'

Mrs Layton had moved on to the Handicraft Competition – knitting, crochet, patchwork, embroidery. Two more Americans wandered over and he introduced them.

'This is Lieutenant Grossman and Lieutenant Hamilton.'

The best conversation opener, she had learned, was to ask where they came from. It seemed to matter to them, far more than to any English person who would wonder why on earth you wanted to know. The first one came from Pennsylvania, the second from California and she definitely remembered noticing him before – at the Mad Monk, at briefings and interrogations and in the Officers' Club. He'd been staring quite a bit, but this was the first time he'd spoken to her.

She was shaky about where some of the American states were located, but she knew that Pennsylvania was east and that California was way out west – the final destination of the covered wagons and the rush for gold. He looked easily tough enough to have made that journey himself – to have handled the Indians, the Rockies, the snakes, the wild beasts, the heat, the cold. Eyes of steel. Strong features.

He offered a cigarette and lit it for her. 'Are you liking us any better now?'

'How do you mean?'

'Well, I guess we take some getting used to, and it seems to me you've been finding it pretty hard going. But this evening you're looking as though you might give us an even chance.'

'I'm thinking about it.'

'That's nice. I was afraid you were just being polite.'

'I am. Mr and Mrs Layton want you to feel at home.'

'It's good of them. I wouldn't have any of us guys over the threshold. Most of us don't know how to behave in decent company.'

'I've noticed that.'

He said, 'You should do that more often, you know.'

'Do what?'

'Smile – like you did just then. Usually you only do it to us when you know we might not be coming back. Or when we've come back and you didn't expect it.'

She flushed. 'I'll try to remember not to smile at *you* next time.'

'Hell, don't do that – I look forward to it.

Every time.' He drew on his cigarette. 'Where are you from in England?'

'Does it matter?'

'I guess not. I was just asking.'

'London – well, a suburb of London.'

'I was in London in '36 but only for a couple of days, then I went off to the Continent.'

'On holiday?'

'Kind of. I could see there was a war coming and I wanted to get to see the places I'd only read about before it started.'

'Where did you go?'

'Paris, Rome, Florence, Berlin.'

'Lucky you! I've never been to any of those. In fact, I've never been abroad at all. Goodness knows when I will now.'

'I go all the time,' he said. 'But I don't recommend the trip.'

She caught his meaning. 'I'm sure you don't.'

Mrs Layton came up. 'Daisy, could you be a dear and do some more sandwiches? We seem to be running out.'

'Need some help?' he asked her.

She shook her head. 'No, thanks.'

'Make any headway?' Gene asked.

He watched her moving away. The corners of his mouth twitched in a slow smile. 'I think she's thinking about it.'

The evening was judged a success and the Laytons let it be known that their home was now open house for any of the crews who felt like getting away from the base for an hour or two in the evenings. They came, hesitantly, in ones and twos to begin with, and stayed to play cards, or chess, or backgammon, or read books, or to listen to records on the gramophone. They brought American recordings with them and played them over and over again. 'Paper Doll', 'Deep Purple', 'Moonlight Serenade', 'Green Eyes', 'I'll be Seeing You'.

Gradually more men turned up, and still more, and Daisy was given the job of limiting the numbers so things didn't get too crowded. At first they kept to the sitting room, but then they took to wandering into the kitchen. They brought presents for Mrs Layton – tins of food and chocolate which she tried in vain to refuse – cigarettes and Scotch whisky for Mr Layton which he didn't, and presents for the children: toys that they'd made themselves and American candy. And they brought photos to show. Photos of girlfriends and parents and brothers and sisters back home, and sometimes, if they were older men, of their wives and their own children. Daisy came to know names: lieutenant this and captain that and major the other became Gene and Frank and Buzz and Charlie and Budd. And Lieutenant Hamilton became Ham.

He asked her if she was still thinking.

'Thinking about what?'

'Whether you like us Yanks any better.'

'You're not so bad,' she said coolly. 'Some of you.'

He called by her office one day on some flimsy pretext. He knew that he hadn't fooled her for a moment, though she gave him the information he'd asked for very politely. He'd been going to ask her out – to what they called the pictures, or maybe to have dinner if he could find anywhere to take her – but he could tell that she was going to refuse. Turn him down flat. He wasn't used to being given the brush-off, in fact he couldn't remember it ever happening to him. What the hell, anyway? There were plenty more girls around.

There was a dance in the Officers' Club. As Sandy Dimmock pointed out to her, it was their sacred duty to attend and to help drink the booze. He escorted her faithfully – two lone blue RAF uniforms afloat in a sea of American olive drab.

She danced every dance – doing her sacred duty. The station band was wonderful and the Yanks were good dancers; it wasn't too much of a penance.

Lieutenant Hamilton was there, dancing with a succession of other girls. She was a bit surprised, and just a mite put out, that he never asked her.

The Red Cross girl was busy telling him all over again what great guys they were, and boring the pants off him. He didn't bother to answer – just went on dancing. He could see the English WAAF dancing with the CO and being charming to him, smiling and laughing at whatever he was saying. He steered the Red Cross girl in that direction, passing close by, but without looking at the WAAF. She didn't look at him either but she noticed him all right – he was damn sure of that.

When he went by her table at the end of the next mission briefing, Daisy looked away quickly and then back in time to smile at his co-pilot, his navigator and his bombardier, following after. They were chalking up the missions and they had a reputation as a top-class crew – one that never turned back, always got through, always bombed on target. She'd been right about their captain being a tough guy.

It was Hamburg this time and it wouldn't be a milk run. Swarms of Luftwaffe fighters, a fiercely defended target, poor weather. She stared out of her office window. The ground crews were hanging around, sweating it out, practising baseball throws, looking at watches, searching the skies. She kept thinking that because she hadn't smiled at him, he wouldn't come back and it would be all her fault. She'd cast an unlucky spell, like the chop girl who acts as a jinx and always brings doom.

Sandy Dimmock wandered in, leaned against the wall, smoking a cigarette, and started telling her about his own Hamburg ops – the flak and fighters, crossing the North Sea on three engines, coming back on a wing and a prayer. She tried not to listen. After a while, she saw the ground crews stop tossing the baseball around and start running, and, at the same time, she heard the sound of the first of the B-17s returning.

The flight lieutenant levered himself off the wall and stubbed out his cigarette. 'Better get down to Interrogation.'

From her desk she watched the first crew come into the hut. From the look on their faces she could see that it had been a very shaky do. It showed in their eyes and in the way hands trembled as they lit their cigarettes, long before they said a word. The next crew came in, and the next, and then another, sitting, in turn, round the tables giving their reports to the interrogation officers. The flak had been ferocious, the enemy fighters had gone for them in howling packs, three B-17s had been seen going down in flames, one had ditched later in the middle of the North Sea. She passed on the co-ordinates to Air Sea Rescue.

His was the very last crew to come in and, by then, she had given up all hope. He walked in and paused by her table to light a cigarette. He did it slowly and deliberately, with hands that were rock steady. As he thumbed the lighter shut, he lifted his head and looked down at her. This time she smiled.

Nine

Briefing was at 0230 hours – the middle of the night – and the target was the lock gates at La Pallice on the Atlantic coast of France where the Germans had constructed U-boat pens. There were fresh eggs for breakfast before – same as guys got given who were going to be executed – and twenty minutes to eat them before biking over to the briefing room. It was already light by the time Hamilton and his crew took the truck out to their plane, the sun coming up, the sky clear, the temperature pleasant. He thought, what a hell of a way to spend a nice day, sealed up in a tin can being shot at. They racketed round the peri track to the hardstand where *Miss Laid* was waiting for them, the painted lady sprawled seductively along the fuselage wearing high heels and nothing else. He'd often wondered whether the Luftwaffe fighter pilots had time to appreciate American nose art as they zoomed in for the kill.

He chucked his parachute pack up through the nose hatch and swung himself after it, Gene following. While the rest of the crew settled themselves they went through the checklist and started up the engines. A green flare from the control tower and they rolled out onto the peri track to join the other Forts taxiing round to the start of the runway. While he waited his turn to take off, he and Gene both stood on the brakes, and he eased into full throttles with his right hand surrounding the four levers, his left hand holding the wheel – all engines roaring. *Miss Laid* shook like a belly dancer. Every take-off was an adventure. A B-17 heavily laden with bombs, fuel, ammunition and men always took to the air sulkily and sometimes not at all, which was usually curtains for the crew. Their turn finally, and he nodded to Gene to release the brakes. They surged forward. Cliff, standing behind, was calling out the air speed for him. 'Sixty-five . . . seventy . . . seventy-five . . . eighty . . . eighty-five . . . ninety . . .' He pulled back the wheel and released it, testing the lift on the wings. *Miss Laid* did a couple of cock-teasing bounces. 'Ninety-five . . . one hundred . . . one-o-five . . .' It was lap-of-the-gods time. Engine failure, prop wash from the guy ahead, running out of runway, could all screw them. 'Hundred twenty . . . hundred twenty-five . . .' He nursed the bomber off the runway, skimming the ground and the tree tips beyond.

'Wheels up.'

Gene hit the switch. 'Wheels coming up.'

'Wing flaps up.' They climbed faster and higher. He looked down at the English fields and the woods and the farms and the cottages, all laid out peacefully in the morning sunshine. They'd started harvesting and he could see sheaves of wheat stooked against each other. The idyllic scene slipped away beneath the wings. Gene and Cliff had their eyes wide open, necks swinging on the lookout for other aircraft on a collision course. At the rallying point, he slid into formation, wing tip to wing tip with the other bombers so that no fighter could dive between them. They turned towards France.

An escort of Thunderbolts showed up to keep a friendly eye on them but as soon as the fighters' fuel got low they had to quit, and the minute they did, the unfriendly German version appeared like bats out of hell – Focke-Wulfs and 109s.

'Pilot to crew. Six fighters coming in eleven o'clock high. Go for 'em, Turret.'

The German fighters picked on a straggling Fort and raked it with fire. Hamilton saw it blow up into bits. No parachutes – just fragments spinning towards the earth. His gunners were firing away like crazy, peppering the sky. So were all the other Forts.

'Got one at four o'clock,' Alvin yelled from the tail.

The bandits were coming in from all angles, in waves of thirty or more each time, spitting fire and flashing past.

'Ball to crew – more of the sonofabitches comin' up at us from below.'

He could hear Milo's guns chattering away

furiously down in the ball, though he couldn't see what the hell was going on under the plane. Another Fort, ahead of them, suddenly burst into flames, and, soon after, another began the long, steep fall downwards, streaming black smoke. One, two, three, four, five chutes out of that one . . . no more after that. The Fort on their right wing was next: one moment it was there wallowing alongside, the next it was gone. The Fort behind slid forward to take its place in the formation. More fighters swept in from ten o'clock, aiming straight at the nose, before rolling away. The top turrets missed but his bombardier clobbered one of the bastards and he watched a wing break off and the German pilot bail out. No time for cheering. His fingers were gripping the wheel, tight as a vice.

'Ball to crew – two fighters six o'clock low.'

Miss Laid lurched and shuddered and he knew they'd been hit.

'Pilot to crew. What's the damage?'

'Right Waist to pilot. There's two bloody great holes back here. Shell went clean between us an' out the other side. Boy, were we lucky.'

'Pilot to Ball. OK down there, Milo?'

No answer.

'Pilot to Waist. Check on him, soon as you can.'

The fighters vanished as suddenly as they'd arrived.

'Tail to crew – flak at eight o'clock level.'

Instead of the fighters, there was a curtain of flak ahead that they had to fly through, praying hard. Tight formation was no defence against flak; it just made it easier to collide. Pretty soon *Miss Laid* started plunging about like a frightened mare.

'Bombardier to pilot. We're on the bomb run.'

'OK. Go ahead.'

They went onto the target and got the hell out again. What was left of the formation turned for home. No more enemy fighters on the way back, which was the good news. The bad news was that Milo had been wounded. They'd got him up out of the ball turret, staunched the bleeding and given him a shot of morphine and wrapped him in blankets.

The Thunderbolts showed up again to escort them for the last bit, after all the damage had been done. When they flew in over the coast of England, the sun was still shining and the idyllic country scene was still there as they came back to Halfpenny Green – cottages and woods, and fields of ripe wheat, another one harvested since they'd left that morning. He sent the wounded-on-board red flare and got priority. With Milo in mind, he brought *Miss Laid* down as gently as he knew how to land her. An ambulance was there as soon as they came to a stop. He waited while they carried the barely conscious ball-turret gunner out on a stretcher. Hamilton touched his shoulder.

'You're OK now, Milo. They'll take good care of you. You'll be fine.'

He stayed as the stretcher was loaded into the

ambulance, the doors banged shut. Beside him, Gene said, 'Reckon he's going to make it?'

'Doesn't look too good.'

The crew chief, Deerfield, came up. 'Any other damage to report, Lieutenant? Aside from the obvious?'

He shook his head. 'Controls still seem to work OK – far as I could tell.'

'We'll check 'em out real good.'

They took the truck over to Operations for interrogation. Hot coffee and spam sandwiches in the waiting room, the surviving crews swopping accounts, asking after missing buddies. The CO was there too, patting backs and boosting morale. In the interrogation room, the WAAF was sitting quietly at her table with the RAF liaison officer. She spotted him as soon as he came in and she smiled right across the room before he even got near her table. He knew she must have been on the lookout, waiting to see if he was one of the lucky ones who'd made it. He thought, forget Lola and the rest of them back home, and all the others over here. She's the one I want.

When the interrogation was over – a long-drawn-out inquisition on every detail of the mission: fighters, flak, shootings-down on both sides, any new enemy tricks – exhaustion took a hold. Instead of going to the mess hall he went to the hut and fell into the sack. Within a couple of minutes he was asleep.

It was evening when he woke up – one of

those long English summer evenings when the light turns to gold and takes hours to fade away. He got up, took a shower, put on clean clothes and went by the enlisted men's hut to see how his gunners were doing. They were still asleep, humped shapes under the blankets. The last bed in the row was tucked in neat and tidy and very empty. He rode his bike over to the base hospital and found a nurse in the corridor.

'What's the news on Sergeant Gambi?'

'Was he in your crew?'

'My ball-turret gunner. How is he?'

'I'm so sorry, Lieutenant,' she said. 'He died about an hour ago.'

Before the Americans had arrived, the Boot Record in the Mad Monk had been held by the RAF. Flight Lieutenant Johnnie Rivers had drunk the pub's glass boot of beer in the shortest time of fifty-nine seconds and his name, along with the closest contenders, was still chalked up on a slate beside the bar. So far no Yank had beaten it, though not for want of trying.

When Daisy walked in with Sandy Dimmock another attempt was being made. The American lieutenant took one minute, twenty-three seconds to do it, to deafening encouragement.

'They're getting closer,' the flight lieutenant said gloomily. 'Is nothing sacrosanct?'

She smiled. 'Maybe that's one record we shouldn't mind losing.'

The Yanks were in a mood that she knew well:

the sort of mood that always followed a string of bad ops. The RAF had been just the same. The ridiculous boot game, the name-carving, the hand-imprinting and smoke-writing on the pub ceiling, the wild sing-songs round the piano were all born of the desperate need to blot out reality. She'd seen the RAF boys falling around in the bar, drunk and incapable, sometimes weeping while they laughed, and yet the next day they always surfaced bright-eyed, perfectly normal and ready for the next op. It had been bad for the Americans – very bad. They'd lost a lot of planes and a lot of men in the past few weeks. And they needed to forget. One of them went over to the upright piano in the corner and began to play, fast and furiously. Presently, others gathered round him and began to sing – Yanks with their arms round girls, all yelling away together, the old locals watching from their benches with their beer mugs in their hands and toothless grins on their faces.

Now this is number one
and the show has just begun
Roll me over, lay me down
and do it again . . .

It had been easier to deal with when they hadn't been so nice, when they'd been so pleased with themselves and so dismissive of the RAF, when she hadn't really cared all that much what happened to them. Now, it was just as heart-breaking as it had been before.

Some more Yanks came in, and she saw Lieutenant Hamilton with his co-pilot.

Roll me over, in the clover
Roll me over, lay me down
and do it again . . .

He'd elbowed a way through the crowd and appeared at her side. 'Hi, there.'

'Hallo.' She managed to make it sound casual. On every one of the last few missions, she'd convinced herself that he'd got the chop.

Now this is number two
and I've got her by the shoe,
Roll me over, lay me down
and do it again . . .

'How's your drink?'

'It's fine, thanks.'

'Don't go away while I get mine.'

Now this is number three
and I've got her by the knee,
Roll me over, lay me down,
and do it again.
Roll me over, in the clover,
Roll me over, lay me down
and do it again.
Now this is number four
and I've got her on the floor . . .

By the time he came back, some other Yanks had moved in on her and it was a group. The singing went on, louder still. 'Roll me over' finally petered out after many bawdy verses and 'Tipperary' started. After that, it was 'Pack up your Troubles' and then 'Roll out the Barrel' – all songs learned from the British.

He said in her ear, 'Let's get out of here.'

She went and found Sandy to tell him.

'Are you OK,' he said, 'or do you need rescuing?'

'No. Not from this one.'

They sat on a bench outside the pub, overlooking the green – cricket pavilion, duck pond, the encircling houses, all still visible in the twilight.

'Why the Mad Monk?' he asked.

'Nobody seems to know. There's a ruined abbey near here. He was probably from there.'

'I guess he was some crazy old guy who wandered in and out for a pint, now and then. Maybe the beer was better in those days.'

'I think it would have been mead.'

'Mead?'

'A sort of early beer.'

'Never tried that.' He looked away, across the green. 'It sure is peaceful here. Hard to believe there's a war on. Too bad it's true.'

She said quietly, 'I heard about your ball-turret gunner, Ham. I'm terribly sorry.'

'Yep. Too bad. He was a good guy. But that's the way it goes. Cigarette?'

They were getting more and more like the RAF in every way, she thought. Little or nothing said about those who bought it. Not callous. The only way to play the game.

He lit the cigarette for her with one of those heavy American lighters with a hinged lid that snapped shut like a trap. 'Sorry, hauling you out here. I wasn't in a singing mood.'

'You need to be half-drunk to sing those songs.'

'I guess so. And they had a head start on me.' After a moment, he said, 'You know, I really don't know anything much about you – except that you're called Daisy and you come from a London suburb. That right?'

'That's right.'

'OK. Tell me some more.'

'Such as?'

'Your family. How many brothers and sisters?'

'No brothers. I have four sisters, all older. Lily, Violet, Primrose and Iris.'

'And you're Daisy. All flowers. That's kind of nice.'

'Our mother's a very keen gardener. Actually, my real name's Marguerite, but nobody calls me that.'

'I like 'em both,' he said. 'But Daisy suits you best. Little and lovely. And you're the youngest. Nineteen or twenty, I'd guess.'

'Twenty.'

'I'm an old man of twenty-two. And my real name's Howard, but nobody here calls me that either. What made you join the air force?'

'Well, I already had two sisters in the navy, and one in the Land Army, and the other's a FANY, so I thought I'd do something different.'

He laughed. It was the first time she'd seen him do that. 'A fanny? No kidding! I guess that doesn't mean the same over here.'

'It stands for First Aid Nursing Yeomanry. Primrose drives ambulances in London. She drove them all through the Blitz.'

'Did they send you out of London – during the Blitz?'

'Heavens, no! My mother wouldn't have considered it, and nor would I. Anyway, it wasn't too bad where we were.'

He drew on his cigarette, flicked the ash away. 'We think a hell of a lot of you British, you know, Daisy – the way you stuck it out on your own – specially now we've seen something of what it's been like for ourselves. It's a beautiful country and it's a great country. And I'm sorry we didn't get here sooner.'

'Well, you're here now.'

He nodded. 'When it all started in '39 I wanted to join the RAF – there were guys doing that. Going to Canada and pretending to be Canadians and getting trained and sent over. Only my parents kicked up a hell of a fuss. I was eighteen and I'd just started at Berkeley so I guess they had a point. But after Pearl Harbor nothing would have stopped me.'

'Berkeley?'

'A college in northern California. University. I'll still have a year to do if I get back.'

She noted the *if*.

'Well, I'd already learned to fly before the war and I was used to flying my father's plane around, so it made good sense. Except I'd planned on flying fighters, not bombers.'

'Wouldn't they let you?'

'Too tall and they needed bomber pilots. Strong guys who could heave a big plane around. It takes some muscle to keep in formation for hours on end. I reckon I could arm-wrestle Joe Louis now – specially with my left.' He flexed the arm. 'That's the one gets to do most of the work – the steering.'

'You must get awfully tired on ops.' She knew they did – she'd seen the grey faces and the dark circles under the eyes when they came back.

'Sure do. All of us. But we get over it fast. Sleep in our cots like babies.' He flicked his cigarette again. 'I wish I'd more time to go see more of the countryside – down on the ground. I'd like to do some more sketching while I'm over here.'

She was surprised. 'Sketching? You don't look the artistic type.'

'Appearances can fool you. It's nothing fancy. Pencil, mostly.'

He took a small book out of the patch pocket of his leather jacket and showed it to her, flipping over the pages. Sketches of life at

Halfpenny Green. Watchers on the control tower balcony, a mechanic working on an engine, a Jeep overloaded with a ten-man crew, a tangled pile of bikes outside the briefing room . . . she could see, even from the rapid glance that he allowed, that they were very well done.

She said, 'Where did you learn to draw so well?'

'Hell, they're just doodles. We had a good teacher in high school, though, and I learned a lot from him. I guess some of it comes naturally. My mother's a pretty good artist. Watercolours, mainly. It's in the family.'

'What else about you?'

He gave her a sideways smile. 'What do you want to know?'

'Well, you could start the way Americans usually start.'

'What way's that?'

'Telling me where you come from. I know it's California but what city or town?'

'Pasadena. Right by Los Angeles.'

'Is that anywhere near Hollywood?'

'Sure. Hollywood's a part of Los Angeles and Pasadena's only a few miles east of LA.'

'Is it a nice place?'

'Yeah. I think so. It's kind of old – by our standards, not yours. Big old houses, nice neighbourhoods, lots of trees . . . it's a good place to live. My father's company's based in LA, though.'

'What sort of company?'

'Magazine publishing. A bunch of different kinds of glossies – architecture, interiors, fashion . . . And a whole lot of smaller ones on hobbies – fishing and horseback-riding and collecting things, that sort of stuff. My grandfather started the company, then Dad took it over. I'm expected to do the same.'

'Are you the only son?'

'Yep. I've got a kid sister but she's not interested. She wants to be a big film star. See, that's what comes of living anywhere near Hollywood. It can rub off on you, if you're not careful.'

'Do you have photos of them?' They usually did and it was polite to ask.

'Oh, sure . . . Yanks always carry them – you know that. I've seen you being nice and kind about it. I'll bore you with them some other time.'

Private planes, big old houses, a dynastic family . . . it spelled wealth, position, power. She knew that some of the Americans did a lot of line-shooting and lie-telling about their backgrounds to impress the girls, but she had no doubt that what he'd told her was perfectly true, and it wasn't her sort of world at all.

'I really ought to be getting back, Ham.'

'Sure.' He stood up. 'I'll walk you right to your door.'

They took the pathway up through the woods and stopped to listen to the distant drone of the RAF setting off on a night op.

'Beats me how they do it,' he said. 'No escort, pea-shooter guns, pitch black. It must take a hell of a good navigator to find the target and make it back to base.'

She told him about hearing the nightingale singing with the bombers. 'But that was in May. I haven't heard him since.'

'Maybe he's flown off to Berkeley Square.'

She smiled. 'Maybe he has.'

As promised, he took her right to the farm-house door. By then it was too dark to see much of him – just the dark shape of him, the outline of the high-brimmed American cap, the faint gleam of its big brass badge.

She said, 'I hope they won't send you on ops again for a while.'

'Sure they will – soon as we get a replacement gunner. The way I look at it is the sooner we finish the missions, the sooner we go home.'

She knew very well – and he would know very well – the frightening odds against that ever happening. 'I won't be around for a bit,' she told him. 'I've got two days' leave.'

'Going home?'

'No. I'm spending it here at the farm. I've offered to give the Laytons a hand with their harvest.'

'If we get a break from flying, I'd be glad to help as well,' he said. 'And I'll bet you some of the other guys would, too. Want me to ask around?'

'Would you? They'll need all the help they can get.'

'Sure thing. Goodnight, Daisy.'

He moved deliberately closer and took hold of her shoulders. She let him kiss her and it was very obvious that he'd kissed lots of girls, lots of times. Of course he had. She pulled away before it went on too long, or got too serious. 'Goodnight, Ham.'

As she opened the farmhouse door, his soft American voice came out of the darkness. 'Seems you're getting to like us a whole lot better now.'

Mrs Layton lent her some working togs, bibbed dungarees and a blouse, and gave her a red and white spotted scarf to tie round her hair. The dungarees were far too big but she tied them at the waist with string and rolled up the legs.

They assembled out in the fields – old farm-workers, land girls, friends, neighbours, villagers. It was already warm, the sun shining down on them from an almost cloudless sky – the sort of fair-weather day that would be ideal for a mission. They cleared the first field of the sheaves left lying behind the binder, heaving them across the stubble into groups and stooking them upright against each other. It was hot and dusty work; the sheaves were heavy and the sharp stubble scratched her ankles painfully. Whenever a bomber took off from the airfield Daisy stopped, shielding her eyes against the sun, to watch each one climbing upwards – just test flights, nothing more. No mission, so far.

While they were working on the next field – a

ten-acre – the Yanks arrived. Thirty or more of them swarming across the field like the cavalry charging to the rescue. She gave a sigh of relief. No mission, then. Ham came straight to where she was standing and lifted the wheatsheaf out of her arms.

'OK. Let's go.'

And go they did. The ten-acre was done in record time and they moved on to the next field – the Yanks fooling around, the land girls giggling, all of them laughing, the sun beating down. At noon, Mrs Layton, with the children helping, carried out jugs of lemon squash and bottles of ginger beer, and cheese and beetroot sandwiches. She'd brought her box camera as well and clicked away with it.

When they stopped to eat, Daisy flopped down in the shade of the hedge. Ham stretched out beside her, propping himself up on one arm – the one that steered the Fort for hours on end, the one that could wrestle with Joe Louis.

'You know, you look pretty wonderful in your WAAF uniform, but what you're wearing right now is a knockout.'

'It's borrowed finery.'

'Well, don't give it back.'

'Actually, Mrs Layton gave the scarf to me. It's a present.'

'Keep it for ever.'

She said, 'Thanks for coming to help, Ham – all of you.'

'Forget it. The guys wanted to. Gets us off base

and keeps us busy. Besides, it meant I could see you, Daisy. All selfish motives, you see.'

She looked away from him across the field, eating her sandwich. She had wanted to see him, too – very much – but she was remembering the way he had kissed her. The lots of girls and the lots of kisses. The Yanks had it all so easy. English girls were there for the picking and the plucking. They swooned into their arms, fell at their feet, never said no. She didn't want to be like that. Only she knew that she was falling in love with him and, soon, she wouldn't be able to help herself.

'I know what you're thinking,' he said.

'Oh? What?'

'You're thinking to yourself – here's another Yank aiming to score, like all the others you've been fending off since we got here, and you're thinking that this particular Yank's probably even worse. Am I right?'

'Something like that.'

'Yeah . . . well, that's too bad. I guess I just have to hope you'll learn to trust me, in time. Only I don't know how much time there is left.'

'That's not fair, Ham. Trying to make me feel bad.'

He smiled. 'Fair means or foul, Daisy – whichever it takes.'

They worked on until the light faded and all the wheat was stooked, to be carted later for threshing. Mrs Layton had set out food on trestle tables in the barn – rabbit pies and some lethal home-made potato wine. One of the old men brought out a fiddle and sawed away, other villagers started to caper around, the Yanks watched and clapped in time and stomped their feet, and pretty soon they were all capering too.

Outside the barn, the sky was black velvet studded with diamonds. Daisy walked with Ham across the lawn by the house, the fiddling and the clapping and the stomping fading into the distance.

He stopped under a tree and took her in his arms. It went on much too long and got much too serious, but instead of pulling away, she stayed.

Ten

By November the weather was a joke. Day after day of overcast skies, rain, fog, not a peep of sun: grey, damp, cold, miserable, the whole base sinking slowly under a sea of mud. But still they flew, and in conditions when even the birds stayed home and watched them take off with their wings clapped over their eyes. He and Deerfield, the crew chief, who was from Arizona, exchanged bitter comments.

'Sure makes me appreciate home, Lieutenant.'

'Yeah . . . I've forgotten what the sun looks like. One thing about the Limey weather, though, Joe – if you don't like it, just wait five minutes and it'll change.'

A couple of times, to Hamilton's intense frustration, the target was so obscured that they had to abort and dump their bombs in the ocean. All that prodigious effort – getting ready, taking off, forming up, flying there, flying back – for no score. Twelve missions done, thirteen to go, and with the bad weather, that could be a heck of a long time to be living under a death sentence. He still stuck to his golden rule: forget about tomorrow; there is no tomorrow. Or next week, let alone next year. To hell with them! Today was all that counted. Today. And Daisy.

He sometimes went over to the farmhouse in the evening. There was always a crowd of other guys there, playing cards and board games, listening to the wireless and to records, wandering around . . . almost no chance of getting her to himself, and he had a feeling that she was deliberately keeping it that way – as though she was afraid of getting in too deep. He could understand that. From where he was standing – potential dead meat any day – he'd nothing to lose, but for her it was different. Get too serious, too involved and it would be tough on her if anything happened to him, whereas he wouldn't be feeling a thing.

Next time he went over, she was in the kitchen, mixing something in a bowl. For once, there was nobody else there.

'Pastry for an apple pie,' she told him when he asked what it was. 'Isn't that a big American favourite?'

'Sure.' He watched her kneading and rolling the pastry and then peeling and slicing the apples. At home, they had a cook and he rarely went into the kitchen. 'Where did you learn to do all that?'

'From my mother.' She went on working at the pie, laying the pastry deftly over the apples, slicing round the edges, cutting slits in the top and making pretty leaves out of leftover bits for decoration.

'Your mother must be a great cook.'

She gave him a quick smile over her shoulder on her way to the oven. 'She is. So are all my sisters.'

'What a family! I hope I meet them some day. And I sure hope you meet mine. How about coming to California when the war's over?'

'It's an awfully long way away.'

'If you marry me you could make it a one-way ticket.'

She was busy with the oven door, her back turned. 'Is that an official proposal, or an idea that's just come into your mind?'

'No. It's an idea that's been there ever since I first saw you.' He dropped the flippant tone. 'I mean it, Daisy. I'm serious.' He knew it was unfair to her and that he was breaking the rule, but what the hell? If she felt about him the way he felt about her – and he was pretty damn sure she did – then she'd be willing to take the risk, wouldn't she?

She turned towards him, unsmiling. 'I expect you *do* mean it now, Ham – when everything's upside down for you and you're so far from home. But how will you feel when the war's over and everything gets back to normal and you go back to your own country and your own people? Your own sort of girl?'

He said, '*You're* my sort of girl, Daisy. Can't you tell? And I thought I was your sort of guy.' She looked away without answering him. 'But maybe I've got that wrong?'

She said low so he could scarcely hear it, 'No, you didn't get it wrong.'

'Then what's the problem? Is it because you're afraid I'll get the chop? You can't face that happening?'

'No, it's not that. It's not that at all.'

He moved closer to her. 'So what is it?'

'I've just tried to tell you—'

But then some guy came barging into the kitchen and then more guys after him. They all clustered round her, planning on staying. He left them to it.

'Beautiful morning, Chief.'

'Sure is, Lieutenant, sir. Makes me glad I'm not goin' home just yet.'

The rain was coming down as though somebody up there was emptying great buckets of water and the wind was blowing it all sideways across the airfield. Nonetheless, take-off conditions were deemed favourable and visibility over the target – Bremen and the submarine installations – was said to be fair. So off they were going into the wild, grey yonder on their thirteenth mission and crossing fingers the number wasn't a bad omen. He and Gene went through the usual checks, started up engines in order – number two, number one, number three, number four – and moved out onto the peri track. *Miss Laid* was even more tricky to handle on take-off than usual and he thought for a while that she was going to refuse at the first fence. But up they went, scraping tree tops and clambering slowly through wet cotton wool – one of a long line of Forts all aiming to meet up and form up in a death-defying, suicidal exercise of precision flying in visibility that had the sweat breaking out on his forehead and the muscles in his arms going rigid. On the last mission, when the conditions had been about the same, four Forts had collided and turned into bits of wing and fuselage and tails and men and parachutes littering the sky.

Their fighter escort joined them near the Dutch coast, keeping a wary distance from trigger-happy formation gunners who didn't know their 47s from their 109s. Fuel time up, they peeled off and headed home. Jesus, he envied those guys. Pretty soon, the expected swarm of German fighters came snarling round, and the carnage began. He'd reckoned that he ought to be immune by now to the sight of a bomber getting jumped and slaughtered but it still got to him every time – the thought of the ten men going with it.

'Pilot to Left Waist. Get those two bastards eleven o'clock high! Watch 'em. Here they come.'

He took what evasive action he could with the ship, which was almost none in close formation. The gunner missed the fighter, but the fighter missed them. He'd be round again, and so would his pals. For every one of them that was knocked down it seemed like two more turned up – meaner and rougher.

'Ball to Waist. My oxygen tank's gettin' kinda low.' Milo's replacement in the ball turret was a nice kid, just out of high school. Still wet behind the ears and there was a hint of panic in the voice.

'Waist to Ball. OK, Bernie. Ready to fill it whenever you are.' That was Ken – three years older and calm and reassuring as a father.

The plane ahead was throttle-jockeying – falling back, catching up, falling back. A nervous rookie pilot, or maybe some kind of engine trouble. Finally it fell right back and four or five 109s fell on it like jackals. He saw it being torn apart as he moved into the empty space. Blood and guts were spattered all over his windshield – German or American, he didn't know.

Alvin's voice came over. 'Tail to crew. Two chutes outta that Fort – that's all.'

The cloud cover cleared over the target – enough for them to see it and enough to give the guys behind the guns on the ground a nice view of the approaching formation. They flew on steadily through the flak – a fancy pattern of shells exploding into black powder puffs and white-hot pieces of jagged metal. The ball turret was the worst place on the ship to be in flak – three-quarters of the glass and metal ball suspended in space under the aircraft with only a small patch of armour plating, the gunner all cramped up like a foetus in a not-so-cosy womb.

'Pilot to Ball. How are you doing down there, Bernie?'

‘OK thanks, Ham.’ Only a faint waver in the reply. The kid had guts.

‘Hang on. We’ll soon be through this.’

‘Bombardier to Pilot.’

‘Go ahead.’

‘We’re on the bomb run.’

‘OK, Bombardier. Handing her over. She’s all yours.’

Three minutes later. ‘Bombs away! Giving her back to you, Ham. Let’s go home.’

The formation made a left turn towards the North Sea. They left the flak behind but the fighters came back like vengeful furies.

‘Bombardier to crew. Bandits eleven o’clock high – get ready!’

They came screaming down, guns blazing. One of them flashed by so close he damn near took their wing off. Another lot came up below from a different direction. *Miss Laid* jumped indignantly as if she’d been goosed and he knew they’d taken a hit somewhere near the tail. Next minute, there was an almighty explosion that knocked him sideways and stunned him. When he’d got his senses back, he saw the side window by Gene had a damn great hole in it and that his co-pilot was slumped forward, blood all over the controls, over the inside of the windshield too, and, he realized, trickling down his own face though he didn’t know if it was the co-pilot’s blood or his. The hole was letting in an icy blast of air.

He couldn’t shift Gene to see how bad it was.

The 109s were still coming at them and he could feel another hit somewhere. Number two engine was trailing black smoke and then wicked orange flames; he shut it down and zapped the extinguisher before the flames could spread to the fuel and blow them apart, but when he tried to feather the prop nothing happened and it went on turning like a runaway windmill. He had another try at shifting Gene. He was unconscious, if not already dead: an inert weight in cumbersome flying gear, collapsed in a small space.

With Cliff's help they raised him enough to see that the blood was coming out of a big wound in his chest and to find out that he was still alive. They got some padding tight over the wound but there was no sense trying to move him out of the seat, it'd probably finish him off. He had to leave him where he was. The German fighters were still buzzing round the formation and all his attention and all his energy was needed to watch them, keep flying the plane, keep in formation and keep on at his crew. The blood was still trickling down his face and over his mask and must be his own, though he couldn't feel where it was coming from.

'Pilot to crew. Watch those bastards . . . they haven't done with us yet.'

Miss Laid wasn't feeling too good – that much was obvious and she was giving him a hard time. The pressure gauges were all to hell, she was haemorrhaging hydraulic fluid, and the windmilling prop was dragging her like a convict's ball and chain. They'd lost a hell of a lot too much fuel for his liking and there was no hope of keeping up with the formation, which meant they'd be easy pickings. He gave his crew the bad news.

Their guardian angels had to be somewhere out there, because, as they dropped back from the formation, the German fighters had miraculously disappeared. But that still left plenty to worry about – such as whether *Miss Laid* was going to consent to stay in the air for long enough to get across the North Sea and whether the fuel was going to last out, even if she graciously felt like doing that. He reckoned the odds were stacked high against either possibility.

'Pilot to crew. Sorry, but it looks like we might not make it all the way back to England. If you want to bail out while we're still over land, go right ahead. Ditching's a bad option, the way things are with the controls, and the swimming's goddam cold this time of year.'

'Navigator to Pilot. What about you, Ham? What're you figuring on doing?'

'I'm staying with Gene. He's in bad shape – too bad to get him out with a chute. I'll try and take him home.'

'OK. I'm staying with you two guys.'

They all chose to stay. Eight good men and true. A hell of a crew.

'Pilot to Waist. Get Bernie up out of the ball, quick as you can. You're coming out of there, kid.'

When they finally reached it, the North Sea was dotted with white flecks which meant it was mighty rough down there. None of it added up to getting *Miss Laid* on the water in one nice neat piece, if he had to try it, or of her floating for long – if at all. The dead engine prop was still windmilling and dragging, the other three labouring away. He cut back on power and they droned on across the ocean, losing height steadily. Whenever he could, he checked on Gene. Still breathing. The fuel warning light came on for number three engine which meant less than fifty gallons left in that tank. Ten minutes later another warning light lit up for number one.

'Pilot to crew. We've got to jettison the heavy stuff. Get the ammo out and anything else you can.'

They opened the bomb doors and hatches. Out went the boxes of fifty-calibre shells, oxygen bottles, the waist, nose and radio guns. Number four warning light winked at him merrily.

'Pilot to Radio. Stay with Air Sea Rescue frequency, Carl.'

'Roger.'

'Tail to Pilot. Bogey coming up six o'clock low.'

Jesus, that was all they needed. 'What's it look like, Bernie? One of ours, or one of theirs?'

'Can't tell yet.'

'Well, don't go shooting it down till you can. We may need it.' If it was an enemy fighter they'd pretty much had it, with only two guns left, almost no ammo and nowhere to hide.

'Tail to Pilot. Hey, think it's a Spit, Ham.'

The kid had better be right.

'Pilot to Navigator. We want the nearest strip you can find, Don.'

'Sorry, Ham. Can't pinpoint exactly where the hell we are, but there's bound to be an airfield near, wherever we hit the coast.'

True enough. There were hundreds of them all over England.

'Bombardier to Pilot. I can see the coast ahead now. Maybe five minutes.'

He'd better be right too – they must be flying on fumes. 'Pilot to Bombardier. Keep your eyes peeled for a place to land.'

'Tail to Pilot. It's a Spit all right. One of the RAF guys.'

The Spitfire with its red, white and blue roundel slid into his peripheral vision and stayed alongside, rising and falling gently. He could see the pilot's face turned towards him and a gloved thumb lifted in a jolly salute.

'Pilot to crew. Nanny's here to hold our hand.'

The coast was coming up closer and closer – a dark streak of land wreathed in primeval mist. He went on letting down, using less and less power, expecting the engines to quit at any moment.

'Pilot to Bombardier. See any landing strips, Lee?'

'Not a thing yet, Ham. Bad viz.'

Goddam the Limey weather! If they didn't find a strip in a minute he'd be putting down in somebody's back yard. The nanny Spit was waggling its wings at him, altering course and descending. He followed it. Nothing to lose. Then another miracle happened: all of a sudden the mist cleared as though somebody had flung back the drapes.

'Bombardier to Pilot. I can see an airfield – over to your left, Ham. Ten o'clock.'

'Gotcha! Fire the emergency flare when we get closer, so they spot us.'

It was a fighter airfield – he could see the Spitfires standing out at dispersal – and the strip wasn't as long as he'd've liked, but it was no time to be fussy. As he'd expected, the hydraulic landing gear wouldn't budge, so it was going to be a wheels-up with screwed-up flaps, but he'd got the open stretch of flat land that he needed. So long as the engines kept going . . . just for another sixty seconds. Sixty seconds – that's all it would take. As he banked the Fort to go straight on in – no messing around with procedure – number three engine quit, giving him a whole new set of problems. He dropped *Miss Laid* on the grass, at the edge of the runway, almost halfway down. They skidded on, tore through a hedge and ploughed into a field of good old English mud. As they slithered to a stop number one engine finally quit too. It was that close.

An RAF officer with a handlebar moustache came squelching up through the rain. 'I say, are you chaps all right?' He was followed closely by a very angry farmer with a purple face who wanted to know what the bloody hell they thought they were doing to his turnips.

The formation returned with gaps. Daisy counted the Forts as they went over and circled to come in to land. Three missing, but she didn't know which three. In the interrogation room she sat beside the flight lieutenant and watched the doorway, waiting for Ham to walk through it. She went on waiting. One of the missing Forts had been seen by another crew ditching near the English coast and Air Sea Rescue were already out looking for them, but it wasn't his.

'Lieutenant Hamilton's crew's not come in yet, Sandy.'

He glanced at her. 'I'll see what I can find out.'

He went off and she watched him speaking to one of the interrogators and tried to gauge by his face if there was any news – good or bad. But how could she tell? Standing there, pipe clenched in his teeth, he had no particular expression, nothing to read. It was too many RAF years of war and too many casualties. Not indifference: simple acceptance of the situation and press on regardless. At last he came back.

'Apparently, Hamilton's plane was hit soon after they left the target and had to pull back out of the formation. They'd lost power in one engine and had some other damage. Nobody saw them go down though, so there's a good chance they'll be able to make it back on their own.'

She'd seen and heard too many combat reports to believe any such thing. A damaged bomber that was forced to pull out of formation on an American daylight raid had almost no chance at all.

'Thanks, Sandy.'

He lifted the phone. 'I'll have another word with Air Sea Rescue. See if they've picked up any more Maydays.'

They hadn't.

When the last crew had left the interrogation room she went back to her office and tried to concentrate on her work. Ground staff drifted in and out – bringing lists, returning files, asking for information, or simply to chat. As she dealt with it all, she listened for the sound of another Flying Fortress coming back alone. *Is it because you're afraid I'll get the chop? You can't face that happening?* She could face it because she must, but it was going to break her heart.

The phone on her desk rang.

'I say, is Flight Lieutenant Dimmock there?'

'Not at the moment, I'm afraid. This is Assistant Section Officer Woods speaking. Can I take a message for him?'

'If you would. Squadron Leader Patterson here – RAF Lampton.'

'Yes, sir?'

'We've got one of your Yank B-17s here. Had to make an emergency landing coming back from an op and picked on us. The captain asked me to give Flight Lieutenant Dimmock a ring.'

'Which captain, sir?'

'Lieutenant Hamilton.'

Thank God! Thank God!

'Are you there, Assistant Section Officer?'

'Yes. I'm sorry, sir. Is Lieutenant Hamilton all right?'

'A bit battered but otherwise OK. The co-pilot's not so hot – we got him to hospital – but the rest of the crew are fine. Their kite's rather shot up, though . . . God knows how they made it back. They're spending the night here as our honoured guests – we'll wine them and dine them and send them on in the morning. Pass the message on, will you?'

'Certainly, sir. Thank you for letting us know.'

'Jolly good.'

The navigator, Don, came into the Officers' Mess. There was a lot of back-slapping and drink-buying and cigarette-offering. Presently, he caught sight of her and came across.

She said, 'It's good to see you back safely, Don.'

'Yeah . . . it feels pretty good. Didn't seem like there was too much hope but then we've got one hell of a good pilot.'

'How's Gene?'

'Well, I reckon he's going to be in the hospital a long time, but they seem to think he'll pull through. He's a lucky guy. Ham stuck with him, even though it looked like the plane was never going to make it. The rest of us could've bailed out, like Ham offered, but we figured we'd stay along for the ride. I'm sure glad we did.'

'Is Ham all right?'

'Sure. He's around somewhere. I guess he'll be in here later.'

She didn't see him, though, until the evening, when he turned up at the farmhouse. She'd been bathing Madeleine and Peter and was reading them a bedtime story. *Once upon a time, there lived a poor woodcutter and his wife. They had two children: a boy called Hansel and a girl whose name was Gretel* . . . She'd got to the bit about them seeing the gingerbread cottage in the wood with the roof made out of marzipan and windows made out of sugar when Madeleine started giggling and she looked up and saw that he was standing in the doorway, leaning against the post, arms folded, listening. He smiled.

'Hey, don't stop. I want to know how it ends.'

She carried on reading the rest of the story – about the kind old woman who was really a witch and locked poor Hansel into a cage to be fattened for eating . . . about clever Hansel who poked a chicken bone through the cage for her to feel . . . about brave Gretel pushing the witch into the hot oven . . . and the happy reunion with the father.

When she had finished she said goodnight to the children and turned out their light. On the landing they looked at each other.

He said, 'I haven't heard that story in years – not since I was a kid. It sure is gruesome.'

'It's one of their favourites.'

'Well, I guess most kids can take it.'

She said quietly, 'I thought you were dead, Ham. I really did.'

'So did I, for a while. It was a close call.'

'Gene's going to be all right, isn't he?'

'The medics think so. But I guess the flying part's over for him.'

'You stayed with him and brought him back home.'

'We all did. That's what good crews do. Stick together.'

'What about your forehead? The plaster?'

'Hell, that's nothing. It'll mend in a couple of days.'

They went on looking at each other.

'So, what happens now?'

'Well, they're giving us a week's leave. Packing us off to a rest home to forget all about the war. One of those gracious English country houses that've been commandeered by us rough Yanks: beautiful grounds, tasty food and even tastier American girls dancing attendance. I hear they even have hot water and clean sheets, too.'

'It sounds wonderful.'

'Yeah . . . the other guys are looking forward to it.'

'Aren't you?'

'I'm not going.'

'Why on earth not?'

'I'm going some place else,' he said. 'Some little old country pub. The kind that has soft feather beds and big log fires and where the landlord's stashed away a barrel of good beer in the cellar.'

'It sounds wonderful, too.'

Downstairs, somebody had put on a Frank Sinatra record. The song floated up to them, so poignant and so confident: 'I'll be Seeing You'. It would always remind her of Halfpenny Green; and of him.

He smiled down at her. 'And guess what else is going to be wonderful about it, Daisy.'

'What?'

'You're coming with me.'

The pub was called the Cat and Mustard and it was in a village that was very nearly as lovely as Halfpenny Green. He'd been told about it by one of the other guys, he said, and English pubs sure did have some oddball names. It was nowhere near any airfields, nowhere near anything much at all. Sandy Dimmock had wangled her some leave and they had taken the train from Bury St Edmunds, changing to a branch line and a two-carriage train that chuffed unhurriedly through the winter countryside. Black trees, brown fields, patches of frost, a lemon-drop sun.

The only other occupant of the compartment – an elderly woman in headscarf and thick woollen stockings, a big wicker basket covered by a cloth on her capacious lap – had been fascinated by Ham in his uniform. Why didn't his trousers match his jacket? What foreign country was he from? She had wanted to know all about America. Where was it? How big was it? What language did they speak? What was he doing here? Why hadn't he come before? Since neither she nor Ham could understand each other, her questions were all addressed via Daisy, who had acted as interpreter. From time to time, whatever was in the wicker basket had moved under the cloth and the woman had lifted a corner and muttered something soothing.

Daisy had watched the American sitting opposite her in the compartment, politely fielding the barrage of ignorant, if well-meant questions. It didn't seem to matter much any more whether what she was doing was right, or sensible, or wise, or anything else. *He* was all that mattered.

They never did find out what was in the basket.

'What do you reckon?' he'd asked when they had got off the train. 'My money's on a cat.'

'Something edible, more probably. A chicken. Or a duck. Or a pigeon. Or a rabbit.'

'I still say it was a cat. You wouldn't be that nice to something you were going to eat.'

The landlord of the Cat and Mustard was very nice to them as well. He'd lit a fire in the open fireplace in their room and turned down the bed.

'What did I tell you?' Ham prodded it approvingly. 'Feathers.'

There was good beer in the cellar and another log fire blazing in the inglenook in the bar, and, for supper, a pigeon casserole cooked by the landlord's wife with country cheese and apples to follow. And there was mustard on the table and a cat curled up on a fireside chair. Nobody asked any more questions and nobody stared suspiciously at the brass curtain ring she was wearing on her left hand. The locals, absorbed in their darts and their shove-ha'penny and their dominoes, left them alone.

He said, 'Will you marry me, Daisy? Soon as I'm through with the tour?'

'You really mean it?'

'I'll say I do! And don't give me any more of that stuff about me being far from home and your not being my kind of girl. I told you, you're the girl I love and I'll always love. You're the girl I want to marry. And I'm asking you right now.'

'We're from two different worlds, Ham.'

'Sure. You're from the Old, I'm from the New. We'll make our own kind of world together. Whatever kind suits us. So, is the answer yes?' He looked at her and smiled his smile. 'It'd better be.'

The fire was still burning cosily in the bedroom upstairs but she was shivering and shaking like a jelly.

'I'm not cold,' she told him when he asked.

'I'm scared. I've never done this before, Ham. And I'll bet you have lots of times.'

'A few,' he said. 'But never with a girl I really cared about, so I guess you could say this is a first for me, too.'

'I'm still scared.'

'Hell, there's no need to be, Daisy. No need at all.' He took her face in his hands and kissed her gently. 'You'll see.'

Eleven

At Christmas, the Group gave a tea party in one of the hangars for the Halfpenny Green village children. Spam, jellies, candy bars, chewing gum, oranges and ice cream – some of the guys had taken the ice cream up to 25,000 feet in a bomb bay and flown it around to keep it frozen. Most of the English kids had never seen an orange or eaten ice cream. Hamilton watched their round eyes and the shy wonder in their faces. They'd sure had a hard time of it over the past four years. Their faces were all pale and pinched and some of them seemed badly undernourished. He guessed they'd put their best clothes on for the party but they were still patched and darned and shabby. He helped a small boy peel an orange and took it apart for him, but the kid sat and stared at it on his plate. It needed a lot of persuasion to get him to try it: he had to crouch down to his level and take a bite himself before the kid would even touch it.

Across the crowded hangar, he could see Daisy doing much the same with a cute little girl who didn't know what the hell to make of her ice cream. He went on watching for a while – how she was coaxing her so patiently with a bit on the end of a spoon, smiling at her, pretending to eat some herself.

Santa Claus came stomping in wearing RAF flying boots – ho-ho-hoing and clanging a hand bell – all dressed up in a red robe with big white whiskers and a sack over his shoulder. The small boy, nibbling wonderingly at his orange, promptly burst into terrified tears. Hamilton picked him up in his arms.

'Hey, it's only Santa Claus. He's a real nice guy. See that sack he's carrying – he's got a present for you in there. Something special.'

Daisy was looking his way and he looked back at her over the boy's head. He thought – ignoring his golden rule one more time – soon as we're married, we'll start our own kids. They'd talked about that, too, along with everything else they'd talked about during the week at the Cat and Mustard. Lying in the feather bed by the firelight's glow, smoking a cigarette, he'd told her all about the rule and how he'd figured it was better never to think about anything beyond the day. Never to think about tomorrow, or next week, let alone the future.

But then he'd gone on talking recklessly about the future that he might never have. He wouldn't go back to Berkeley; instead he'd start work with his father's company. They'd buy a house on the edge of Los Angeles, in a good neighbourhood – somewhere like Westwood or

Santa Monica or Pacific Palisades. He'd drive her around, show her some places, so she could choose where she'd want to be. Maybe she'd like a house with a view of the ocean.

'Oh boy, you should see the sunsets, Daisy.'

'We have sunsets in England, too.'

'Yeah, I know. I've seen them and they're great. But not like these ones out over the Pacific. The whole sky looks like it's on fire. They can be like that in the desert, too.'

'You have desert? I didn't realize that.'

'Sure. We've got desert, we've got mountains, we've got lakes and rivers, we've got the ocean. California's a big state. I'll fly you all over it in our plane. Take you up north to see Santa Barbara and Carmel and San Francisco and down to San Diego, right by Mexico. We'll fly across Death Valley and go down the Grand Canyon; I'll fly you all the way along right down inside it – that's a hell of a thrill.'

'It sounds terrifying.'

'I've done it lots of times. You'll love it. And I'll tell you what – we'll go to Palm Springs.'

'Where's that?'

'Right out in the desert. We'll stay at the Ingleside Inn. That's a beautiful old place built in the Twenties – all the Hollywood stars used to go there.'

She'd said wryly, 'It all sounds a bit different from Ealing. Are you sure I'll fit in?'

'Sure I'm sure. You'll love it and everyone'll love you.' He'd propped himself up on one elbow, looking down at her. 'I swear you'll never regret marrying me, Daisy.'

He'd spoken as though they were already married, as though nothing stood in the way of their happiness, and he knew that he was tempting fate. He'd broken the rule again and again and again.

She'd pressed her fingers to his mouth. 'Don't let's talk about it any more, Ham. Don't say another word.'

'OK. Suits me fine.' He'd turned away from her to stub out his cigarette. Then he'd leaned over her. 'Not one more word.'

After the children's Christmas party, they biked down to the Mad Monk – round the peri track and down Nightingale Lane to the green. It was a clear, frosty night with a skyful of glittering stars and a brilliant moon shining on the village. The landlord and his wife had decorated the inside of the pub with coloured paper chains strung all along the bar and round the walls, and there was a Christmas tree in the corner by the old piano festooned with coloured lights and shiny glass ornaments and fake cotton-wool snow.

Ham came back from the bar with their drinks. He clinked his glass against hers. 'Hey, maybe this time next year you'll be having Christmas in California. If I can fix getting you over there somehow.'

'I can't imagine Christmas in warm weather. It must be so different.'

'Yeah, I suppose it is. It can get kind of cool at night but we almost never get frost, though there's plenty of snow up in the mountains – you can see it from the city. And you can go skiing, if you want. It's not far up to Big Bear – only a couple of hours' drive – and we've got a great cabin up there.'

'I've never skied. Have you?'

'Since I was a kid. I'll teach you.'

'I'd like to try. Is it difficult?'

'Easy – once you get the hang of it.'

'How about Christmas decorations? Do you have those?'

'Sure we do. Lots of them. Trees, lights, all the trimmings. We just don't have the White Christmas, like in the song – not in Pasadena, anyway.'

Ray, Ham's new co-pilot, came up then and somebody went over to the piano and started to play 'White Christmas'. She watched him drinking his beer and talking to the co-pilot. She didn't mind where she went, or what it was like, so long as he was there. He was all that mattered. Absurdly, she envied the watch on his wrist because it was always with him. When she'd told him that, he'd laughed, but actually she'd been perfectly serious. And now they'd broken the golden rule yet again. They shouldn't have talked like that about the future. They shouldn't have thought about it at all.

The season of goodwill didn't stop any missions;

they flew them just the same. Hanover, Brussels, Paris, Chartres – dropping leaflets. They were the easy ones: the pieces of cake. Then back to Bremen again for another stab at the U-boats, dropping bombs instead of paper, and to Münster and to Ludwigshafen. Those were the tough ones. *Miss Laid* was out of action being patched up, so they took another Fort with somewhat better manners. Ray, his new co-pilot, was a decent guy but he wasn't as good. He missed Gene by his side in the cockpit, the way they'd worked together.

1943 turned into 1944. The Allies had landed at Anzio, north of Rome, and were having a hell of a tough time from the sound of it. In England, it stopped raining for a while and snowed instead and then it froze. Everything froze: water, mud, people, planes. Their twenty-first mission was to Caen in France. Twenty-one, as Don reminded him unnecessarily on the way out to their morning rendezvous with a newly patched-up *Miss Laid*, was getting close to the finishing post. Get through this one and they'd be on the home straight. At the hardstand one of the armourers wanted to take a photo of them. Waiting around while he did it froze their asses off, but they obliged. Hell, they even smiled, though they'd have been smiling a lot more if the guy had waited to take it when they got back. They took off into an overcast sky – nothing new in that – and into what the weather crystal-gazer had called snow flurries, which *was* a novelty.

He'd never heard of them but he was soon getting acquainted. *Miss Laid* was in a bad mood and he didn't blame her. She was probably remembering what had happened last time he'd taken her out.

The enemy fighters left them in peace for once, but as soon as they hit the French coast the flak started: puffy black Jerry smoke signals sent up to greet them on the target approach. *Welcome to Germany. Come on, you guys. This way.* He'd seen a lot worse on other missions, but somehow he had a bad feeling about this one.

Daisy had seen them leave from her bedroom window. The night before she'd gone to bed with a headache and sore throat and had woken up feeling much worse. She'd heard the bombers starting up and then begin to taxi round the peri track, and hauled herself out of bed to watch. The runway had been swept but snow lay over the rest of the airfield. As the first bomber had begun its take-off run, she had opened the window wide to hear and see better. Oblivious of the bitter cold, she had watched each take-off, counting them. *Miss Laid* was the sixth. The Flying Fortress with the languorous beauty painted on her port side – Ham's side – had raced along the runway, engines bellowing. Daisy had seen her wheels bounce a little and then leave the earth and she'd watched her clamber slowly into the sky, higher and higher, smaller and smaller, until she had vanished into cloud.

She had gone back to bed and buried herself under the green silk eiderdown, still counting as each bomber took off. Twenty. Not so many as on the big raids. Probably somewhere in France: one of the easier ones.

When the Forts returned, she awoke instantly from a fitful sleep and dragged herself out of bed again. The bombers were circling the airfield and began coming in to land. She counted carefully. One, two, three . . . six, seven, eight . . . eleven, twelve, thirteen . . . fifteen, sixteen, seventeen, eighteen. *Eighteen.* That was all. And none of them had been *Miss Laid.* She waited for the other two, listening hard for the sound of more engines. Waiting and listening. More than an hour later, Mrs Layton found her collapsed by the open window.

He hid in the wood until it was dark. At the base, they'd been given a lecture on what to do if they landed in enemy territory. Some guy who'd bailed out over France and made his way down to Spain and back to England had given them some helpful tips, and he tried to remember them. A French family caught helping an escaped American or British airman would get shot, so don't go approaching them. Head for the nearest wood. Wait until dark, then move off as far away as possible from search patrols. Find a remote village. Watch it for signs of Germans, then, if there aren't any, walk through the place without speaking to anyone. Let the French make the first move. There'd been other helpful hints too from instructors, about how to land without breaking your legs, how not to get towed along by the chute like a fish on a line, how to get rid of it fast, and how to hide it.

He'd landed more or less OK, shed the chute OK and there was a wood close by where he'd stuffed it well out of sight under some leaves. All OK, except that he was bleeding badly from a big gash in his leg. He'd taken a look at the wound and seen it was ugly. He'd no idea how it had happened. No real idea how he'd got out. He'd been lucky, and luckier still that he hadn't been barbecued in the process. All he could remember was *Miss Laid* getting hit by flak and bursting into flames. One moment they'd been flying along, the next the wings were streaming fire, the cockpit was full of flames and they were corkscrewing down through space. He and Ray had fought their way to the hatch and the co-pilot had gone first. There'd been no chance to help any of the other guys, no chance at all, and he didn't know what had happened to them. All he could remember was the roaring crackle, the searing heat of the flames, and, he thought, the sound of screaming which might have been himself. He'd been falling right alongside *Miss Laid*, faithful to her to the end, and then there'd been a mighty jerk as the chute opened up. He'd seen another Fort passing overhead – spotted the big black and red Mickey Mouse painted on its nose: Joe Bronsky and his crew going by. He'd thought, they'll have been looking out for chutes so they'll know some of us got out OK. Daisy'll know there's a chance.

Daisy lay in bed upstairs at the farmhouse. She could hear voices and laughter from the sitting room downstairs – the crews had come over as usual. They'd be playing cards, chess, backgammon, putting on records. The door must be open because she could hear each record, in turn, quite clearly: 'Green Eyes', 'Paper Doll', 'Moonlight Serenade', 'I'll be Seeing You'.

He spent that night in the wood and the next day considering his options. Option one, he could stay there for a while and hope the leg got better. Not such a great idea. The temperature was well below freezing and the wound was giving him hell; soon he wouldn't be able to use it at all to go in search of any villages, remote or otherwise. The only sign of human habitation he'd spotted so far was a lone farmhouse maybe a mile or so from the wood, down in a valley among some orchards. A farm meant a barn and a barn usually meant hay, or straw, some kind of shelter and a place to hide up. That was option two and he liked it a whole lot better. He ate the chocolate from his escape kit, saving the Horlicks tablets. Later, when it was almost dark, he swallowed a Benzedrine tablet before he set off slowly and painfully across the fields, dragging his injured leg and leaving a spotted trail of blood across the frozen earth.

It took him over an hour to reach the farm. By that time the moon was up and he could make out the silhouette of the house and a walled yard, with the expected barn at one end. It was a rundown, poor sort of place; he could tell that from the stink of a midden, from the encrusted dirt under his feet, and from the way the barn door, pegged shut by a nail through a hasp, was hanging crookedly by one hinge. Inside, there was another smell – the pungent aroma of chickens; he could hear them clucking around in the darkness and the nervous flutter and flap of wing feathers at his entrance. When he flicked on his Zippo lighter and moved the flame around there was a whole lot more clucking and chicken eyes staring back at him, heads poking nervously this way and that.

An old ladder led up into a loft. He managed to pull himself up it, rung by rung, and rolled sideways onto the flooring above. As he had hoped there was hay – hay that was old and musty but soft to lie on and good to hide in. He crawled into a corner and covered himself up.

The hens woke him at daylight; they were moving about below, yacking among themselves like a bunch of old women. Presently, he heard the sound of the nail being pulled back through the hasp and the crooked door being heaved open, and then a young girl's voice, clear and high, speaking to the hens in French. He lay there listening. The wound in his leg was a throbbing, fiery pit of pain and he knew that he was in bad trouble. There was no question of him holing up for a day or two and then scampering over the fields and far away. No question, right now, of even getting to his feet and walking anywhere at all. He dragged himself by his elbows across the hayloft to the top of the ladder and peered down. The girl was feeding the hens – throwing handfuls of meal out of a tin bowl onto the barn floor, scattering it wide as though she was sowing biblical seeds, and the hens were running around, pecking away like crazy. She was about ten or twelve, he judged, and dressed in a threadbare wool coat with a scarf tied, peasant fashion, round her hair and old-fashioned laced-up boots on her feet.

He debated what to do, and, as he did so, some basic instinct must have made her look upwards towards the loft. She saw him. Her mouth gaped and her face froze with shock and terror. Christ, what the hell was the French for don't be frightened . . . He said quickly, '*Je suis américain. Pilote. Pas dangereux. Je suis blessé.*'

She dropped the bowl with a loud clatter and ran out of the barn. The hens scattered and then regrouped, resuming their feeding frenzy.

Influenza turned into pneumonia and Daisy was moved to the base hospital, in a room at the end of a ward. She was on the critical list for several days, unaware of her parents visiting, unaware of anything much at all. When she was off the danger list, Flight Lieutenant Dimmock came to see her; he ignored the rules and sat on the end of her bed, pipe in hand. His face, as usual, told her nothing.

She said at once, 'Is there any news, Sandy?'

'Nothing very good, I'm afraid. Awfully sorry.'

'Tell me what happened.'

'Are you sure you want to know?'

'Quite sure.'

He fiddled with the pipe, peering into the bowl, poking at it with the end of a matchstick. 'Hamilton's plane was hit by flak soon after they crossed the French coast and was seen going down in flames. No parachutes spotted, unfortunately.'

'That doesn't necessarily mean—'

'I'm afraid it does in this case, Daisy. Some Intelligence chap in France sent a message across. Apparently, the wreckage was found on the ground by the French Resistance people before the Germans got there, and it's been definitely identified. No survivors.'

'The crew? Were they all identified?'

He blew carefully down the pipe's stem. 'Tricky that. Not a whole lot left, apparently. If you see what I mean.'

She saw only too well. She'd been to such funerals.

He went on, 'Usual procedure for that sort of case, I imagine. The crew buried together in one grave. The Germans are pretty good about doing it all decently, one gathers. Proper respect, and so on. Another Fort bought it that day, too. Joe Bronsky's lot. Remember him?'

Yes, she remembered him. Dallas, Texas. Big D. Nice Joe. He was a regular at the farmhouse evenings, showing the family snaps, telling her all about his home and the Lone Star State. The other plane missing must have been Joe's.

Sandy fished in his pocket. 'I got this for you. They were clearing out Hamilton's stuff to send back to his next of kin, and I palmed it when nobody was looking. Against all the regs, of course, but I thought you'd like to have something of his.'

It was the sketchbook that Ham had showed her. The pencil drawings he'd made of life on the base, with some additions that she'd never seen – including one, near the end, of her sitting at her table in the Interrogation hut. She hadn't even known that he'd done it. She closed the book.

'Thank you, Sandy. And for coming to tell me.'

'Least I could do.' He put his pipe away in his pocket and stood up. He turned at the doorway. 'It's not much comfort, of course, Daisy, but it must happen so damn fast, I doubt they ever know much about it. I've always believed that.'

When he'd gone, she lay staring at the ceiling. She wished that she had died too.

An American nurse came breezing in, all bright and smiling. 'Some guy just asked me to give you this. He didn't say his name. Hey, let me plump up those pillows for you.'

She was made to sit up, the pillows pummelled, the sheets retucked, an envelope put in her hand. When the nurse had left the room she opened it. Inside, there was a photograph of Ham and his crew. They were grouped on the starboard side – the side without the painting of *Miss Laid*. There was snow on the ground and they were wearing heavy winter flying kit. She realized that it had probably been taken just before they had left on their last mission. In their final hours. He was standing at the end of the back row, fisted hands on hips, heavy sheepskin collar turned up, the brim of his cap pulled down so that only a part of his face was visible – the middle part. She could see just his eyes, his nose and his mouth – the corners curved in the smile that she knew so well.

The French doctor was an elderly man and had difficulty getting up the ladder into the hayloft. He had brought his bag up too and proceeded to examine Hamilton's leg, poking and prodding. His English wasn't great but his meaning was crystal clear.

'Not good, my friend. Very bad. Hospital is necessary, but also now impossible. The Germans will know this family has helped you. They shoot them. Perhaps me too.'

The wound was agony after all the prodding. 'If I could walk, I'd go.'

'Of course . . . but it is much time before you walk. So, here you must stay. I will do my best but I promise nothing. Perhaps I cannot save the leg. Or you.'

The doctor disinfected and rebandaged the wound. 'Another American has been discovered by the French, but he is dead. The parachute did not work. He has been buried so that the Germans will not know anyone escaped. But it is believed that everybody else was in the plane. Nobody knows about you.'

'Did they find the wreck?'

'Oh, yes. All burned. Nobody was living. You are the only one.'

Soon after the doctor had gone down the ladder, the little girl appeared, bringing some hot soup in a tin can. He didn't know her name, or the name of the family, or where he was. It was better not, they had said. There were four of them – the girl, the girl's parents, and another older woman – the grandmother. They had all come running to the barn when the kid had first spotted him and stood staring up with white and frightened faces while he struggled again with his French. '*Je suis un pilote américain . . . je suis blessé . . . pouvez-vous m'aider?*'

They hadn't looked as though they were going to help him at all – more as though they were going to go running straight to the nearest Germans. There'd been a big argument between the husband and wife, a long gabble of agitated, incomprehensible French with a lot of hand-waving. Finally, the man had shrugged and the wife had come climbing up the ladder and taken stock of the situation. Her husband had been sent to fetch hot water, scissors and some old sheeting. His pants had been cut open, the gash laid bare and washed and bound with strips of sheet, while he did his darnedest not to groan and yell out loud.

Later, the old grandmother had brought bread and cheese and blankets and a bucket for him to use, hauling herself stiffly up the ladder and sliding them towards him across the hayloft floor with a toothless grin and a lot of nodding. None of them spoke English but he could make himself understood in his rusty French – enough to thank them, and let them know how grateful he was. He had nothing for them except the Horlicks tablets, which he gave to the girl. The doctor had come after a day or two.

He went on lying up in the hayloft, drifting in and out of consciousness, and they went on bringing him food and once in a while some lung-busting French cigarettes. Every so often, the doctor would clamber back up the ladder to clean and dress the leg. His watch had been smashed up when he'd bailed out and he found it hard to measure the passage of time; the days seemed very long, the nights endless. Hours of dark and pain and cold. If it hadn't been for his thick sheepskin jacket, he reckoned the cold alone would have killed him, never mind the wound.

A lot of the time he thought of Daisy. Bronsky and his crew would have seen the two chutes – he was sure of that – and they'd have reported it at debriefing. Daisy would have heard all about it. She wasn't the sort of girl to give up easily: she had more guts than that. She'd keep on hoping, keep on believing, keep on waiting. He wished to God he could somehow get a message to her but it was impossible. Sometimes he thought about the Cat and Mustard and the feather bed and the firelight and of how they'd talked about the future. He knew she'd been afraid of him breaking the golden rule and tempting fate and maybe he had, but fate hadn't done with him yet. He was still alive and he could still get through this and find a way back to England.

Other times he thought about his parents, who must have been told by now that he was missing; he knew how cut up they'd be, his sister, too. The MIA letter wouldn't have said anything about chutes, so they'd have no reason whatever to hope. Once he thought about Lola back home, who still kept on writing to him. He figured she wouldn't be shedding tears for long. And he thought a lot about his dead crew: Ray, Don, Lee, Carl, Ken, Alvin, Cliff, Merle, Bernie. He mourned them as brothers. The bond between them had been a kind that he knew he'd never experience again. He was sorry about *Miss Laid* too. For all her faults, she'd gutted it out with them as long as she could.

Whenever the little girl came to feed the hens

she would nip up the ladder and sit beside him. He taught her simple English words and phrases and she corrected his French, giggling when he made bad mistakes. Once she brought him a deck of cards and he showed her how to play gin and how to cut and shuffle the deck like a river-boat gambler. Alone, he played endless games of solitaire. During the day he sometimes heard American bombers go over, and, at night, the RAF.

The leg improved slowly until he was able to stand on it, and then to hobble. They brought him a stick so that he could begin to walk. He practised walking up and down the hayloft – up and down, up and down, up and down – until he could do without the stick and knew he was ready to leave. When the doctor came again, he said so.

'And where will you go, my friend?'

'Away from here. Head south for Spain, I guess.'

'And in which direction is south? Do you know that?'

'I'm a pilot, doctor. I can steer by the sun and the stars. Also I have a compass. They give us one in our escape kits. And a map.'

'Ah . . . such efficiency. But you have only American uniform and no identity papers. You would not go very far, believe me, before the Germans arrest you. If you have a little patience, I can perhaps organize clothes and papers for you. There are people I know who will help you.

Spain is not perhaps the best idea; there are other ways.'

He said, 'Thanks but I wouldn't want to put anyone in danger.'

'By yourself, my dear friend, you will not succeed. The clothes we can find quickly, the *carte d'identité* is more difficult. For that we need a photograph of you and film is very difficult to get.'

Hamilton produced the grainy photo of himself in a civilian jacket – the escape-kit one that all American air crews had taken for that very purpose.

'Will this do?'

The doctor took it, looked at it and smiled. 'Now I know that you will certainly win the war for us.'

A tin bath out in the yard was home to two ducks. The farmer's wife and daughter carried it into the barn, took out the straw and filled it with water from the pump. The grandmother brought a pitcher of hot water and a bowl, a sliver of soap, a cut-throat razor and a hand mirror. They left him while he took a bath in the cold water and shaved in the hot and when he'd finished and put on the civilian clothes provided by the doctor, they came back and the three of them stood admiring the way he'd cleaned up. The grandmother took away his American clothes. They would burn them, she told him, except for the sheepskin jacket. It was too good to waste so they would bury it and mark the place secretly, so that after the war he could come back for it if he wished. He wondered if he would ever be able to find the farm again.

A few days later, he left in a baker's horse-drawn cart carrying a French identity card that gave his occupation as a cook. He had been given French francs, a train ticket and an address in Rennes to memorize, where he would be given shelter and more help. He did not know how to thank either the doctor or the family adequately for risking their necks for him; his French wasn't up to it, but he sure hoped they understood what he felt. When he gave the little girl a goodbye hug, she started crying. The farmer shook his hand, the wife kissed his cheek, the old crone of a grandmother clasped his hands tightly in both hers and tears trickled down her withered cheeks.

Daisy went home to convalesce. The weather was still cold but the crocuses were out in the garden, the daffodils coming up fast and buds starting to open on the trees. The English spring was beginning: a spring that Ham would never see. And summer would follow, and autumn and then another winter. And next year and the year after and all the years after that which he would never see either, and which she would have to live through without him.

She had been home for a week when Vernon came to visit his mother. He called round to see her and sat with her in the old nursery upstairs beside the gas fire – the room she and her sisters had played in, and where their children's books and toys and games had been left undisturbed. This was also the room where he had helped her with her homework, patiently trying to explain the mysteries of logarithms and geometry and algebra.

He looked tired and as though he had lost weight. His clothes hung on him, as ill-fitting as always – bony wrists protruding from too-short sleeves, trousers finishing above his ankles to show odd socks. He reminded her of Worzel Gummidge, the scarecrow in the children's book that she had sometimes read to Madeleine and Peter at bedtimes, and she half-expected to see tarred-string braces and bottle-straw boots on his feet. When she asked him how his job was going, he mumbled something vague and said it was pretty boring.

'Your mother says they work you too hard.'

He gave a helpless shrug. 'You know what she's like.'

'You *do* look a bit tired, Vernon.'

'Do I? Well, there's a lot to do . . . you know, with the war on.'

'Communicating?'

He nodded, staring at his shoes. 'All that sort of stuff.'

She wondered what he really did. Whatever it was he'd never tell her and she wouldn't ask any more questions. 'Well, don't forget to eat sometimes. You look as though you could do with a few square meals. No wonder your mother's worried.'

He lifted his head. 'It's *you* that's the worry, Daisy. You've got over the pneumonia, but that's not all, is it? You're very unhappy. I can see that. Will you tell me what the matter is? I can keep a secret.'

She smiled. 'I know you can.'

'Then tell me. Perhaps I can help you.'

'Nobody can help,' she said. 'I have to work it out for myself.'

'Tell me, just the same.'

And so she told him. All about meeting Ham and falling in love. About the week away at the Cat and Mustard, the plans and the hopes and the unbelievable happiness. And then what had happened.

'His plane was shot down. He and his crew were all killed.'

'Are you sure they were? All of them?'

'Oh yes. The other crews always look for parachutes, for men bailing out. Nobody saw any and the wreck was found in France with the crew inside. Or what was left of them.'

He shook his head. 'How dreadful! I'm so sorry, Daisy. No wonder you're so unhappy.'

'When I heard what had happened, I wanted to die as well. I didn't want to live without him.'

'You must have loved him very much.'

'He was the love of my life – that's the phrase people use, isn't it? The one that will never *ever* happen like that again.'

'Yes, I think that's what people call it.'

'There's something else, Vernon. I'm pregnant. Three months to be exact. What with being ill, I didn't realize for a while . . . When I did, though, I stopped wanting to die because I knew I had something to live for. His child. A part of him.'

He was silent and she thought she had shocked him deeply.

At last he said, 'Have you told your parents, Daisy?'

'No – not yet. I've been trying to think what to do for the best. Whether to go away and have the baby somewhere else . . . what on earth to do. I'll be thrown out of the WAAF of course, but I've got some money a godmother left me, so I could manage on my own.'

He said quietly, 'You could marry me, Daisy. Right away. I'd love your child as if it were my own. And, like I said, I'm quite good at keeping secrets.'

She touched his arm. 'Thank you, Vernon. But that wouldn't be right. Or fair on you.'

'It would be all right by me. Very all right.' He knelt down clumsily on the old nursery rug in front of the gas fire and took both her hands in his. 'I've loved you all these years, but I've always known that there was no real hope . . . that you'd never feel the same way.'

'I'm awfully fond of you, Vernon.'

'It's not the same thing though, is it? There's a big difference between being fond of someone and loving them. But I'd be content with that, and I'd never expect anything more from you. I'd take care of you and the child, give you both my name and a home . . . and my unconditional love, for always.'

She shook her head. 'No, Vernon . . . but thank you, all the same.'

He said, 'Have you thought about what it would mean to have an illegitimate child?'

'Yes, of course I have. I don't care what people think of me.'

'I didn't mean that. I know you wouldn't care about yourself, Daisy. But think about your child. About the stigma he, or she, would always have to bear. Imagine the child growing up and being shunned by other families, going to school and being mocked and taunted by other children, ostracized all its life. It doesn't have to be like that. We could say we were married in secret three months ago at a register office. Nobody would ever need to know the truth – except you and I.'

It was her turn to fall silent.

'I need time to think . . . do you mind?'

'Of course not. Take all the time you want.'

She said slowly, 'I'd want the baby to know.'

'That would be up to you, Daisy. Maybe one day, you could tell the truth – if you thought it would be the right thing to do.'

The address in Rennes was a small restaurant – *Le Faisan d'Or* – and the patron and his wife were expecting him. Hamilton was given a cubbyhole under the eaves and it was explained to him that, when the time was right, he would be passed on to the next safe house. Eventually, with luck, it would be arranged for him to be picked up off a beach at night by a British motor boat, or possibly by an aeroplane landing in a field. But it would all take time, he must understand that. He must be patient and do exactly as he was told and stay inside, out of sight, at all times. Meanwhile, he was to work in the kitchens – it would give him something to do to pass the time, and if his *carte d'identité* should be demanded, then, *voilà*! he was a cook, just like it said.

During the time that he was there, Hamilton learned a whole lot about French cooking: how to make sauces and cassoulets and carbonnades and fricassées, and how to cook a perfect omelette. He even got used to eating trotters, cheeks, tongues, livers, kidneys, brains – things he'd never touched before. Sometimes German soldiers came to the restaurant and he watched them through the hatchway from the kitchens as they guzzled away. The patron ritually and ceremoniously spat in their soup before it was carried out.

His next safe house was close to the Channel port of St Malo – the neat little home of two elderly spinsters who feigned loony senility in front of the Germans, but, behind closed shutters, were sharp as tacks. He played cards with them every night, gambling with matchsticks, and they beat him every time. When the war was over, he promised to honour his debt in real money. The ocean was so damn close now, England only the other side, but, again, he was told that he must be patient. There were rumours that the Allies were preparing to land somewhere on the north coast of France, but nobody knew where or when – least of all the Germans.

He had been moved on, yet again, when the invasion finally happened. More rumours, more waiting – several teeth-grinding weeks of it – until, with the sight of American and British planes daily overhead and the sound of gunfire only a few miles away, he decided, the hell with it. He started walking towards all the noise and fury. As he reached a village, a tank came rumbling round the corner. He was lucky: it was American.

An American army truck gave him a lift to Cherbourg and he hitched another on a plane to England. He spent three days at an officers' club in London being interrogated before they let him go on leave. He checked into the Savoy Hotel and phoned the Laytons' number in Suffolk. Mrs Layton answered the phone. She remembered him at once and sounded knocked sideways to hear that he was alive, not dead. Kept saying how wonderful it was, how sad they'd been, how she almost couldn't believe it – they'd been so sure he'd been killed. All of them had thought so. Daisy too.

'Is she there? I'd like to speak to her – give her the news myself.'

A pause. 'Daisy's not with us any more, Ham. She was very ill indeed – with pneumonia – soon after you were shot down. She nearly died. They kept her in the hospital at the base for several weeks and then sent her home to convalesce.'

He was shocked. He'd never thought of anything happening to her. 'Jeez . . . is she OK now?'

'Yes, as far as we know. But she's left the WAAF.'

'Oh? Why did she do that?'

Another pause. 'She got married, Ham. To somebody she'd known a long time . . . a friend of the family. We had a letter from her the other day, telling us. Of course, she thought you'd been killed. Your people told her there was really no hope, you see. They said that you and all your crew were presumed dead.'

For a moment he couldn't speak. He couldn't believe what he'd heard. Within a few months she'd gone and married some other guy . . . Jesus Christ! A few months! Was that all he'd meant to her? Was that all the time it had taken her to get over him? She hadn't even waited to be sure he really *was* dead, not just presumed so. *Jesus Christ!*

'Ham? Are you still there?'

He collected himself. 'Yes, Mrs Layton, I'm still here. Do you have her address?'

'I'm not sure . . .'

He said levelly, very calmly, 'I'd like to have it . . . to write and congratulate her.'

He got the address and went down to the hotel bar to get drunk. There were other Yanks in there, and after a few drinks he got talking. He found out they were Glenn Miller's band and someone took him over and introduced him to the great man himself. Then he carried on drinking.

When he'd sobered up the next day, he wrote a letter to Daisy. He couldn't help sounding bitter, though he tried not to lay it on too much. Within a couple of days he had a reply.

Dear Ham, Your letter was a very great shock. I had believed you to be dead. Your plane was seen going down in flames and they told me that nobody had got out. The wreckage was found later in France and all the crew were reported as killed.

I know that you will be surprised and hurt that I have married so soon. I want you to know that I had my reasons, that there is no going back and that I believe that, in the end, it will be for the best.

I'm so glad and so thankful that you are alive, Ham. And I'll never forget you.

Daisy.

Oh yeah, he thought. Oh yeah . . .

They wouldn't let him back into combat. If he was shot down again, they said, he could give away too much about the French who'd helped him. The Gestapo had too many ways of finding things out to run the risk. Instead, he was sent back stateside. He travelled home on the liner *Queen Mary*, which had been spending the war ferrying troops across the Atlantic. She went unescorted and lickety-split – too fast for any goddam U-boat to catch her. At dawn, as they approached New York, he went up to stand in the bow and get the first sight of the Statue of Liberty and the city's skyline beyond: the great sight that he'd never believed he would see again. It choked his throat right up.

There was a girl standing beside him at the rail – an English girl, he discovered, who'd married a Yank colonel and was going to join him. She looked happy and excited – eyes shining, a beautiful smile on her face. It could have been Daisy, he thought, and it could have been him.

He watched his country coming closer and closer – the skycrapers, the quayside, the customs sheds, the people. The New World. *His* world. To hell with the old one! Forget it! That was yesterday. This was today. And, come to think of it, now, at last, he had a tomorrow.

The wireless shop was in the middle of the high street, in between a greengrocer and an iron-monger. It sold wirelesses, gramophones, electrical goods and records. Daisy passed it whenever she was shopping, and, one day, she stopped and went inside. Yes, the counter assistant told her, they had a copy of that particular recording, and, if she would care to step into the soundproof booth at the back of the shop, she would be able to try it. He showed her how to work the turntable and left her alone. She pressed the button, the needle arm moved across and descended.

She listened with the tears running down her face.

PART III

Twelve

In September the watercolour evening classes started up again and Monica and I continued our Thursday visits to the coffee bar. I had already told her about discovering the old airfield, Halfpenny Green, in Suffolk, and as much as I wanted her to know of the rest – not that there was much to tell. Privately, I'd been doing some counting on my fingers and worked out a few dates. I had been born in late September 1944 and, therefore, probably conceived in late December 1943. Joe Deerfield had implied that the crew in the photo had already done a number of missions to earn their tough reputation before they went missing, and so they would have been flying from Halfpenny Green throughout the last half of 1943. I'd done some more reading on the Yanks in my airfields book. Twenty-five missions made an American tour – later on in the war they upped it to thirty, but not then. How long a tour took depended on the planners and the weather, but it must have stretched over months, maybe a year or more. The crew chief had said that the photo had been taken early in 1944, probably

January, just before the crew had been shot down.

It made sense. Ma obviously hadn't yet realized she was pregnant which was why the pilot had never known about me, and when he had come back from the dead, months later, she'd already got married to Da. I had given that bit of the story a lot of thought. For the first time, I'd stopped thinking about me and thought about her instead – about how wretchedly miserable it all must have been for her. To have believed the man she loved dead, and then to hear that he was alive after all – but to find it out too late. I began to see things through her eyes. *I never forgot him or stopped loving him. Not for a single day.*

She'd married Da for my sake and she'd given up her American for both our sakes. It must have been a heart-breaking sacrifice.

Over the coffee cups, Monica said, 'Any luck with any of the American mags?'

'Not yet. Two of them sent me their latest issues with the photo and my letter in them, but I haven't heard a thing so far.'

'Don't give up. How about giving the American Embassy another go? Now that you know a bit more. You might get someone more helpful.'

'I already have. It's hopeless. They just repeat all that jargon about having to apply to the Pentagon and fill up forms. And go on about their Privacy Act.' In fact, the American voices at the other end of the line had been even less helpful and more openly hostile. I wasn't keen to give it a third try.

'What about the woman in the newspaper – the War Children one?'

'I rang her and told her about Suffolk and the little bit I found out. She said she'd pass it on to her contacts in California – see if they could come up with anything. I don't see how they can, though. There's practically nothing to go on.'

Monica put down her cup. She said briskly, 'Of course, you know what you should do next, Juliet.'

'Do I? What?'

'Go to California.'

'*Go* there?'

'That's what I said. Get on a plane and go.'

'What's the use? I wouldn't know where to start when I got there. Besides, he's probably not living there any more. He's probably already dead.'

'I thought you wanted to find this chap?'

'I do.'

'Then stop making excuses and being so negative. Get out there and find him.'

Adrian invited me to dinner at his favourite fish restaurant – secluded, discreet, quiet, positively no flash trash. He was sitting at his usual table in the corner and rose to his feet to kiss my hand.

'Wherever did you find that coat, darling?'

'Petticoat Lane market. It's an old Balmain, believe it or not.'

'I do believe it. One of your better buys. It suits you very well.'

Praise from Adrian about any item of my clothing was praise indeed. Usually, he kindly refrained from comment.

Over the sole, I mentioned Monica's suggestion.

'Well of course you should go, darling – if you've still got that bee in your bonnet. I did hope the trip to Suffolk might have got rid of it, but clearly it hasn't. It's still buzzing around. Pack your bags and catch a plane. You've never been to America, have you? Now's the time. Especially when one considers that you're half American.'

'I don't consider myself anything of the kind. And I can't up sticks just like that . . . I've got a commission to finish. And there's the evening classes. I can't let them down.'

'Don't they stop for the Christmas hols? You could go then. Spend Christmas in California. Eric and I did that once. Rather a pleasant change. They go right over the top with the decorations – it's quite a sight. Who do you know there that you could stay with?'

'I've got an old schoolfriend who lives in Santa Monica but I haven't seen her for years.'

'Santa Monica's right next to Los Angeles but very civilized. A sort of Wimbledon-on-Sea but much nicer. You'd like it. Write to your friend and invite yourself for Christmas.'

'Rather a cheek. And there's Flavia to consider.'

'Flavia is grown-up, darling, and she has her live-in lover to keep her warm. I'm sure your old friend would be delighted to see you. How is your *Véronique*?'

'Wonderful, thank you.'

'You must try the monkfish next time. It's superb.'

I started making feeble excuses again. 'I don't see much point in going to California, Adrian. I've got so little to go on. Almost nothing.'

'It's more than you had at the start. You've had a positive identification from the photo. You know that his first or last name is almost certainly Ham something – Hamlyn, Hampton, Hampshire, Hammond. American first names often sound like last names, so it could be either way round. You also know that he served as a pilot in the United States Eighth Air Force during the Second World War and that he was in England in 1943 and early 1944, based at Halfpenny Green in Suffolk. And that he came from California. That's quite a lot.'

'California is a *huge* state. I looked in my atlas. It goes a long way down the Pacific coast of America. He'd be a needle in a haystack.'

'But you know something else about him, too, darling.'

'Do I? What?'

'You told me that the crew chief from Arizona who recognized him in the photo said they used to joke about our ghastly English weather because they were both used to living in much warmer temperatures. Now, northern California can get quite chilly and rainy at times, which rather suggests to me that your father came from down south – the Mexico end. A reasonable deduction, don't you agree, my dear Watson?'

'I suppose so.'

'Furthermore, he was a bomber pilot and an officer of the American Air Force – not some barn-storming backwoodsman. A college man, I'd say, from a town or city in southern California. Santa Barbara, Los Angeles, San Diego . . . there aren't that many, you know. There's an awful lot of mountain and desert, if you take another peek at your map. So you'd be well placed in Santa Monica to do some sleuthing. If I were you, I'd find a native out there to help. Hopeless, I agree, to try on your own. Employ someone who knows how to go about tracing people. A private detective or an attorney, or some such. Your friend might know somebody she can recommend.'

'It would have to be somebody I could trust not to go trampling around, making waves.'

'That sounds a bit mixed-up, darling. I take it that what you actually mean is that you'd like to find out about your father without him finding out about you? And, if you succeed, you'll just come winging home and get on with your life, as usual?'

'Something like that.'

'As I told you before, it would never work. If

you trace him, you'll have to meet him. Why else bother?'

'Curiosity. Compulsion.'

'It's not quite as simple as that, though, is it? Your mother kept your existence a secret from him. So far as he knew, the minute she thought he was dead she'd waltzed off and married someone else. He must have been rather upset about that, to say the least. However, in the end, she told you the truth because she thought you should know it. She wanted, as they say in the well-worn phrase, to put the record straight.'

'I suppose so.'

'Well, darling, it can't really be put straight until, and unless, he knows too. Can it?'

A new commission, doing illustrations for an alphabet book, kept me busy during October and November – the usual sort of easy-to-recognize things: apple, banana, castle, dog, elephant. No bunnies this time: in modern and more realistic times R was for rat.

I had kept in touch with Chris, my school-friend, over the years. She had met her American husband, Dan, in London when he was working there for an American bank and when they had moved back to his home state, California, we had written to each other fairly regularly. Even so, it was more than ten years since I'd last seen her. I wrote to her now, with the same old half-truth. My mother had died early in the year, I told her, and I was trying to trace an old wartime American friend of hers from California – probably from somewhere in the south. I had been thinking of coming over in December to see if I could track him down. It all sounded pretty lame to me but Chris answered almost at once, with her usual enthusiasm. It was wonderful to hear from me. I must come and stay – for Christmas if I could. It was the only time she got homesick for England and it would be great company to have me there. What was the name of my mother's friend? She'd see if she could find out anything, meanwhile.

I told Flavia about the invitation, leaving out the fact that I had instigated it, and, of course, the real reason. Oh, what a tangled web we weave . . . 'Do you mind if I go, darling? If I'm not here for Christmas?'

She laughed. 'Of course not, Ma. Christmas was three months ago for me. We're already thinking about Easter. You must go. It sounds wonderful.'

I'd forgotten about magazines working so far ahead in the seasons. 'What about you? What will you do?'

'Don't know, really. Callum's auditioning for another TV series, so he might be working. We'll see. We might splurge some of Grandma's money on an exotic holiday.'

I didn't like the 'we', but Flavia's inheritance had had no strings attached and she could spend it how she chose – or Callum could spend it for her. Last year we'd both gone to Oxford – without Callum, who had gone to visit the family he never talked about. In fact, we'd spent almost every other Christmas together for as long as I could remember: sometimes in London, other times in Oxford, once with Adrian and Eric in France, or with other friends. The exceptions had been when Flavia had spent them with her father – tricky for her, I knew, with his new family and Caroline's demanding lifestyle, but she coped.

I booked my ticket with British Airways: Heathrow to Los Angeles. The return fare at that time of the year was horrendous and I had to raid my savings. Then I rang Drew and brought him up to date.

'Well I hope you know what you're doing, Ju.'

'No,' I said. 'I've no idea but I'm going to do it anyway.'

'I wouldn't, if I were you.'

'That's the whole point, Drew. You're not me, so you're not in this situation.'

'You could be in for a big disappointment . . . unnecessary heartache.'

'I'll risk it.'

'I hope you haven't said anything to Flavia.'

'No, I haven't.'

'Thank God for that. Let me know, anyway, how you get on.'

I called Stella Morrison – champion of the War Children. Her California contacts had drawn a big blank so far. I told her about Adrian's theories and she agreed that they made sense.

'It all helps to narrow the field. Like I said, Juliet, it's partly luck. By the way, I meant to tell you that most American telephone directories are on microfilm so you can look them up in the library and go through possible names. If you do happen to get any leads while you're out there, I'd advise you to play it very carefully. Stick to your old-friend-of-the-family story – people will be much more inclined to help and it's close to the truth. And even if you're certain you've found your father, don't go telling him straight out. You might give him a heart attack.'

'I'm not sure I'd want him to know at all.'

'Wait and see.'

I said, 'How did your father react when he learned about you?'

'He took it wonderfully – accepted me at once, without question. But some of them don't. It can turn quite nasty.'

'How did *you* feel?'

'Terrified – at first. Very awkward. It's quite a strange happening, you know. Very traumatic. Of course, you can never get the past back – what's gone is gone – but it meant a lot to me to find him – a sort of natural instinct, I suppose. The need to *know*.'

I gave her Chris's phone number in Santa Monica in case her contacts over there came up with anything. She wished me good luck and good hunting.

* * *

I worked flat out on the alphabet book. After R for rat, there was snake, tomato, umbrella, violin, windmill, xylophone, yacht and – inevitably – zebra. If the choice had been mine, I think I'd have tried some fresh alternatives, but I did my best to make the illustrations different. The tomato was being squeezed whole out of a ketchup bottle, the umbrella was dragging an old lady into the air, showing her red bloomers, the violin was played with a saw by a mad-looking musician, a miller whirled round on the windmill's sails, the yacht was crewed by monkeys, the zebra's stripes were hidden, puzzle-like, among trees. The xylophone stumped me, though: all I could think of was to make it of candy with the sticks as lollipops.

Callum's detective series was shown on television and I went downstairs to watch the first episode. I wasn't expecting more than the previous blink-and-miss-him appearances, but this time he had a larger part as assistant to the lead detective. It was a dogsbody role but he did it very well, and he looked extremely good in a belted raincoat with the collar turned up. It really seemed as though the big break he needed was finally coming nearer.

The evening classes stopped for the Christmas holiday and I had finished the illustrations and delivered them, on time, to the publisher. Flavia insisted on driving me to the airport and waiting until I'd checked in. As I went off into the departure lounge I looked back to see her still there, waving and smiling. I wondered whether she would still have been smiling if she had known the crazy thing I was doing.

On the plane I sat next to an English woman flying out to stay with her married daughter, who lived in Los Angeles. She didn't think much of the city but she liked the Americans and she loved the California climate. Santa Monica, she assured me, was very nice. Very nice indeed. I listened politely to her chatting on about her American son-in-law who was a doctor and had no faults except that of transplanting her only daughter six thousand miles away. Her two grandchildren, similarly, only had one failing: speaking with an American accent. She had nothing against it, per se, but she would have preferred them to speak proper English. Fortunately, her daughter still did – unlike some expatriates she had met over there who had gone completely American. Personally, she thought that a great mistake – especially when Americans seemed to love an English accent. She'd lost count of the number of times she'd been told so and asked to repeat things. Eventually, to my relief, she fell asleep.

We flew steadily west, going backwards in time – perhaps that was appropriate, since it seemed to be what I was aiming to do. We went past Iceland, across the tip of Greenland, down over Canada, and on, for more long hours, across the United States of America. Forests, plains, rivers, lakes, mountains, deserts . . . to insular English eyes the immense scale of the North American continent was staggering. *From sea to shining sea* meant three thousand miles in between, not a mere few hundred, and two completely different oceans.

We came into Los Angeles from the east, descending gradually in smoggy afternoon sunlight over a vast sprawl of Monopoly houses lining grid-patterned streets. I could see red, brown and grey roofs, the blue glitter of swimming pools, a hazy cluster of downtown skyscrapers, and, across it all, a Scalextric labyrinth of multi-lane freeways, flyovers, highways and toy cars racing along.

The woman beside me had woken up and was patting her hair in place. 'Did you do your immigration and customs forms? They can be quite unpleasant if you don't fill them in properly.'

I stepped off the plane into the New World: an American voice squawking over the tannoy, American spelling on the signs, a gigantic photograph on a wall of the American President beaming a welcome to visitors, and a very long queue for a very small number of immigration officials. When my turn came at last the man behind the desk, unlike his President, was unbeaming and far from welcoming. He examined my passport, turning pages very slowly, and stared at the green and white forms I'd filled in. Then he stared at me.

'What is the purpose of your visit to the United States, ma'am?'

'I'm visiting a friend.'

'Where?'

'In Santa Monica.'

'At this address you've given?'

'Yes, that's right.'

'How long are you intending to remain?'

'Two weeks.'

'Do you have adequate funds to support your stay?'

'Yes, I do.'

'In what form?'

'Travellers' cheques and some dollars. I've put the amount on the customs declaration form.'

'Have you a return ticket?'

'Yes.'

He clicked his fingers and I fumbled in my bag.

The return ticket was scrutinized, the passport reopened. 'It says here you're an artist.'

'That's right, I am.'

'What kind of artist?'

'I illustrate books.'

'Are you looking for work here in the United States?'

'No, I'm here for pleasure – like I said. To see an old friend.'

Finally, he reached for his stamp, passport and forms were handed back.

'Enjoy your visit, ma'am.'

I collected my suitcase from the carousel. In the customs hall I was ordered over to a bench and told to open the case. The official, an immensely fat woman, was as frightening as the immigration man. She went through the contents of the suitcase, turning things upside down. The Marmite, the Harrods Christmas pudding and mince pies were all confiscated.

'You did not declare any of these items on your form. It's against the law to bring foodstuffs into the United States.'

She went off with the illegal foodstuffs and disappeared through a door. I slumped wearily on the bench beside the open case, wondering if I and them were going to be deported on the next plane out. At that moment, I was past caring. The flight had taken more than ten hours and back in England it was long past my bedtime. After what seemed like a very long time, the customs woman came back with my provisions.

'You can keep them. And you can shut the case now.' She didn't tell me to enjoy my stay.

The ring of waiting faces in the Arrivals Hall belonged to strangers and just as I was wondering what to do next, I heard my name being called and saw one of them waving and smiling at me. I would have known Chris anywhere by her teeth – slightly prominent and with a gap between the two front ones – except that now they weren't and there wasn't, and her hair was blond, not brown, short, not long, and she was thin not plump. The English jumpers and skirts had been superseded by designer jeans, a cream polo neck, a pale blue suede jacket and an outsize shoulder bag to match. We hugged.

'Julie . . . you haven't changed a bit!'

'*You* have, Chris. You look so glamorous!'

'I've been made over – California style. Teeth, face, boobs, liposuction, hair, the works . . . you have to keep up in this place. How was the flight? What kept you so long in there?'

Underneath the before-and-after makeover, I could tell that Chris was just the same and the speech was still more English than American. 'The flight was fine, thanks, but immigration and customs took a while. I'm sorry you've had to wait.'

'They can be pigs here. So many undesirables trying to get in to live the American Dream, not to mention the drugs and the diseases.'

We went outside and the sunlight was dazzling. Blue skies, palm trees waving in a little breeze; back home it would be pitch dark and probably raining. In December it felt as warm as a nice spring day in England, and people were dressed in casual clothes and bright colours as though they were on holiday. Chris's car was a metallic bronze convertible with cream leather seats.

'It's a Chrysler. Fantastic, isn't it? I love it to bits. I'd put the top down if it wasn't so cold today.' We swung out of the car park with a screech of tyres, past the pay kiosk and out onto a highway. 'Sorry I can't take you the scenic route. There isn't one from LAX.' We zipped past multi-storey hotels and concrete office blocks and joined a six-lane freeway. Chris drove with one hand on the wheel, changing lanes at random, and, apparently, without looking before she did so. The inky, nail-bitten fingers of long ago now sported unbelievably long red talons.

'This American guy you're trying to find – Ham something. There are all sorts of names with Ham in them in the phone book, but that gets you nowhere. Did you find out anything else?'

'I know a bit about him, but it's not very much. I was thinking of finding someone to help over here – a private detective, maybe.'

She glanced at me curiously. 'What's the big deal about tracing him? Did your mother leave him something in her will?'

'No, nothing like that. He was an old friend from wartime days . . . a bomber pilot with the American Eighth Air Force when she was in the WAAF. She left me a letter about him, and a photo.'

We changed lanes abruptly again. 'Sounds like he was a bit more than a friend . . . don't you think?'

I said truthfully, 'She never spoke of him before, so it's rather a mystery. I'd like to track him down, if it's possible.'

'Well, I think I know just the man to help you. We're having some people in tomorrow evening and I've asked him along so you can meet him.'

'Who is he?'

'His name's Rob Mclaren.'

'A Scot?'

'Well, I suppose his family must have been once, but now he's a full-blown Yank. They all come from somewhere else – unless they're American Indians and there aren't too many of those around. He's a freelance journalist. Contacts everywhere. He'll know which strings to pull.'

'I'd sooner steer clear of anything to do with newspapers.'

'He's not a muckraker, if that's what you're worried about. He does stuff for the broadsheets and upmarket mags like *Time*. All pretty high-brow. See what you think of him, anyway.'

She glanced at me again. 'You know, I can't imagine your mother two-timing your father, Julie. They always seemed the perfect couple to me.'

'She didn't. And they were. She knew this American before.'

'So he's come out of the past? Big surprise. Did she ask you to trace him – in that letter?'

'Not in so many words. I'm just curious. She never talked much about her time in the WAAF and I never asked her. I wish I had. Maybe if I find him, he can tell me something.' I smiled at her. 'And it was a lovely excuse to come and see you, Chris. I brought the Christmas pudding and the mince pies. And the crackers.'

'Bless you! Now we can have an English Christmas. I love America the rest of the year, but not right now. They don't do it the same as us. It's Happy Holidays and bloody Santa Claus instead of Father Christmas, and they don't have Boxing Day. Did you bring the Marmite too?'

'The biggest pot I could find.'

'You're a star! I ran out ages ago.'

We left one freeway for another and I shut my eyes while Chris did some more rapid lane-changing. After a while we veered off up a ramp and turned onto a street lined with garish neon signs: Taco Bell, Pizza Hut, Donuts, Burger King, Jack-in-the-Box. The people on the side-walks were nearly all dark-skinned, black-haired Mexicans.

'Most of them are here illegally,' Chris said. 'They get all the grotty jobs nobody else wants to do.' She swung into another street. 'We're more scenic now. There's the Santa Monica mountains in the distance.'

We crossed a boulevard into the residential area of Santa Monica. Adrian's Wimbledon-on-Sea had wide, tree-lined streets with clipped grass verges and beautiful homes set among hot-house greenery with flowers blooming exotically in midwinter – bougainvillea, azaleas, hydrangeas, birds of paradise. The architecture was mostly California Spanish, occasionally neo-Georgian, sometimes, incongruously, English mock Tudor. And everything looked so *clean* – as though it had all been jet-washed. No dirt, no dead leaves, no litter, no dogs' mess. And the air, away from smoggy LA, was crystal pure.

'Wait till it gets dark,' Chris said. 'You can't see

them now, but the Christmas lights are a knockout.'

We came to Georgina Avenue and Chris and Dan's house – one of the California Spanish ones with a wavy terracotta-tiled roof, shady balconies, blue shutters against whitewashed walls, cascades of red bougainvillea, great green fans of luscious palms. On the front lawn there was a metal notice stuck in the grass: *Armed Response*.

'That's the American version of *Beware of the dog*,' Chris said. 'It means we keep a gun.'

I followed her into the house and into an open-plan living room where there was more greenery in Ali Baba-sized pots, ceramic-tile flooring, ethnic rugs, squashy white leather sofas, a stone fireplace of inglenook proportions and a very tall Christmas tree – every inch of it smothered with silver and gold ornaments and big red velvet bows.

Chris switched on the fairy lights which pulsated like a traffic-hazard warning. 'Isn't it ghastly? It's not real, of course. It unscrews and you just get the damn thing out every year and screw it back together. I'll say one thing, it saves a lot of time and trouble. Come and look at the pool – that really *is* something.'

Shuttered doors led out to the garden at the back. Well, not a garden, exactly, more a paved area with more potted palms and a kidney-shaped swimming pool with mosaic sides and sapphire water.

'There wasn't one when we moved in. It takes up most of the yard, of course, but I said to Dan, if we're going to live in this climate then I'm damn well having a pool so we can make the most of it.'

Chris's daughter, Kim, appeared – a smiling teenager with long blond hair and perfect teeth, wearing a candy-pink jogging suit and trainers. Ricki, the son, was still away at college and due back on Christmas Eve. By the time Dan came home from the bank it was dark and he took me out in the street to show me the neighbourhood decorations. I saw what Chris had meant and it put English efforts to shame. Candles shone in every window and thousands of coloured lights twinkled along eaves and balconies, round archways, over porches, up palms, through bushes, down steps and paths . . . and, best of all, on the roof of the house across the street, a glittering, full-size Santa Claus sitting in his sleigh, whip held aloft, was driving his four reindeer up across the Spanish tiles towards the California night sky.

'Well, what do you think of California?'

It was the fifth time I'd been asked the same question during the evening and I gave the same jet-lagged answer. 'I haven't had time to see much yet, but I'm sure I'll love it.'

'Bit different from the Old Country, weather-wise?'

'It certainly is.'

'We've the best climate of any state in America . . . some say the best in the world. Sun all the year round, never gets too cold. You can swim in the ocean in the morning and go skiing in the afternoon, did you know that?'

'No, I didn't. Good heavens! How amazing!'

'Sure thing. The mountains are only a coupla hours' drive away. Laurel and I have got a time-share up at Big Bear and we've been going there for years. The kids have been skiing since they could walk.'

Chris had asked a roomful of people and kept introducing them in turn. *This is Glen, this is Janey, this is Art, Saul, Cary, Melanie, Bill . . .* This was Greg, the owner of the house opposite with Santa Claus and the reindeer galloping across the roof. The guests were all well groomed, well dressed, squeaky clean – as though they'd just stepped out of their power showers, jet-washed all over like their sidewalks and their streets. How filthy dirty Europe and Europeans must seem to them. How backward our inefficient ways and unhygienic habits. Lucky Americans! They'd started from scratch, which had given them a big advantage. No Old World hang-ups about sticking stubbornly to ancient traditions, or guilt about taking new short cuts. No putting up with woeful inefficiency or pathetic inadequacy, or plain filth.

Their houses were designed to save all unnecessary labour and everything in them worked properly: baths, showers, heating, cookers, decent-sized fridges, proper-sized washing machines, garbage shredders, remote-control garage doors, automatic garden sprinklers . . . Chris hadn't slaved for hours in the kitchen and worn herself out getting food ready for the party. Instead we'd simply got in the love-it-to-bits Chrysler, driven to the nearest delicatessen and collected the gourmet delights that she'd ordered over the telephone: a mouth-watering variety of dishes all prepared and ready to serve. Nor had she had to do messy battle on her knees in the fireplace. The false logs burst into cheery Christmassey flames at a flick of a switch and looked almost indistinguishable from the real thing. There seemed to me to be an awful lot to recommend the American way. And they'd just elected themselves a young and glamorous new President, made in the Kennedy image. Europe was looking rather tired and old.

A woman called Sherry approached. 'Say, that's a real cute blouse you're wearing. Where did you find it?'

I decided not to tell her that I'd unearthed the Forties polka dot in a charity shop in the North End Road and that it had cost 75 pence. One has one's pride, after all. Her husband, Walter, joined her. He wore rimless spectacles and a very intense expression.

'How are you liking California?'

I could see that he expected a proper answer. 'It's wonderful. So sunny and so clean.'

I must have said the right thing because he looked pleased.

'We keep environmental cleanliness at the forefront of our agenda. Of course, we've been addressing the air-pollution problem here for some years but I think we're finally finding real solutions.'

'You mean to the smog?'

He stopped looking quite so pleased. 'That's an ongoing challenge, of course, and one that we take very seriously. We also have to consider other potentially harmful sources – smoking, for instance.'

'Smoking? But surely that can't do much harm? Not compared with smog.'

'Maybe you haven't heard of passive smoking, Juliet?'

'I'm afraid I haven't.'

'Inhaling the fumes from someone else's cigarette has been proven just as harmful as smoking yourself. Smoking will be banned in restaurants soon. It should be banned from *all* public places – and soon will be in the state of California. In my opinion, it should be outlawed completely.'

'Completely? You mean, in people's homes as well?'

'I most certainly do. Sherry and I could never travel to Europe because of the way they allow smoking there.'

Sherry nodded her supportive agreement. I thought, bewildered, of what they were missing in order to avoid smoking passively – all the wonders and glories of Greece and Rome, the culinary delights and beauties of France and Italy and Spain, the ancient history of green and pleasant England. It seemed to me that a trip on the California freeways could prove far more risky, not to mention the perils of keeping a gun as a response to intruders. Walter went on, expanding on the subject, citing grisly statistics.

Then, thankfully, Chris was at my elbow again, with another guest. 'Julie, this is Rob Mclaren. Remember I mentioned him?'

'Of course.' I held out my hand. 'How do you do?'

I waited to be asked what I thought of California; instead, he said, 'Chris tells me you're trying to trace some guy.'

'Yes, as a matter of fact, I am.'

'She thinks maybe I could help. So, tell me about it.'

I wasn't prepared and he wasn't at all like I'd expected – or had hoped. A lived-in face, grizzled hair, stocky build, navy blue checked jacket with an open-necked shirt sprouting more grizzled hair, lighted cigarette in hand with smoke spiralling, which had the happy side effect of removing Walter and Sherry immediately to the very opposite end of the room. Tabloids surely, not broadsheets. Scoops and gossip columns.

'Well, it's a bit awkward at the moment . . .' I

indicated other guests still close by, braving the cigarette smoke.

He took me by the elbow and marshalled me over to a free corner of the room. 'OK. Let's start somewhere. Is this somebody you know?'

'No, I've never met him. He was a friend of my late mother's during the Second World War, in England.'

'Chris says you don't know his full name. Right?'

'Only that he was called Ham. It could be part of his Christian name or surname – I've no idea which.'

He said drily, 'We don't have Christian names in the US – we have first names. Same as we have Happy Holidays, not Happy Christmases. All part of our Constitution – no established religion. So far, not so good. What *do* you know about this guy, then?'

'He's American and he served as a B-17 bomber pilot with the Eighth Air Force in England during the war.'

'Do you know where?'

'A place called Halfpenny Green, in Suffolk.'

'Halfpenny Green? Crazy name.'

It was my turn to sound dry. 'Crazy names aren't unusual in England.'

'I know. I've been there. When was he over? What date?'

'The last half of 1943 and early 1944 when he was shot down on a raid and bailed out over

France. He was posted missing, believed killed, but he survived.'

'Was he a POW?'

'No, he managed to hide and evade capture.'

'What else?'

'I've got a photo of him – with his crew.'

'Do you know any of *their* names?'

'I'm afraid not.'

'How do you know he lives in California?'

I felt as though I was being grilled on a courtroom witness stand, Perry Mason style. *Will the witness please answer the question. Do you, or do you not* . . . 'I don't know for sure. But I met someone at his Bomb Group reunion in England this summer who'd been a crew chief at Halfpenny Green and he recognized him from the photo. He's the one who remembered he was always called Ham and that he originally came from California – apparently, they were always joking about the awful English weather.'

'You don't say?'

I said coolly, 'We had a lovely summer this year – actually.'

'Sure you did. What else?'

'Well, it seemed to me more likely that he was from southern California if he was used to warm weather. I gather it can get quite cold up north.' He was staring at me, without comment, smoking his cigarette. *Will the witness please confine herself to the facts, not her own opinions.* I floundered on. 'But, of course, he may have moved somewhere else. For all I know, he might be dead. I realize it's pretty hopeless and I certainly don't want to put you to any trouble.'

I'd made up my mind by then that I didn't want to put him to anything at all.

'You're not,' he said. 'Not yet, anyway. I'll let you know if you do.'

Another guest came up – a svelte blonde, and from the perfect look of her she'd had the complete California makeover too. She laid a hand on the sleeve of the checked jacket with talons even longer than Chris's. I'd since discovered that the nails were all false and stuck on by the manicurist. Yet another brilliant trouble-saving device.

'Hi, Rob . . . good to see you again. Hey, you haven't called me in months.'

'Hi, Deanne. This is Julie from England.'

'Oh, hi there! From *England*? Say, what do you think of California?'

By midnight the party was more or less over, the stragglers drifting towards the door. Rob Mclaren came over.

'Here's my card. I'll call by around eleven o'clock and take you to lunch. We can talk more then.'

He was gone before I could argue. The card said: *Robert F. Mclaren, Journalist*. The address was in Malibu.

Chris said later, 'Well, how did you get on with him?'

'Look, I really think it would be better if I hired a private detective.'

'Didn't you like him?'

'I don't think we were quite on the same wavelength.'

'That's not what women usually feel about Rob. He told me he's picking you up in the morning for lunch.'

'Did he, indeed?'

'You'd be a fool not to go, Julie. If anyone can find your mystery man for you, he will. Rob knows everyone worth knowing in LA and a lot more who aren't worth a dime. Give him a chance.'

I felt ungracious. 'I'm sorry, I didn't mean to sound ungrateful, Chris. It's very good of you to try and help.'

'Look, here's one of Rob's articles in the LA *Times* – take a look. See, he's serious.'

She thrust the newspaper at me. It was a piece on the dreadful war in Bosnia and I could see that it was high-class journalism. I handed the paper back. 'OK. I'm convinced.'

'He was over there in the summer. He gets around.'

'Then I don't know how he could be bothered with helping me.'

She smiled. 'I wouldn't worry about that, Julie. He wouldn't do it if he didn't want to. Come on, let's you and I have a nightcap. Dan's gone off to bed, so we can have a good old chinwag.'

She poured brandies and we sat on the squashy leather sofa beside the fake log fire. The

Christmas tree lights twinkled away prettily. We talked about the shared memories – school-teachers, the other girls, the boys we'd known, the men.

Chris said, 'I never liked Mark, you know. Always thought he was a pompous prick. I could never understand what you saw in him.'

'We both got it wrong, that's all.'

'Yep . . . easily done.' She waved her near-empty glass at me. 'Dan hasn't been the only one with me, you know. I've gone off piste a few times, but nothing too serious. Most people do here.'

'Do they?'

'What do you think all the makeovers are for? Hey, you've never mentioned any other man in *your* life, Julie?'

'That's because there isn't one.'

'Oh, come *on*! No-one since Mark? I can't believe that.'

'There *was* one, but he was married and that was an even worse mistake.'

'God, don't talk to me about married men and affairs! I know all about them. They won't leave their wives and they won't leave their mistresses . . . they want it both ways. And they're trailing all that unhappy baggage . . . guilt, children, lies. I've always avoided them like the plague. How long did your thing go on?'

'Oh, years . . .'

'Grim. And since then?'

'I've stayed *hors de combat*.'

'Don't you get lonely?'

'Not really. I've got friends and my work, and Flavia's downstairs.'

She wagged a finger at me. 'You shouldn't rely on her, Julie.'

'I don't – at least, I hope I don't.'

'She's living with that actor guy, isn't she? You said about him in one of your letters. So she's got her own life. Which leaves you free to do as you damn-well-pleasy.'

'I more or less do. Which I couldn't if there was a man around.'

'Point taken. But I'd still miss having one. Maybe you'll meet a guy here. There's plenty of divorcees to pick from in California – Rob, for one.'

'I'm not on a man-hunt, Chris.'

'Actually you *are* – in case you'd forgotten.' She leaned towards me. 'Do tell me, why are you so bloody keen to find this other guy, Julie? I don't buy the old-friend-of-your-mother's story. There's *got* to be something more to it than that. Come on, you can trust *me*.'

I couldn't confide in her for the same reasons I hadn't told Monica. I didn't want to and I couldn't risk it. The spoken word is the fled arrow. Maybe one day – but more likely never. 'There really isn't anything more, Chris. It's just like I said.'

She looked hurt and I could see that she didn't believe me. I felt ashamed to be repaying her kindness by hiding the truth. The web was getting too tangled, too deceitful, and I almost felt like giving up.

Later, alone in my bedroom, I took out the photo and studied it yet again – the face part-hidden by the cap's brim and the turned-up sheepskin collar. The smile.

And I knew I had to go on.

Thirteen

Rob Mclaren called by late in the morning the next day, driving some kind of modern black Jeep and wearing a leather jacket and jeans. At least we had a casual attitude to clothes in common.

'We're going to Canter's on Fairfax so I hope you like Jewish food.'

'I'm not sure I've ever had it.'

'Well, this is the best Jewish food in LA. The best outside New York, in fact. Great bagels, great deli, great soups . . . great place. It's been there ever since the Thirties and that's a long time over here.'

Fairfax Avenue was a long street with a Mexican-Asian mix of shops and eateries – a sort of California Soho. From the outside the Jewish restaurant didn't look anything so special. Inside there was a bakery and a deli counter near the door, and, beyond that, a cavernous, rather gloomy room with old-fashioned booths, brown leather benches, wipe-over tables and middle-aged, boot-faced waitresses. One of them brought menus and slapped them down.

I opened it. *Chicken Matzo Ball, Brisket of Beef,*

Chopped Liver, Matzo Brey, Gefilte Fish, Noodle Kugel . . .

He said, 'You can have the non-Jewish stuff, if you like. There's all sorts. Pastas, salads, burgers, chicken – no pork, though. They draw the line at that.'

I was all for Jewish since that was what the place was about – you don't go to an Indian restaurant and order fish and chips – but the long menu with its unfamiliar dishes was daunting. 'What do you recommend?'

'The chicken kreplach soup then the hot corned beef on rye. It comes with pickles and potato salad.'

'That sounds fine by me.'

'I'll get a bottle of wine too.'

He ordered and the soup and wine appeared almost immediately. 'Let's talk a bit more about this guy. If he served as a bomber pilot in '43/'44 he'd most likely have been around twenty to twenty-three years old then. Which makes him in his seventies now. Soup OK?'

'Very nice.' It was. So was the wine.

'What did your mother tell you about him?'

'We never talked about him at all. I didn't know he existed until she told me about him in a letter she left for me when she died.'

'So what did she say about him in her letter?'

'That he was a bomber pilot that she'd met during the war when she was in the Women's Auxiliary Air Force.'

'OK. What else?'

'I can't think of anything else.'

'Think harder. There's always something else. Have you got that crew photo you mentioned?'

I gave it to him. 'That's him there. According to the crew chief I met in England.'

'Nice-looking guy – what you can see of him. Can I keep this?'

'Yes, I've got copies. I sent some to American Bomb Group Association magazines – in case anyone recognized him. No luck, so far.'

He looked at me hard. 'You've been trying your darnedest, haven't you?'

I thought he was going to ask me the old question – *why?* – but he didn't. He put the photo away in an inside pocket of his leather jacket. 'Well, if you get any replies, watch out for some wacko stringing you along; there's plenty of those around. How about the letter your mother left you? Are you going to let me see it?'

I shook my head. 'I'm sorry.'

'Too personal?'

'Yes. Look, if you'd sooner not bother with this, I'd quite understand. There's not much hope of tracing him, is there?'

'Sure there is. I'll find him for you.'

I said, not really believing him, 'Actually, I've got something else that I think must have belonged to him.'

'What's that?'

'A sketchbook. It was in her desk.'

'Let's see it.'

I took the book out of my bag and gave it to him.

He turned pages. 'What makes you think this was his?'

I hesitated. 'My mother said something about him having artistic talent.'

'Well, this guy sure did . . . OK if I keep it too?'

'If you let me have it back.'

'Trust me.'

I didn't but there didn't seem much choice. 'There was another thing in the desk – together with the sketchbook.'

'Oh?'

'An old record of a wartime song.'

'Which one?'

'Frank Sinatra singing "I'll be Seeing You".'

'Great song. Great singer.'

'I don't see how it can help, though.'

He smiled – the first time I'd seen him do so. 'If we come across some guy and he starts crooning it, we'll know for sure he's the one.'

We finished the chicken soup and the waitress brought the hot corned beef on rye, with side dishes of giant pickles and potato salad. Unexpectedly, she smiled too as she set them down on the table. It was a warm and motherly smile that transformed the boot face. 'There you are, folks. Enjoy.'

'Cast iron outside, pure gold inside,' Rob Mclaren said. 'Never judge a book by its cover. Do you like the corned beef?'

'It's nothing like when it's out of a tin.'

'I've seen that crap in England – I can't eat it. This is the real thing.' He refilled the wine glasses. 'Are you married, Julie?'

'No. Divorced – a long time ago.'

'Me, too. Twice over. Most women won't put up with me – not on a permanent basis. I'm a selfish kind of guy and they soon figure that out. Any kids?'

'One daughter.'

'Same as me again. Beth's teenage now. Lives with her mother down in Orange County but I see her pretty often. How about yours?'

'Flavia's twenty-four. She lives in the flat below me.'

'In London?'

'Suburbs of. Putney.'

'Yeah, I know . . . I've some friends there. I get over to London several times a year. It's a great city. Boyfriend?'

I said stiffly, 'You mean, me?'

'No, I meant your daughter.'

'Yes. An actor. He lives with her.'

'But you're on your own?'

'Yes.'

'Can't be necessity, so it must be choice.'

'That's my business.'

'Sure. Potato salad OK?'

'It's very good, thank you.'

'They know how to make it here. What do you do for a living – when you're not out hunting for guys?'

'I illustrate books.'

He looked at me. 'That's kind of interesting. What sort of books?'

'Mainly children's. Sometimes other kinds. And I teach watercolour painting at evening classes.'

'I guess that keeps you busy.'

'Yes, it does. Look, Mr Mclaren—'

'Rob.'

'Rob. Do you really think you can find him?'

'I just said so. Didn't you believe me?'

'No. There's so little to go on.'

'As a matter of fact, there's quite a lot.'

'The American Embassy in London wouldn't help – even if they could have. You have a Privacy Act.'

'Yeah, that's right, we do.'

'It's almost impossible to find out anything about veterans.'

'Going down your route it would be.' He speared a pickle with his fork. 'But I have an old pal in the Vets' Administration here in LA who owes me a big favour. That's the difference. How long are you over here?'

'I'm booked to fly back the week after next.'

'OK. Christmas is two days away and this guy's taking a couple of days off work. After that he'll be back at his desk. It's not like England where every goddam thing shuts down till January. You'll get some news before you leave.'

'The thing is . . .'

'What thing is what?'

'If your friend *does* manage to trace him – for

certain – I don't necessarily want this man to know I've been looking for him.'

'Hang on a second, Julie. Tell me that again, will you? When you find this guy, you don't want him to know he's been found?'

'I'm not sure it would be such a good idea, you see.'

'You mean you've come six thousand miles in search of someone you don't even want to meet? No, frankly, I don't see.'

'I realize it sounds ridiculous.'

'It sure does. Still, I guess you've got your reasons.' He waved the half-eaten pickle at me on the end of the fork. 'All right. Let's get this thing straight. You want to know if he's still breathing? And you want to know his full name and where he lives and his occupation. What else?'

'Anything else there is to know.'

'You mean what sort of a guy? A good guy or a hopeless bum? Before you decide if you want to meet him?'

I said coldly, 'No, I didn't mean that at all. It's difficult to explain.'

'And you're not doing too good a job at it, but never mind.'

'There's something else that I need to know.'

'Yeah?'

'You're a journalist, a newspaperman.'

'Yeah.'

'Are you doing this because it might make some sort of gossipy news story?'

He said, 'I don't do that stuff.'

'But you must know people who do.'

'Sure, but I'm not going to spill the beans on you. You're not looking as though you believe that either, but you're just going to have to trust me, Julie.'

'Actually, it's *Juliet*, not Julie. That's just Chris who calls me that.'

'Julie suits you better. You're not the balcony type.'

I could see he'd go on using it, regardless. 'I meant to ask you, as well . . . what sort of a fee will there be? For your friend's time, and yours?'

'*Fee?*' He looked amused. 'I hadn't thought about that one. I'll let you know. And, by the way, *Julie*, you're going to have to learn to lie a whole lot better.'

After the lunch he offered to drive around to show me some of the sights. I wasn't sure I wanted him to, but, on the other hand, I didn't want to be rude since he was being so helpful.

'Can you spare the time?'

'No, I should be working. But I'll make an exception in your case.'

He drove the modern Jeep round Los Angeles much as William had driven the wartime version round Halfpenny Green airfield. We cruised up and down the wide streets of Beverly Hills so I could gawp at the multimillion movie-star houses – the *Gone With the Wind* mansions, the turreted French chateaux, the English Gothic halls, the Italian palazzos and Spanish haciendas. After that we went very slowly down Rodeo Drive so I could see where the Beverly Hills residents shopped for the bare necessities of life: Cartier, Tiffanys, Dior, Armani, Louis Vuitton, Gucci, Prada, Versace . . . Then the Art Museum and the old tar pits; Culver City and the MGM studios, disappointing, tacky Hollywood with Grauman's Chinese Theatre and the stars' footprints.

'Like to see Malibu, where I live?'

'Is it far?'

'No. We'll take Sunset down there.'

The very long, romantically named Boulevard ended at the ocean where the sunsets happened and he turned the Jeep north along the Pacific Coast Highway, tall cliffs on one side, golden beaches on the other, the Santa Monica mountains ahead. After a few miles, we came to a row of old painted wooden houses on the beach side – lovely sun-bleached blues, greys, pinks, yellows. He pulled up in front of one of them. 'It ain't much, but it's home.'

Downstairs there was a bedroom, a bathroom, a storeroom; upstairs was all one big open room with a kitchen corner, table and chairs, a studio couch, shelves and shelves of books, a desk with a computer, a telephone, tottering piles of papers and more books, an ashtray full of cigarette ends. And a spectacular view of the Pacific ocean through a huge plate-glass door.

He slid open the door. 'Take a closer look.'

The telephone rang then and he went to

answer it. I stepped outside onto a wooden deck cantilevered out above the beach and the rocks below and leaned at the rail, watching the rollers sweeping in and breaking over the rocks, the white spume flying up, the blue water sparkling.

After a while, he joined me. 'You should see the sunsets,' he said, standing close behind me – a little too close for comfort. 'They can blow your mind.'

We went back inside and he fetched wine and glasses, uncorked the bottle, handed me a glassful. 'I live and eat and work in this room,' he said. 'I wouldn't trade it for any of those dumps in Beverly Hills.'

I gestured towards the overloaded desk. 'Speaking of work, I'm afraid I must be interrupting yours.'

'Yeah, you are,' he said. 'But it's the holidays. I can spare some time.'

'Well, it's awfully good of you.'

He smiled. 'No, it isn't, Julie. I wouldn't do it if I didn't want to.'

Chris had been quite right about that.

He lit a cigarette with a steel lighter that snapped shut like a trap, and stared at me for a moment. I was back in the witness box again. 'OK, Julie, suppose we stop pussyfooting around and you tell me the truth.'

'I have done.'

He sighed. 'You're such a lousy liar. This guy you're looking for is your father, isn't he? That's what your mother told you in that letter – the one you won't let me see. It's time to level with me. That's if you want me to help you.'

I hesitated.

'Come on. Play fair, Julie. Spill the jolly old beans.'

I could see there was no alternative with him. 'All right. That's what she told me. I suddenly found out that I was the daughter of a total stranger. An American. It was a bit of a shock.'

'An *American*!' He whistled. 'Jesus! That's *terrible*.'

'I'm sorry. I didn't mean it like that. What I meant was that he belonged to another continent – somewhere thousands of miles away, somewhere I'd never been and didn't know.' I gulped at the wine. 'I simply couldn't believe it at first . . . I thought my mother's illness had made her imagine the whole thing. When I finally realized that it was true . . . it seemed like a nightmare. But I suppose, at my age, it shouldn't really matter who my father was, should it?'

He said, 'I reckon it matters at any age, Julie. It's about our identity. We all like to be clear on that.'

His sympathy seemed genuine but I still didn't trust him. 'All I know is that I want to find him. After that, I don't know a thing.'

He nodded. 'OK. Let's take this one step at a time. And the first step is showing me that letter. After that, you can tell me the rest of it.'

It was getting dark by the time he drove me

back to Georgina Avenue. He stopped the Jeep outside the house.

'I'll call you after the holidays. Tell you what's happening.'

I said politely, 'I hope you have a good Christmas.'

'Hell, I gave up Christmas years ago. It's just another day to me. I guess it'd be OK in England – so long as it snowed and you guys were all dressed up like in Dickens. Otherwise, forget it. In California it's a joke. Fake snow, fake ice, fake everything, and that includes fake goodwill to all men.'

I smiled. 'Well, thanks for the lunch and the tour. And the talk.'

He nodded towards Santa and his reindeer glittering away on the roof across the road. 'That guy's going to have to get a move on. Time's running out.'

'He hasn't moved an inch since I've been here.'

'Maybe he'll get going tomorrow. Keep him under close surveillance.' He clasped my shoulder briefly. 'Merry Christmas, Julie.'

'Happy Holidays, Rob.'

The Jeep roared off down the avenue.

The next day, Christmas Eve, the King's College carol service was broadcast live from England, early morning California time. Chris sat listening with the tears trickling down her cheeks. It made me feel quite weepy myself – the angelic-sounding choirboys, the readings in clear English voices, the vision of the dear old beloved country in the deep midwinter and so far away.

Ricki, Chris's son, arrived afterwards. He was tall and handsome with an easy, warm smile and lovely manners. I could see that Chris was very proud of him. Fifty years ago thoroughly nice American boys just like him were being shipped off to England. I thought of the thousands of white crosses in the cemetery outside Cambridge.

On Christmas Day itself the sun shone brightly from blue skies. We opened presents by the tree, drove to the Episcopalian church and then went back and ate the turkey and the Harrods Christmas pudding and the mince pies. And then we pulled the crackers, read out painful riddles and put on ridiculous paper hats. Except for the weather and the lack of Brussels sprouts, it was much like an English Christmas – to Chris's deep satisfaction.

Flavia phoned in the afternoon – late in the evening London time.

'Happy Christmas, Mum.'

'Thank you, darling. How's yours been?'

She'd had a wonderful day, she said. She and Callum had gone to some friends down in the country and only just got back. The weather had been pretty awful – rainy and dull – but it hadn't mattered a bit. She sounded pleased and excited and I wondered what was coming next.

'The most *wonderful* news, Mum . . .'

They're engaged, I thought. He's asked her to marry him, at last, and I've got to sound thrilled about it. I started to get the words ready. *Darling, how lovely! I'm so happy for you . . .*

'Callum's been offered a screen test in Hollywood. Isn't it amazing? Some American director guy was over here and saw him in that TV series. They want him to audition for a big part in a cops and robbers movie. Isn't it marvellous?'

She went on telling me all about it. The American had been staying at a hotel in London and had just happened to switch on the TV when the detective series was being shown. A complete fluke. He'd rung Callum's agent the next day. Apparently, he thought Callum had the sort of looks and charisma that it took to go places in Hollywood.

'Callum's flying out next week and they're putting him up at some swanky hotel in Beverly Hills.'

'Can't you come too?'

'No . . . too busy at work and it'd be too expensive. Besides I'd cramp his style a bit, don't you think?' She seemed amused and far from resentful.

I said, 'Wish him luck from me. And tell him to phone me while he's here, if he gets the chance.'

When I told Chris she was mightily impressed. 'Wow! He must have something.'

'He does. He's extremely good-looking and very charming – when he chooses to be. He can act quite well too, and do almost any accent perfectly.'

'My God, Julie, he might be a big star one day. How thrilling! If he calls, ask him straight over here.'

On the day after, instead of a bracing English Boxing Day walk, Chris and I went shopping in a big shopping mall – two levels of enticing stores crammed with desirable things, all under one convenient roof. I bought American jeans, a cashmere sweater and a pair of loafers – far cheaper than in England. Chris shopped till we both dropped and went to lunch at a restaurant full of glamorous women pecking at low-calorie salads and sipping mineral water. Nobody, I noted, was smoking – bearing out Walter's pious prophecy. We drove back a different route, taking the palm-tree-lined Palisades on the cliff top at Santa Monica, overlooking the ocean. People were out jogging purposefully along the grass verge wearing sun visors and track suits – arms pumping away like pistons. And little groups were engaged in curious on-the-spot exercises, limbs moving in measured unison.

'T'ai chi,' Chris said. 'Chinese yoga and meditation. Chi is a vital force that animates the body. I'm not sure about the T'ai bit. It's supposed to teach you about the genesis of movement from the body's vital centre and give you a calm and tranquil mind. I went to a couple of classes once but it didn't do a thing for me.'

Then we passed a man: an unshaven, straggle-haired man dressed in dirty clothes and lying asleep on the grass. Then another man slumped on a bench. And another sitting with his back against a palm tree, staring blankly into space. And another curled up, foetus-form, with his arm wrapped pathetically over his eyes.

I said, 'Chris, those men . . . they look like down-and-outs. Surely they can't be. Not *here*.'

'They are, poor sods. We've got loads of them in Santa Monica. They come from all over. It's the climate – they survive a lot better than in colder places. They're mostly veterans who've dropped out or been kicked out. It's very sad.'

'You mean they fought in the war?'

'Not the war you're thinking about. The Vietnam war.'

'But I thought the US government took such good care of its veterans.'

'It does, generally. Very good care. But those 'nam guys are different. They had a bloody raw deal. They made them go and fight a shitty war, and when they came back all screwed up nobody wanted to know them – not even their own families sometimes. They were outcasts. Shunned for having done what they were ordered to do.' She glanced at me. 'Don't look so worried, Julie. You won't find *your* man panhandling on the streets. His war was a good one. He'll have had something to be proud of.'

'A *good* war?'

'Well, World War Two was a simple choice, wasn't it? Us against the Nazis. Right against wrong. White against black. Vietnam was something quite different. Nobody here's proud of what happened, I can tell you.'

We drove back to affluent Georgina Avenue where Santa Claus was still driving his reindeer merrily over the roof and where everything was so clean and so neat and so ordered. But I couldn't get the pitiful image of the ragged homeless vets out of my mind.

Fourteen

Three days before New Year's Eve, Rob Mclaren phoned.

'That guy still on the roof?'

'Yes. No sign of movement.'

'What a dipstick! He blew it.' A pause, a more serious tone. 'We've got a possible, Julie. A Hammond Wright who lives down in Orange County – place called Garden Grove. He was a pilot in the Eighth, served at Halfpenny Green, Suffolk, England in '43 and was shot down early '44. He adds up. I think we should go down and check him out.'

I should have felt excitement, instead I felt total panic. 'You mean, *meet* him?'

'That's exactly what I mean. Come on, Julie. It's the only way we're going to find out fast. No need to spill all your beans. We'll give him the wartime-friend-of-your-mother angle. You can ask him some questions, show him the photo . . . see what he says. After that, it's up to you how you play it.'

'When would we go?'

'The sooner the better. I'll call him now.'

He picked me up an hour later in the Jeep

and we headed south on the San Diego freeway.

'What did he sound like?'

'OK. He thinks he might remember your mother, but he's not sure.'

Thinks. I remembered Adrian's prophetic words. *A wartime romance . . . young people thrown together. He probably can't even remember her name*. And my own response.

'I'm sure he'd remember her. She wasn't the sort you'd forget easily.'

He said, 'Do you look like she did? Or, to put it another way – did she look like you?'

'People always said so.'

'Then maybe you'll jog this guy's memory.'

Garden Grove was less than an hour away – a pleasant place with quiet streets, modest homes, far removed from the excesses of Beverly Hills. A bedroom community, Rob called it. The street in question had one-storey houses – chalet-style with shingle roofs and a small patch of lawn in front. He stopped the Jeep outside number 2006 which had a neglected look: uncut grass, an unswept path, a dead palm in a pot beside the front door. I felt slightly sick. Rob put a steadying hand on my arm.

'Take it easy, Julie.'

'I'm trying to.'

'And, by the way, I'm a very old friend of yours – that's what I pitched him.'

We went up the concrete path – me skulking behind Rob – and rang the bell. Nothing happened. My heart was imitating a sledgehammer, my knees jelly. Rob gave me a bracing grin, pressed the bell again, and then the door opened.

He was a big man, almost bald and overweight, a Father Christmas belly sagging over his belt, creased clothes, a stain on his shirt front. I searched his face for any resemblance to the face in my photo but found none. And I waited for him to smile, but he didn't.

Rob said, 'Mr Wright? I'm Rob Mclaren and this is Julie Porter from England. The one I told you about who's trying to trace her late mother's old wartime friend.'

'Yeah . . .' He peered round Rob's shoulder and looked at me. He seemed neither friendly nor hostile – somewhere in the middle. 'Well, I don't know if I can help you, but I guess you'd better come inside.'

We followed him into a depressing living room. The slatted blinds filtered out any sunlight and the furniture and furnishings were all dark colours – brown, orange, black – with a grubby shagpile carpet. There was another palm in a pot – this one alive, but only just. He gestured towards a moquette sofa.

'Sit down. Can I get you folks something to drink? I've got beer, Coke, maybe some tea – if I can find it.'

Rob asked for beer, me for Coke – I didn't want it in the least but it seemed a good idea to accept. He went off and came back clutching cans and glasses in his fists and put them clumsily down on the coffee table.

'I'm on my own these days. My wife took off six months ago. Haven't gotten used to coping yet.' He handed Rob the Coors beer and poured the Coke into a glass for me. 'You married, Julie?'

'No. I'm divorced.'

He shook his head. 'I guess it happens to most of us. Enid and I were married more than thirty years. It was one hell of a shock when she walked out, I can tell you. No other guy, she said. She just wanted a change – to do something else with the rest of her life. I don't know what.' He shrugged despairingly.

I said, 'I'm very sorry.'

'Not your fault. And I can't see how it was mine.' He poured his own beer and settled back in his armchair. 'Well, what's all this about? Rob here gave me the gist but you'd better fill me in some more.'

I did and he kept nodding while I spoke. 'Sure, sure . . . I was at Halfpenny Green then. My crew and I did eighteen missions before we got shot down. A 109 sneaked up under us before we knew it. Gutted us like some goddamned fish.'

'Were you over France?'

'Yep. Somewhere near Caen. Three of us got out OK and the French hid us for a while. They passed us along from one hiding place to the next till we finally got away back to England.'

It could be him, I thought. It could be him.

And I prayed it wasn't. I said, 'Do you remember my mother, Daisy Woods – the WAAF who worked with the RAF liaison officer?'

He frowned and rubbed at the side of his nose. 'You know, I've been thinking ever since Rob called and it's coming back to me. I'd clean forgotten her name but there *was* an English WAAF on the base – I do recall that for sure. She was a real pretty girl. I guess we all tried our luck with her – that's the way it was in those days. You never knew how long you'd got and you sure wanted to make the most of it while you were still alive.'

Rob said, 'How lucky did you get?'

'With the English WAAF? Didn't even get to first base, so far as I remember. There were other English girls who were a whole lot easier – no shortage, I can tell you. They liked us Yanks a lot. And we liked them. They had a lot of guts.' He looked at me. 'You said you're looking for a particular guy who knew your mother? Someone she told you about but you don't know his name? That's kindofa long shot.'

I handed over the photo. 'He's in this photo, with his crew. The one at the back on the far right.'

He groped for spectacles in the breast pocket of his shirt. I held my breath, heart pounding, remembering Stella Morrison's wise warning: *the reality can be a let-down*, and Adrian's . . . *there's no guarantee that you'd care for this man*.

After a long, long moment, Hammond Wright

said, 'I don't remember any of these guys. You know, there were a lot of crews coming and going – specially going – and it's a hell of a long time ago.' He tapped with his forefinger. 'This one, you said? He won't look like that now. None of us do. Do you want to see a picture of me and my crew?' He got up and went over to the wall and unhooked a framed photograph. 'This is us.' The forefinger jabbed again as he held it out in front of me. 'And that's me there in the centre. You wouldn't know me, would you?'

I stared at the tall and slim young man in his flying kit, grinning amiably at the camera. There was no easy or polite answer to the question. Instead, I asked another. 'Did you have a nick-name? For instance, did they call you Ham?'

'Ham? No, never. I was always known as Mack. Still am, by most people. It's only Enid calls me Hammond. Or used to.' He returned the photo to its hook on the wall and sat down again. 'I've just remembered something else. Funny how things come back when you start talking. There was a family who lived in the farmhouse by the airfield – I think they owned the land and they farmed what was left of it. I can't recall their name but they used to invite the crews over some evenings. I went once or twice and I remember the English WAAF was billeted there. Must have been your mother. We'd go over sometimes and chat her up. Didn't go there too often, though. Like I said, we were after the easy girls and they were in other places – Ipswich and Cambridge and London. We went those places whenever we could.'

'Can you remember if she was specially friendly with any of the Americans who went to the farmhouse?'

'Can't say I do. There were always guys buzzing round her.'

'Do you think any of your old crew would remember?'

'Like I said, only three of us survived. I kept up with my navigator, Dean, but he died last year. I don't know what happened to my bombardier. We lost contact long ago.'

'Do you remember a pub in the village called the Mad Monk?'

'Sure do. It was a great place. There was a piano and we used to sing these Limey songs – "Roll me over in the Clover"', "Roll out the Barrel", stuff like that. And they had a contest to see who could down a glass boot full of beer the quickest.' He wagged his head. 'Oh boy . . . I've forgotten what the record was but I know I wasn't far off it.'

We finished the drinks and left. He came with us to the door and shook hands.

'Sorry I couldn't help, Julie. Are you going back home soon?'

'In a few days.'

'Well, give my regards to England. I always had a soft spot for the old country. Never been back in all these years – couldn't afford to. Now, I guess I never will.'

As we drove away, Rob said, 'Just as well it wasn't him. Bit of a sad case.'

'Poor man. I felt so sorry for him.'

'Yeah . . . I'd've been sorrier for you, though.'

I said, 'I've no right to expect some sort of handsome hero figure – I know that.'

'It's only natural. You'd sooner look up to your father than down on him.'

He asked me if I'd mind calling by on his daughter who lived with her mother in the same neighbourhood. 'My first ex. The second one didn't hang around long enough for us to have any kids.'

The house was as bright and cheerful as the other had been depressing, and the daughter a smiling, vivacious girl of about fourteen or fifteen who quite obviously adored her father.

'Mom's gone to the store,' she told him. 'She won't be back till later.'

'That's OK, sweetheart. It's you I came to see. This is Julie Porter from England.'

Her eyes widened. 'From England! Hey, that's cool!'

She wanted to know if I'd ever met the Queen or Princess Diana and was disappointed that I hadn't. 'I wish I could go there. I keep asking Dad but he never takes me with him. He's real mean.'

'I'll take you one day, kiddo.'

'Swear it.'

He tugged her ponytail. 'OK, I swear it.'

She looked from one of us to the other. 'Hey,

are you guys . . . you know, Dad . . . you and Julie?'

Rob said, 'Forget it, Beth. Julie's not stupid.'

'Oh, I kinda hoped . . .'

'Sorry about that,' he said, as we climbed back into the Jeep. 'She's always hoping.'

On the way back to Santa Monica, I said, 'What about *your* father, Rob?'

'What about him?'

'How do you get on with him?'

'I don't. He's dead. Died years ago when I was still a kid. And I didn't see too much of him when he was alive. They were divorced early on.'

'Still, he was your father.'

'Far as I know. I guess we all have to take it on trust.'

'I did – until last year.'

He looked at me. 'There's no mileage in feeling bitter, Julie. Your mother kept it from you for your own good.'

'Why tell me in the end, then? It hasn't done me much good.'

'She figured you could take it – now you're a big girl. And she wanted you to know about it. The guy meant a lot to her. He was something special. That should mean something to you, too.'

Later, I asked him about the Vietnam vets I'd seen on the Santa Monica Palisades.

'What about them exactly?'

'Why were they treated so badly when they came back?'

'I guess you could say they were the fall guys. It was a no-win situation. A no-hope, hopeless war. We couldn't win militarily, nor could the other side. Everyone had to wait till finally America defeated itself by losing the will to fight. That's something most Americans would much sooner forget – that and the nasty, cruel things that were done. Only those poor old vets are still wandering around like walking wounded, reminding everybody.' He glanced at me. 'No good looking shocked, Julie. Your country has a few skeletons rattling in the cupboard. That's the way it goes.'

He drove me back to Georgina Avenue and handed me out of the Jeep onto the sidewalk. 'I'll let you know as soon as my pal's come up with another possible.'

'Do you think he will? It's not long till I have to leave.'

'Have patience. He's going through the files, making calls, asking questions – it takes time.'

I said, 'I'm sorry, Rob. I'm grateful to him – and to you.'

I was – very. He'd been a rock to cling to, getting me through the ordeal of Hammond Wright. He'd understood my terror and he'd been kind.

He touched my cheek – only for a second. 'Think nothing of it, Julie. Just keep your eye on that bozo over the road.'

'I've been watching him.'

'He could make a sudden move. You don't want to miss the take-off.'

I went indoors and Chris looked up from the sofa. 'You look happy. Was it the right guy?'

'I'm afraid not.'

'Rats! I thought from the way you were smiling . . . Anyway, I've got some nice news. Flavia's boyfriend just called. He's in town and I invited him over this evening. Kim and I can't wait to see him.'

He arrived by chauffeur-driven limousine, dressed in his customary black. Chris had her hand kissed, Kim was given a smouldering Heathcliff look, Dan and Ricki man-to-man handshakes. We air-kissed. Somewhere on the flight over he had acquired an American accent. They all wanted to hear about the audition and he obliged with a short excerpt which he did very well. I watched him, thinking that there was already an aura about him, a little sprinkling of magic stardust. The soap days were probably over.

'How's Flavia?' I asked him later when we had a moment alone.

He dropped the American accent. 'She's fine. Been busy at the mag with summer. They're doing a Rustic Renaissance feature – you know the sort of thing: rough-hewn plaster, rag rugs, yokels' smocks on hooks, wild-flower meadows . . .'

'When will you hear about the audition?'

He shrugged. 'When they've seen all the

others. Days, weeks, months . . . who knows? They're footing the bill for me to stay on a couple more days – a few parties lined up. I think LA's bloody fantastic.'

'That's a very good word for it.'

He looked at me with his gorgeous green eyes, through the thick black lashes. 'Not really your sort of place, is it Juliet?'

'Not really.'

'It's mine, though.'

'Yes, I can see that it is.'

'I'm not really the sort of man you want for Flavia either, am I? Be honest.'

'I'm afraid you'll make her unhappy, Callum – in the long run.'

'I know you are,' he said. 'You could be right.'

The limo collected him later and he slid smoothly into the back and waved as though he'd been accustomed to such things all his life.

Dan and Chris had been invited to a New Year's Eve party and tried to persuade me to go with them but I ducked out, pleading tiredness. The truth was that I'd never much enjoyed New Year parties. To me, there always seems something sad about the old year going and something frightening about a new one arriving. And with the passing of this particular year, my mother was slipping further away into the past. Or that was how it felt. Kim and Ricki had gone off to another party and so I had the house to myself – me and the fake Christmas tree and the gas log fire. I sat watching the realistic flames flickering and the fairy lights winking and blinking, and thought of Ma. What had she really wanted? Simply to tell me about the man she'd loved so much who was my father? Or for me to go out and search until I found him? I'd never know the answer. And finding him seemed so unlikely. Almost impossible without some of the luck that Stella Morrison had spoken of.

The phone trilled in bursts, American style, and it was Rob Mclaren.

'Julie? Why aren't you out celebrating?'

Hearing his voice had made me smile. 'Why aren't you?'

'I've given up New Year parties as well as Christmases.'

'So have I.'

'Good. That means you won't be hung-over tomorrow. We're going to follow up another lead. This guy's called Hamlyn. Craig Hamlyn. Lives in Palm Springs, out in the desert.'

'It sounds a long way.'

'Only a couple of hours' drive.' A pause. 'You getting cold feet again?'

'Just a bit.'

'I'll hold your hand all the way, and you can hide behind me like last time.'

'Thanks.'

'Pick you up around nine in the morning.'

The line clicked silent. I went on watching the flickering flames and the twinkling lights, and thinking about Rob and how much I was getting to like him.

He was at the door dead on nine and he held out a hand to me. 'OK, Julie. Let's go.'

I put my hand in his.

As we drove off in the Jeep he asked if I'd eaten anything.

'I had some coffee.'

'We'll stop and get some breakfast. You can't do this sort of thing on an empty stomach.'

He swung into the parking lot of an IHOP. 'This place is pancakes and all kinds of stuff that's bad for you. You'll love it.'

We sat in a booth and a pretty Mexican waitress brought coffee, big menus and glasses of iced water. There were flags strung along the ceiling and Muzak playing. Two enormously fat women had somehow managed to squeeze themselves into the next-door booth and were working their way steadily through a mound of waffles and cream and strawberries. The Muzak, for some reason, was playing 'Begin the Beguine'.

'What do you recommend this time?'

'Pretty much everything,' he said. 'How about buttermilk pancakes with eggs, bacon, and sausage links? You can have fruit on top.'

'On top of the *eggs*?'

'No, the pancakes. Or instead of buttermilk, you could have chocolate chip, banana nut, buckwheat . . . Or you can have any kind of omelette – country, chicken fajita, Santa Fe, cheese, avocado . . . Or Belgian waffle – they're good. *Or* a T-bone steak and eggs, with pancakes on the side. The choice is yours, ma'am. Me, I'm going for hash browns and eggs over easy.'

I settled for the eggs and bacon with buttermilk pancakes on the side, which came in pairs and were each the size of a small dinner plate. He pushed a rack of syrup jars in my direction. 'Take your pick – maple, blueberry, strawberry, butter pecan.'

Which to choose? I went for the maple and poured it all over the pancakes.

Rob started on the hash browns. 'I called this guy and got his wife first. She took some persuading but she put him on in the end. He checked out OK. B-17 pilot, Halfpenny Green, '43/'44, shot down, and all the rest of it. He says he can't remember there being *any* English WAAFs on the base. Anyhow, he said we can stop by so long as it's p.m. They play golf in the mornings.'

'What did you say about me?'

'Same as before. And I'm still your old and trusty friend. Have you got the photo?'

'Yes.'

He patted his jacket pocket. 'I've got the sketchbook. That's the clincher. Last time we didn't even need to show it. It stuck out a mile that that guy was the wrong one.'

'How could you be so sure?'

He signalled the waitress for more coffee.

'Hell, Julie, there's no way someone like that could be *your* father.'

We left via downtown Los Angeles – through shadowy skyscraper canyons, then fast along the San Bernadino freeway out of the city and on across miles of scrubland – the kind of arid, rocky-outcrop terrain that you see in Westerns. I half-expected a posse of gun-toting cowboys to materialize over the horizon in a cloud of dust, and come thundering full tilt towards us. On the Jeep radio some man was playing a guitar and crooning a country song.

I ain't seen yooo since last July and I'm lonesome,
sad and bloo-hoo,
And my phone it still ain't a-ringin', so I guess it still
ain't yoo-hoo.

Palm Springs lived up to its name. There were palms galore and there must have been springs because it was a green and fertile oasis in the middle of a desert, lying at the foot of the San Jacinto mountains. Hotels, condominiums, haciendas, lakes, lawns, swimming pools, golf courses, flowers, sunshine . . . and a perfect air temperature somewhere in the high seventies.

It was too early to call on the Hamlyns and too soon to eat anything else after the pancake-house breakfast, so we went to a bar where Rob ordered two margaritas.

'Mexican courage, Julie. You're looking

panicky again. As though you might make a run for it – if I let you.'

'Where would I run to?'

'Nowhere. You'd die out in the desert.'

As soon as I'd finished my drink, he ordered another. 'When we get there, turn up the phoney English accent to max. It'll impress the wife and she needs impressing.'

'Phoney?'

'Most Yanks can't believe it's for real. There's a theory that if you wake up an Englishman in the middle of the night, shouting *Fire! Fire!* he'll drop the accent and start talking normally – like an American.'

Between the margaritas and the joking, I felt better. Even so, as we arrived at the gated condominium where the Hamlyns lived, the panic came back, together with the sledge-hammer heart and the jelly knees. I wasn't sure if it was because I so hoped he was my father, or because I so hoped he wasn't. I was so afraid of being disappointed by him. *Why run the risk? It could be such a big mistake*. A security guard admitted us through the gates into the compound. The condo was shining white stucco with flowers in dazzling, regimented bloom, dense emerald-green grass, more palms and exotic greenery, immaculate grounds.

'This is retirement living,' Rob said. 'No kids, no noise, no hassle and a golf course right in their back yard. A dream come true.'

We found the condo number and Rob rang

the bell. He smiled at me. 'Hang in there, kid.'

A woman's voice crackled from a grille beside the door and he answered. There was a click and the door swung open.

Mrs Hamlyn was as immaculate as her surroundings. She was probably well into her sixties but nothing had been allowed to slide – hair, make-up, clothes, figure were all in apple-pie order. Cowardly as *The Wizard of Oz* lion, I hung back and left Rob to do the talking; he turned the charm full on. We were conducted into a living room that was a far cry from the one in Garden Grove. The furniture and pictures and ornaments looked as if they had been transplanted direct and complete from an expensive show house, the potted plants were flourishing, not a single thing was out of place.

'Craig will be joining us momentarily,' Mrs Hamlyn said. 'He's been taking a shower. We only just got back from the golf club.'

I could see the golf course out of the big picture window: acres of verdant lawns, sandy bunkers, velvet greens, silvery-blue eucalyptus trees and electric golf carts crawling slowly about like white beetles. 'It looks a lovely course.'

'Oh, it is. That's why we came here. Craig and I took up golf a few years back, when he retired, and we're just crazy about the game. We play every day.' She was looking me over as she spoke and I don't think she was too impressed. I'd made the big mistake of wearing linen and my skirt and blouse had turned to rags. 'Coming from England, I'm sure you'll like some tea. We're quite familiar with British customs. We had tea at the Ritz Hotel in London when we were last over there.'

'That's very kind of you. I'd love some.'

'Do you prefer Earl Grey or Lapsang Souchong, Mrs Porter? I have both.'

'Earl Grey would be very nice, thank you – if it's not too much trouble.'

She looked past me. 'Oh, Craig, this is Mrs Porter from England. And Mr Mclaren.'

I turned, heart in my mouth. He wasn't quite as tall as the one before – but with more hair and not a pound overweight. To the pristine slacks and the leisure shirt and the slipper-like loafers on his feet, I added an American Air Force cap to see if the face was right. It could have been, except for the mouth which wasn't. The lips were too thin and the corners turned down, not up. But then, I reasoned, mouths probably change over the years. A long marriage to Mrs Hamlyn might have caused his to droop a trifle. We shook hands. His wife left the room – presumably to make the tea – and we sat down on the uncomfortable show-house chairs.

He said politely, 'What part of England do you come from, Mrs Porter?'

'From London.'

'We were over there last summer. We stayed in London for a few days, then went on to Stratford-upon-Avon and Oxford and some other places.'

'You didn't by any chance go to the Bomb Group reunion at Halfpenny Green, did you?' I couldn't remember him at all, but then there had been a lot of people. I could easily have missed seeing him.

He shook his head. 'We've been to a couple of those over here, but we don't care for them. I've never gone back to Halfpenny Green, I'm afraid.' He shifted in his chair – perhaps he found them uncomfortable too. 'I understand your mother was a WAAF with the Royal Air Force during the war?'

'Yes. She died last year and I'm trying to piece some missing parts of her life together. I was hoping to come across people who remembered her then. She was stationed at Halfpenny Green.'

He frowned. 'I got there in late '43 but I don't recall any British WAAFs.'

'Actually, she was the only one left when the Americans took over. She worked with the RAF liaison officer.'

He had steepled the tips of his fingers and was tapping them precisely together. His wrists were thin and bony. 'Did she? I don't remember him either.'

'I wonder if you knew a pub called the Mad Monk in the village? I think my mother went there sometimes.'

'I was teetotal in those days. I still am. I never went to pubs. Flying and alcohol don't mix, in my view. Some of the crews didn't agree with that, of course. A lot of them got drunk regularly, I'm sorry to say. They frequently paid the price.'

I couldn't imagine Ma falling deeply in love with this man and remembering him for the rest of her life. Could anyone describe him as *wonderful*? Nor could I imagine him piloting a heavy four-engined bomber – he seemed more suited to the controls of a golf cart.

'How long were you at Halfpenny Green, Mr Hamlyn?'

'Four months. We had engine trouble on a raid over France and had to force-land. I managed to evade capture and got out through Spain. I was posted back stateside and spent the rest of the war over here.'

I brought the photo out of my bag. 'I don't suppose you'd recognize any members of this crew? They served at Halfpenny Green.'

He took it reluctantly, glanced at it, and returned it. 'No. I don't. You have to realize, Mrs Porter, that there were around fifty crews stationed on the base at any one time. That's a lot of men – five hundred, to be precise. They were arriving and leaving constantly, flying different missions, living in different quarters . . . And it was fifty years ago.'

I said apologetically, 'Yes, of course. It was asking a lot.'

Rob produced the sketchbook. 'This wouldn't ring any bells either, would it?'

He flicked over a few pages. 'It looks like it

could be Halfpenny Green, but I've never seen any of these drawings before.'

Mrs Hamlyn reappeared wheeling a tea trolley equipped with gold-rimmed cups and saucers, matching teapot, strainer and milk jug. They were Royal Doulton, she said. She had bought them in Harrods china department on their last trip and had them shipped back home. We made polite conversation about the Royal Family, the terrible English weather, the wonderful London taxis, the beautiful Oxford colleges, William Shakespeare, Anne Hathaway's cottage, and so on. After a suitable interval, Rob and I stood up to leave. At the door we all shook hands again.

Craig Hamlyn said to me, as an afterthought, 'I did happen to come across somebody a while back who was at Halfpenny Green around the same time as myself. We were at a fund-raising gala in LA and got talking, by chance. We planned to get together another time but we haven't gotten round to it and I doubt we will. Maybe he could help you, Mrs Porter. I think I've still got his card somewhere.' He fished out a crocodile wallet and thumbed through it. 'Here we are . . . he's a pretty big shot. You can keep the card if you like.'

I stared at the name on the card. Later, out in the Jeep, I showed it to Rob. He grinned.

'Well, how about that!'

'Is he really a big shot?'

'Sure is. This guy's loaded, and I mean *loaded*.'

I hadn't bargained for him being stinking rich, or even rich at all. That side of it had never entered my head. I said faintly, 'I think I need another margarita.'

'And I know where to find the best one in town.'

The Ingleside Inn was an old and beautiful Spanish hacienda hidden away among a grove of trees at the foot of the mountains. It had wooden verandas, louvred shutters, purple bougainvillea smothering tiled roofs, cool terracotta floors, old-fashioned ceiling fans. And style.

'All the rich and famous used to come and stay here in the Thirties,' Rob told me. 'Movie stars, moguls, millionaires . . .'

The bar was nightclub dark, apparently lit by glow-worms, and with near invisible patrons located only by the glint of gold or the flash of jewels or the clunk of heavy bracelets on drinking arms. Rob said, 'This is a great post-face-job location. The bruises don't show.'

We sat on stools up at the counter and Rob ordered from a barman who materialized from nowhere like a genie from one of his bottles. The margaritas, when served, were small, ice-cold and utterly lethal.

I started whingeing. 'If this man's such a big shot there isn't a chance that he'll agree to see me.'

'He will if you call him up yourself. It's the only way it's going to work this time. No more hiding behind me.'

'I don't think I could do it.'

He lit a cigarette. 'If it means enough to you, Julie, you'll do it.'

'How come he's so rich?'

'Howard Hamilton owns a whole bunch of magazines, that's how.'

'He'll think I'm after the money. That I'm some kind of ghastly impostor.'

'How can he? He won't know a thing – unless you tell him. Play it the same way you did today. Check him out. See if you think he could be the one. Then decide what you want to do.'

I said bitterly, 'You make it all sound so bloody simple, Rob. It isn't – not for me.'

'Yeah, I know that. But if I didn't keep kicking your ass we'd never get anywhere. Have another margarita.'

'Isn't it time we went back to Los Angeles?'

He looked at me, straight in the eyes. 'Why not stay over till tomorrow?'

'*Tomorrow?* Chris is expecting me today.'

'Call her.'

I turned my head away from his eyes, which were sending mine a pretty clear message. 'What would I say?'

'That you'll be back tomorrow. You're over twenty-one, Julie.'

I fiddled with the margarita glass. 'Where would we stay?'

'Right here.'

'Here?'

'It's a very good place.'

He went away to see about it and came back. 'It's all fixed.'

'Two rooms?'

He flicked the ash off the end of his cigarette. 'One. That's all they've got.'

I didn't believe a word of it. 'I haven't even brought a toothbrush.'

'Nor have I. We'll buy them. Have that other drink. Then we'll go get something to eat.'

In the swanky restaurant we ate lovely food and drank more margaritas.

He said, chin propped on his hand, staring at me, 'Do you always fix your hair like that, Julie? All screwed up with that clip thing?'

'Yes. It keeps it out of the way. Otherwise it's a mess. And, since we're being personal, don't you ever wear a tie?'

'Not if I can help it. If I wear a tie, will you let your hair down?'

'All right. It's a deal.' I propped my chin on my hand, too, and stared back at him. 'Do tell me, Rob. What does the F stand for?'

'The F? What the heck are you talking about?'

'Robert F. Mclaren. What's the F?'

'Finlay. That's the maternal side.'

'So you're a Scot, through and through.'

'No,' he said. 'You've got that wrong. I'm an American. My people came here to get away from Scotland. In this country we're all descended from somebody wanting to get away from somewhere – usually for damn good reasons. We're built on desperation and dream-chasing and making good. That's the big difference between us and you.' He raised his glass to me. 'Otherwise, I guess we're pretty much the same.'

The decor in the supposedly one remaining bedroom was Mexican. Carved mahogany furniture, woven rugs on a tiled floor, soft lanternlight, white muslin hangings. A ceiling fan was humming quietly to itself, around and around and around.

I said, outside far too many margaritas, 'Actually, I'm forty-eight, Rob.'

'So what? I'm fifty.'

'I don't look like I did.'

'I sure as hell don't either.'

'And I haven't done this in ages.'

'It's like riding a bicycle; you never forget.'

'I really don't think—'

'You do a lot too much thinking, Julie. Look on it as something you owe me – the fee you were offering.'

'In advance?'

'OK by me.'

'Full and final settlement?' I had some trouble with the word 'settlement'.

'Sure. Whatever you want to call it.' He unfastened the tortoiseshell clip and loosened my hair slowly with his fingers.

'That's not fair, Rob. You're not wearing a tie. And that was the deal.'

'Scout's honour,' he said. 'I will.'

Fifteen

I called Howard Hamilton from the hotel bedroom the next morning. If Rob had not been there to ignore all my feeble excuses – including a hangover – punch out the number and hand me the receiver, I'm not sure I would ever have found the courage. I listened to a phone ringing in some Bel Air mansion.

'There's no answer.' I started to put down the receiver but he grabbed hold of my wrist.

'Not yet. It'll be a big place.'

Three more rings and a man answered – with a Spanish accent. 'Mr Hamilton's residence.'

Rob was watching and waiting. Flint-eyed. Pitiless. A far cry from the way he'd been the night before. Very far. 'May I speak to him, please?'

'What is your name?'

'Mrs Juliet Porter. I'm from England.'

'One moment.'

The moments passed while I kept clearing my throat, suddenly chock-full of frogs. I looked at Rob. 'He doesn't seem to be at home.'

'No use hanging up. I'll just call the number again.'

'It's all right for you . . .'

'Yeah, I know. You've said that before. Keep holding.'

A voice came on the line: deep, soft, American. 'Mrs Porter? This is Howard Hamilton.'

I cleared my throat yet again and managed a froggy croak. 'I'm sorry to trouble you, Mr Hamilton.'

'It's no trouble. What can I do for you?'

'I'm on a visit from England . . .'

'So I understand. We haven't met, have we?'

'No. We haven't.'

'I'm rather wondering how you got my number since it's unlisted?'

I croaked on. 'From Mr Craig Hamlyn. I went to see him recently and he gave me your card with your address and number on it.'

'I'm sorry. His name's not familiar to me.'

'Apparently, you were introduced at a fund-raising dinner in Los Angeles. I believe you were both stationed at Halfpenny Green in England during the war.'

There was a short and significant pause. 'I do remember him now. So, where do you fit in, Mrs Porter?'

'My mother served in the British WAAF. She was also at Halfpenny Green. Her name was Daisy Woods. I wondered if by any chance you knew her?'

A longer pause; *much* longer. I held my breath.

'Yes, I knew your mother. Many years ago. How is she?'

'I'm afraid she died last year.'

Silence. Then, 'I'm so sorry to hear that, Mrs Porter. How very sad for you.'

'Thank you.' I chose my next words with care. 'She left a letter for me when she died.'

Another pause. 'Yes?'

'And a photograph of an American bomber crew. There were no names, but, naturally, I was rather curious. Unfortunately, when she was alive she never talked about her wartime service and I never asked her – it's a part of her life that I wish I knew much more about.'

'Is that why you went to see Mr Hamlyn?'

'Yes. But he didn't remember her at all and he didn't recognize anybody in the photo. I was hoping you might, and that we might meet.' More breath-holding on my part and another long pause the other end.

'I'd be glad to, Mrs Porter. Where are you speaking from?'

'Well, I'm in Palm Springs at the moment, but I'm staying with friends in Santa Monica and returning there this morning. I fly back to England the day after tomorrow.'

'Let's make it today, then. Come here as soon as you get back to LA.'

I put down the receiver, fingers numb from gripping it to death.

Rob said, 'You look as though you've seen a ghost.'

'Not seen one. Heard one.'

'How did it sound?'

I collapsed on the bed. 'Rather wonderful.'

On the drive back to Los Angeles Rob told me everything he knew about Howard Hamilton.

'It's a family company. The grandfather started it with a couple of magazines, then the son added a whole lot more and then the grandson – this guy, Howard – took over in the Sixties and made it even bigger.'

'Is he married?'

'Divorced once, then married again. The second wife was killed in a car smash a while back. He hasn't remarried yet, but there can't be a shortage of willing number threes. One thing I didn't know about him is that he was a bomber pilot with the Eighth in England, or I'd've cottoned on before. I've never heard him talk about it.'

'You mean you've *met* him? You didn't tell me that.'

'I'm telling you now.'

'What was he like?'

'A very nice guy. But nobody's fool. You'll have to play it straight down the middle with him.'

'If he *is* the right one, I'm not telling him who I am. I've never meant to do that.'

'Sure. I know.'

'Especially considering he's stinking rich.'

'What's the big difference?'

'Like I said, he'd be bound to think I was after the money.'

'No, he wouldn't, Julie.'

'Well, if you were a billionaire, or whatever he is, and some strange woman turned up on your doorstep claiming to be your daughter, when as far as you know you'd never had one, wouldn't you be a bit suspicious?'

'Yeah – unless she was like you. I told you, he's not a fool. He'll figure out exactly what you are for himself.'

Later on, as we were getting closer to the city, I said, 'Does he have any children?'

'Two sons.' He glanced at me drily. 'And maybe one daughter.'

Bel Air was a large and lushly wooded estate in the Los Angeles foothills that put even Beverly Hills in the shade. We went in at the western entrance under an impressive archway. The zillionaire mansions were well hidden from vulgar prying eyes by verdant trees and shrubs, by high walls and by impenetrable security gates.

'Money,' Rob said. 'Can't you smell it?'

We drove for half a mile or so up through exclusive opulence before Rob stopped the Jeep and cut the engine.

'This is it.'

I looked at the tall iron gates – metal-lined so that nothing could be seen of what lay behind them. 'Are you sure it's the right one?'

'Yeah. Quite sure. There's the number on the pillar. And see that panel below it? There'll be a button to press and a grille to talk into so you can tell them who you are. Be sure to smile nicely at the security camera. If they like the sound and look of you they'll let you in. Otherwise they won't.' He felt in his jacket pocket for the little sketchbook. 'Don't forget to show him this.'

I put the sketchbook away inside my bag but went on sitting there. 'Maybe I ought to go back and change first, Rob. I look an awful mess in these clothes.'

'Nice try, Julie. Just get on with it.'

'You could come in with me.'

'Not a chance. Not this time. You're on your own.'

I swallowed. 'I don't think I can do this, Rob.'

'Sure, you can.'

'I'm too scared. I simply haven't the guts. Let's just leave it for now.'

He said, 'We're not going. You hired me to find this guy for you, and I figure we've probably found him.'

'I didn't *hire* you.'

'Yeah, you did. And you've paid me up front. Remember?'

He got out of the Jeep, went round to my side, opened the door and hauled me bodily out onto the sidewalk. Then he kissed me.

'I'm off home now to do some work. Call me when you want to be picked up and I'll come straight over.'

'I don't want to do this, Rob. I'd much sooner forget the whole thing. Really.'

He took hold of my shoulders and revolved

me firmly in the direction of the gate. 'Get going, Julie. Buzz that buzzer.'

I walked towards the pillar, on my way to the scaffold.

He stayed there, watching, arms folded across his chest. 'Just *do* it.'

I found the button and jabbed at it. The same Spanish-accented voice floated tinnily out of some holes.

'Your name, please?'

'Juliet Porter.' If there was a camera it was well hidden and, anyway, there was nothing to smile about.

'Please enter, Mrs Porter.'

The gates began to swing open. Behind me, Rob, the callous louse, had started up the Jeep engine and was driving away, leaving me all alone.

A driveway led down to a building. This was no Beverly Hills fanciful flight into the past but an ultra-modern structure of glass and stone and concrete. I walked towards it, passing a straw-hatted Mexican gardener clipping back shrubs, another sweeping with a large broom, another raking stray leaves off perfect lawns. The front door, when I finally reached it, was bronze and massive. There was no bell to push, no knocker to knock, and no handle to turn. As I stood there, wondering what to do next, the door was opened by a manservant, also Mexican and dressed in a white jacket and trousers and white buckskin shoes.

'Please come inside, Mrs Porter.'

I followed him down a long, light corridor. The floors were slate, the walls limestone, the full-length windows on each side a single pane of glass. Outside, ornamental trees grew in giant pots beside rectangular pools of water. I was shown into a circular room where the ceiling soared, pavilion-like, to a high point in the centre. The floor was pale wood, the furniture all white, three walls were hung with enormous canvases of modern art – bold works in bold colours using bold brushstrokes. The fourth wall was almost entirely made of glass. I went over and gazed out onto a stone terrace and a sparkling swimming pool below. The wooded hillside dropped away to a golf course even lusher than the one I had seen in Palm Springs and with similar white beetles crawling over it.

I didn't hear him come into the room and I didn't see him because I was too busy admiring the view.

'Mrs Porter?'

I turned around very slowly, afraid to look.

He was standing a few feet away from me – tall, upright, silver-haired, dressed in a blue shirt and cord trousers. I knew, at once, that it was the man in the photograph – even without the sheepskin jacket, the American cap, and all the rest of the flying kit. Even before he smiled.

There was a moment's silence and then he held out a hand. 'I'm Howard Hamilton. Glad to meet you.'

No wonder Madeleine Lucas had remembered his smile. I shook his hand politely. 'How do you do.'

He was still looking at me, still smiling. 'You're very like your mother.'

'Yes, I've always been told that.'

I was invited to sit down on one of the white sofas, offered a drink which I refused, though I could have done with a large brandy. He sat back in a chair opposite me, one leg crossed over the other, elbows resting on the chair's arms, apparently totally at ease. The clothes might have been casual but they were certainly very expensive. There was a perfect white orchid plant growing in a moss-covered pot on the glass table between us and I pretended to be enraptured by it for a moment, rather than be caught staring at him. I knew he was watching me intently and that he would weigh up every word I said.

I stalled cravenly, gushingly. 'You have a beautiful home, Mr Hamilton. And what a lovely view! The golf course looks wonderful.'

'I don't play myself,' he said. 'My late wife did, but I've never cared for the game.'

For some reason, I was glad to hear it. I couldn't picture him driving around in those little electric carts but it wasn't hard to imagine him at the controls of a heavy bomber. In fact, it was very easy.

He said, 'Well, where should we start?'

Where, indeed? I had to look him in the eye

then and hope that he couldn't read my thoughts. This total stranger was my father – I was certain of it – but I still couldn't grasp the fact that I was a part of him, just as much as I had been a part of my mother. More nervous throat-clearing on my part.

'Take your time, Mrs Porter. I'm in no rush. Are you sure you wouldn't like something to drink?'

'Well, perhaps something soft.' Rob would have laughed out loud if he'd been there. If only he were.

He called over his shoulder and the manservant appeared silently. 'Jose, Mrs Porter would like something soft to drink. What do we have to offer her?'

'Iced tea, sir? Or mineral water? Or fresh orange juice? Whatever the señora wishes.'

I said, 'Iced tea would be lovely.'

'Would you prefer it hot? Jose knows how to make English tea.'

'No, iced would be fine.'

The manservant left. I had used up my stalling time; he was waiting patiently and politely for me to speak.

I got rid of another frog. *Play it straight down the middle with him.* 'As I told you on the telephone, Mr Hamilton, my mother left me a letter and a photo when she died. I found it in her desk, at her home in Oxford.'

'Do you have them both with you?'

'Yes. The letter's . . . rather private. Would you like to see the photo?'

'Very much.'

I took it out of my bag and gave it to him. He stared at it for a moment in silence, turned it over, turned it back again.

'How did she get this?'

'I don't know. She didn't say. As you can see, there's no date, or place or any names. I wondered if it was your crew? If you were the captain?'

He looked up at me. 'Oh yes, Mrs Porter. It's my crew. This was taken in January 1944, just before we left on our last mission. One of the ground crew took it and we weren't too thrilled to be kept standing around in that cold. You'd never know it, though, would you? We're all of us saying cheese. I'm on the far right, at the back, next to Ray, my co-pilot.'

I said, 'Yes, I can see that. Please keep the photo, if you'd like to.'

'Thank you.' He put it away in the breast pocket of his shirt and looked at me. 'You told me that your mother had never talked to you about her wartime service.'

'No, she didn't. I didn't even know the name of the bomber station in Suffolk. I don't think she ever mentioned it.'

'Then would you mind telling me, Mrs Porter, how you managed to trace me from an unidentified snapshot almost fifty years old? I'm as curious as you must have been.'

'It's rather a long story.'

'Just give me the outline.'

Again, I was saved by the return of Jose with the tea borne on a tray. I took the tall glass from him and drank, playing for more time while I thought out what I was going to say next. The tea was ice-cold, lemon-scented, delicious.

'Whenever you're ready, Mrs Porter.'

I said, 'Well, in the end I traced the airfield from the name of a pub – the Mad Monk. My mother spoke of it in a letter to her sister. Perhaps you knew it?'

'I certainly did.'

'It's an unusual name – even for England. I went to Suffolk and drove around until I found it. It's not called that any longer, so it took a while to track it down.'

'What's it like these days?'

'It's called the Cricketers and it's been done up. Remodelled, I think you'd call it. Restaurant tables, fancy menu, new bar, carpeting.'

'In my day, there was just the old bar, warm beer, a dartboard, and a brick floor, if I remember rightly. There was a piano, too, and a lot of singing.'

'"Roll me over in the Clover"? "'Roll out the Barrel"? "Tipperary"?'

He smiled. 'How did you know?'

'Someone told me. The piano's gone, I'm afraid. But there are still some photos of the old air base hung on the wall, and some signatures carved on a board.'

'I can remember guys doing that . . . I never did myself, though. So, you found the old pub. Did you find the airfield?'

'Yes. I went along Nightingale Lane and up by the water tower onto the perimeter track. It wasn't difficult to find.'

He said, 'There was a short cut down through the woods, from the base to the village green. Your mother told me she'd heard a nightingale singing there once.'

'I'm afraid they've probably gone too.'

He said softly, as though to himself, 'Maybe to Berkeley Square.'

'As in the song?'

He smiled again. 'You've got it. So, the airfield's still there?'

'Very much so. Do you remember Mr and Mrs Layton who owned the land and farmed there during the war?'

'Sure. I remember them well. They used to ask the crews over to their home – nice people. As a matter of act, your mother was billeted with them.'

'Yes, I found that out too. Mr and Mrs Layton have both died but their grandson, William, lives in the house with his family, and he's looked after the old airfield buildings. Most of it's still there – the control tower, the hangars, the runways.'

'That's great.'

'They get a lot of visitors – Americans who served there during the war.'

'I've never been back,' he said. 'Never wanted to.'

'Actually, there was a big American reunion while I was there and the Laytons invited me to the lunch they were giving at the farm. Somebody recognized you from that photo. A Joe Deerfield.'

'Joe! He was my crew chief. From Arizona. How was he?'

'Fine. He remembered you well.'

'We both used to grumble like hell about the English weather.'

'That's what he said. He couldn't remember your proper name, though. Just that your crew called you Ham and that you came from California.'

He rested his head sideways on one hand, watching me. 'So on the strength of that you came to California, Mrs Porter, and you went to see Mr *Ham*lyn.'

'And a Mr Hammond Wright in Orange County who was at Halfpenny Green, too. He's the one who told me about the singing in the pub. But neither he nor Mr Hamlyn knew the photo.'

'If you don't mind my asking, how did you manage to trace both these gentlemen?'

'The people I'm staying with introduced me to someone who has a friend at the Veterans' Administration.'

'I see. You must have been *very* curious, Mrs Porter.'

I pulled the sketchbook out of my bag. 'I think I may have something else of yours.'

He took it from me, went through it slowly, pausing for a long while when he came to the drawing of Ma at her table, holding her fountain pen. At last he said, 'I did these at Halfpenny Green . . . hell, I'd forgotten all about them. Where did you find this?'

'In a drawer in my mother's desk. There was a record there, too – an old 78. Frank Sinatra singing a wartime song. She kept them both together.'

Silence. And then he closed the book and looked at his watch. 'I'd like to take you to lunch, Mrs Porter. There's a place just around the corner. We can talk some more there.'

A place just around here? 'I'm not very smartly dressed.'

He smiled. 'Nor am I. But they'll take us just as they find us, I assure you.'

The manservant, Jose, drove the Rolls-Royce to the Bel Air hotel. We walked from the car over a wooden bridge beside a lake with swans. Pink-washed walls, terracotta roofs, awnings and archways and trellises, crimson bougainvillea, scarlet poinsettias, the orange plumage of birds of paradise, oleanders and orange trees dappling the sunlight. In the dining room white columns supported a pergola roof laced with greenery. It was open to the skies but cunning heating made it June in January.

'Do you like lobster?' he asked. 'It's usually excellent here.'

I was happy for him to choose for me, not much caring what I ate or in any state to grapple with the menu. He ordered wine from the hovering sommelier and when it had been poured raised his glass. 'To you, Mrs Porter. I'm very glad we've met, at last.'

At last? 'Please call me Juliet,' I said.

'Thank you – Juliet.' He set down the glass slowly. 'Now what can I tell you about your mother?'

'Anything you like.'

He nodded. 'Let's see, then. We met at Halfpenny Green in the spring of 1943. I saw her around the base and in the pub but it was quite a while before I got to have a conversation with her. She wasn't too keen on us Yanks at first. We were a cocky bunch – till we'd settled down and found out a few home truths. Then we learned fast. Your mother worked with the RAF liaison officer – I can't remember his name, I'm afraid. She used to sit beside him at mission briefings and in the interrogation room after. There was always a lot of urgent communication going on between the US and the RAF.' He paused while the waiter served a salad. 'I finally got to talk to her at the Laytons' home – the first evening they invited some of the crews over.' He smiled. 'It was Lieutenant Hamilton at first till she found out that maybe we weren't such bad guys, after all. Then she called me Ham, like everybody else.'

'Do you remember Madeleine – the daughter at the farmhouse? She would have been about seven years old then.'

'Sure. She had a brother called Peter. I remember them both well. They were nice kids.'

'She came to the reunion at Halfpenny Green when I was there. She gave me a photo of my mother that her mother had taken. It would have been in the summer of 1943. During the harvest. I brought it with me – in case you'd like to see it.'

I passed over the photo of Ma in her too-big dungarees tied up with string and the spotted scarf round her hair. He stared at it. 'I remember exactly when this was taken. Some of us went over to the farm to give the Laytons a hand with the harvest . . . your mother was helping, too. She'd borrowed these overalls and they were much too big for her . . . it was the first time I'd ever seen her out of uniform.'

'I found the scarf when I was going through her clothes – she still wore it sometimes.'

He gave me back the photo. 'Why did she die?'

'Cancer. She didn't tell us, though.'

'Us?'

'The family. My brother, Andrew, my daughter, Flavia.'

'And her husband – your father?'

'He died several years ago.'

The waiter brought the lobster thermidor, served it deftly and went away.

'How old is your daughter?'

'Twenty-four.'

'Married?'

'No. Not yet. She lives with someone at the moment. An actor.'

'My two sons are married and I've six grandchildren. They all live nearby so I get to see them pretty often.'

It was obviously a happy family set-up. Happy and healthy and wealthy. How would the two sons and their wives and the six grandchildren take the news of an interloper gatecrashing the enchanted circle? I could imagine how. Even without all the wealth, the Hamilton family would be bound to have mixed feelings; *with* it, they were definitely going to think I was after a share, or, worse, that I was some sort of con artist.

'You're not eating very much,' he said. 'Would you prefer something else?'

'No, it's very good, thank you.'

He was still watching me all the time, observing, assessing . . . mistrusting? 'How about your husband? You haven't mentioned him.'

'We were divorced a long time ago.'

'I know what that's like. My first wife, Lola, and I divorced early on – soon after the boys were born,' he said. 'Then my second wife died in a car crash six years ago. Some junkie hit her on the freeway. I've been on my own since then. How about you? Do you live alone?'

'Not exactly. Flavia and I share a house in south London. She lives downstairs with her boyfriend and I live and work upstairs.'

'What sort of work do you do?'

'I illustrate books and I teach art.' *I can draw because of you.*

He set down his fork. 'What medium?'

'Usually watercolour.'

'That's a tough one,' he said. 'One of the toughest. I've tried it. I usually go for pencil, or pen and ink. Charcoal sometimes, crayon, maybe chalk. But these days I mostly collect instead. Modern American artists. It's interesting discovering new talent.'

'Yes, it must be.' The oil paintings I'd seen had probably been some of his discoveries. I had no doubt that he had a very discerning eye.

I struggled on with the lobster. It *was* very good but it was rich and I had no appetite. And, of course, I drank too many glasses of wine. I could feel my head begin to swim, hear my words begin to slur. He, on the other hand, drank very little. We skipped dessert and had coffee which helped. But what was the point of prolonging this meeting for much longer when I had already made up my mind not to tell him? It was painful for me, and probably tedious for him. His love affair with my mother had happened almost fifty years ago. He'd had two wives since, sons and grandchildren, a golden life out here in California, far away, in every respect, from the grim and grey wartime

England he'd known, and especially from Halfpenny Green. *I've never been back. Never wanted to.* So far as he was concerned, the past was past.

I looked at my watch. 'It's been a lovely lunch and so kind of you, but I really ought to be getting back.'

'I don't think we've quite finished yet, have we?' he said. 'Let's go back to the house – if you can spare me a little more time.'

It would have been ungracious to refuse. Jose drove us back again in the Rolls and I was given a tour of the house – room after beautiful room of uncluttered and sophisticated elegance. Adrian would have approved no end.

'A Swedish architect designed it,' he told me. 'It's built of four components – glass, slate, architectural concrete and limestone from the Lake District in England.'

I wondered how many millions it had cost and I thought of the ugly, rambling Victorian house in Oxford with its dodgy plumbing and its sulky heating and its old-fashioned everything. The home Ma had lived in happily for so many years. Would she have been as happy here? Yes, she would, because she would have made it her own and she would have been happy anywhere with him.

He opened yet another door. 'This is where I spend most of my time.'

It was a very different sort of room with bookshelves, worn leather armchairs, a TV screen, music centre, family photographs on a desk and artwork on the walls. Not the giant canvases but small drawings that I recognized instantly as his; some watercolours too. He took one down – a California scene of Spanish houses, purple bougainvillea, palm trees, the blue ocean in the background. It was uncannily like my own work. 'Santa Barbara,' he told me. 'Just north of LA.'

'I like it very much.'

He looked down at me with his half-smile. 'Is that an honest opinion, Juliet, or are you just being a kind teacher?'

'It's honest.'

He rehung the picture. 'Sit down. I want you to listen to something.' I waited while he hunted in a cupboard, hit buttons. Then he sat down as well and the voice of Frank Sinatra began to sing. We both listened in silence. At the end, he said, 'It's the same recording that your mother kept, isn't it?'

'Yes, it is.'

'It always reminds me of her.' He got up, walked away from me and stood staring out of the window. I stayed silent, waiting, and, after a few moments, he started to speak.

'I fell in love with Daisy when I first saw her in the Mad Monk. It took a while for her to feel the same way about me, but in the end she did. We were going to be married – just as soon as I'd done my tour. We'd got it all planned. She'd come back here. I'd give up Berkeley and go straight to work for my father. We'd look for a house in a good neighbourhood around LA. I was going to show her around and let her pick whatever pleased her. We talked it all through. In spite of the golden rule.'

'Golden rule?'

'A strict rule I had – a superstition, if you like. So many crews were getting killed, it didn't do to think about the future too much, let alone talk about it. It was like tempting fate. And I guess that's what we did.' He crooked one arm against the windowpane, rested his forehead on it. 'I got shot down on our twenty-first mission. Posted Missing In Action, presumed dead. There was another crew that might have seen parachutes come out of our plane but they were brought down themselves soon after. I didn't know that until a lot later. Everyone else figured we were all burned to crisps in the wreck found on the ground. My co-pilot, Ray, and I had got out – somehow – but he didn't make it. I was the only one. I'd been injured in the leg and a French family hid me for months. Then I got passed from place to place until, finally, I met up with the American army after they'd landed in Normandy.' He paused for a moment. 'As soon as I got back to England, I tried to phone your mother at Halfpenny Green. I still thought somebody would have seen the chutes and that she'd have kept on hoping. It was then I found out that she'd already got married. I wrote her an angry letter and she wrote back, saying she'd thought I was dead. I was bitter as hell, Juliet. I couldn't forgive her for doing that – for marrying some other man so fast. When I got back here, I got married even faster. But I'll tell you something. I've never forgotten her.'

I said, 'She never forgot you either. She went back to Halfpenny Green when she knew she was dying – I found her signature in the book there. She kept your photograph and your sketchbook and she played the record. She was listening to it in the days before she died.'

He turned round. 'I think you should show me her letter, Juliet. Don't you? It's only fair.'

It seems only fair to him now . . . Though perhaps it's not so fair to you? If I opened this particular door, it could never be shut again.

He said gently, 'You're my daughter, aren't you? That's what she told you.'

I gave him the letter and he read it, and then I could see that he was reading it through again and again. Just as I'd done myself. At last, he said, 'Thank you for showing this to me.'

'There's no proof, of course. She was taking strong drugs . . . she may have got confused.'

'She wasn't confused, Juliet. It happened exactly the way she told you – only I never knew the truth until now. I was too busy being mad at her and I was too damn stupid not to realize that there had to be some good reason.' He looked at me. 'But you weren't going to tell me that you were the reason, were you?'

'No. I wasn't.'

'Why not?'

'I wasn't sure you'd believe me. Or that you'd be pleased.'

He said quietly, 'It's the most wonderful news I've ever had in my life. Wait till we tell the rest of the family.'

'Could we keep this to ourselves for the moment, do you think? Just between us?'

'But I want them to know, Juliet. I want you to meet them, them to meet you. For you all to get acquainted.'

I said, 'It might be a shock for them. They might not be quite so pleased about it as you. They might resent me – and I'd *hate* that. Don't you see? Don't you understand?'

He went on looking at me for a moment. 'You're so like her, Juliet. That's how she'd probably have figured it. All right, we'll play it your way. I guess we should take a while to straighten out everything between us, in any case. One step at a time. But I know the family would all love you and I'm not promising to keep it a secret for ever. And I'm not letting you go out of my life.'

'We can meet again, if you'd like to.'

'You bet I'd like to. I get over to London regularly and I stay at the Connaught. They do a pretty good lunch there too. Maybe next time you'll be able to eat it.'

I managed to smile. 'I'll certainly try.'

'How about my granddaughter, Flavia. Does she know about me?'

'No, I haven't told her.'

'I'd still like to meet her.'

'I'll introduce you.'

'As what?'

'An old friend of her grandmother's.'

'Well, that's true enough. Tell me something, Juliet. The other guy – the one Daisy married – did he make her happy?'

'Yes. He was a good man. Kind and gentle. They'd known each other since they were children – he lived next door, you see. And I think he'd always loved her . . . that's why he offered to marry her.'

'In the letter she says he was a wonderful father to you. Is that true?'

'Yes. I loved him very much.'

'Did she love him?'

'In a different way,' I said. 'Not like she loved you.'

I asked him later whether he had ever gone back to France.

'Not for twelve years – after Lola and I were divorced. I found some of the places where I'd been hidden – a restaurant in Rennes, two old ladies near St Malo. I owed them money that I wanted to repay, but they'd already died. It took me a while to find the first place – a farmhouse near Caen – and the family that saved my life. The old grandmother had died and the farmer, too, but the wife was still alive and the little girl I'd known had grown up and married. She and her husband ran the farm. They dug up my old flying jacket for me.'

'You mean you still have it? The one in the photo?'

'Sure.'

He went away. After a moment or two he came back carrying the jacket. It looked worn and battered and there was a jagged tear in one sleeve.

'I guess that happened when I bailed out. Otherwise, it's in pretty good shape. They'd buried it in an old tin trunk.'

I said, 'Do you mind putting it on?'

'OK. Let's hope it still fits.'

It did. He turned the heavy sheepskin collar up round his ears and made fists of his hands at his waist, just like he'd done in the photo. Then he smiled at me. And it wasn't sunny California any more. It was a freezing cold day in England and he was standing in the snow at Halfpenny Green, nearly fifty years ago. Oh Ma, I thought. Oh, Ma . . .

When I left, he held my shoulders, looked down at me in silence for a moment, and kissed my cheek. 'Thank you, Juliet.'

'For what?'

'For finding me.'

'I think she wanted me to.'

'Yes,' he said. 'I think so too.'

Jose drove me back in the Rolls. Halfway there I asked him to take me to the beach house in Malibu instead of to Georgina Avenue. Rob opened the door. He took me upstairs to the living room, sat me down and handed me a fistful of Kleenex. I mopped my eyes, sniffed and snivelled.

'I'm sorry, Rob.'

'Don't be,' he said. 'Just tell me about it.'

'Well, it *was* him. The photo is of him and his crew, and the sketchbook is his. He knew my mother. They were in love and going to get married, then he was shot down over France, and everybody thought he was dead. When he finally got back to England she'd married someone else. There's no doubt about it.'

'Did you tell him who *you* were?'

'I wasn't going to. I'd made up my mind to say nothing – to leave the past alone. But then he told me his side of the story. How bitter he'd been – how he couldn't understand how she'd gone and married someone else so soon. I wanted him to know why she'd done it, but I hadn't the courage to tell him. You know what a coward I am, Rob.'

'You've got plenty of guts, Julie. Or you wouldn't have come here in the first place.'

'Anyway . . . Then he asked to see the letter. I *still* wasn't going to show it to him, only he suddenly said that he'd already guessed that I was his daughter.'

'So you handed it over. What did he say then?'

The tears started again and Rob passed more Kleenex. 'He said it was the most wonderful news he'd ever had in his life. He wanted to tell his family, and for me to meet them.'

'That's great, Julie.'

'No, it isn't. I asked him not to say anything.'

'I'm wondering why the hell you did that.'

I was tearing the Kleenex to shreds in my hands. 'I told you why before, Rob. Can you imagine how they'd feel? A half-sister suddenly appearing out of the blue? And with all that money around? They'd think I was some blood-sucking impostor, preying on their father. They'd hate me.'

'On the other hand,' he said, 'they might like you, Julie. They might like you a hell of a lot. Same as I do.'

I did some more mopping. 'Well, I'm not prepared to take the risk. I want to leave things as they are – for the time being. He says he comes to London quite often and we're going to meet again then.'

'I guarantee he'll make you change your mind. A guy like that's not used to taking no for an answer. That's why you happened.'

'Don't forget I'm a chip off the old block.'

'Yeah . . . that's true. But my money's on the old block.'

'I can't think about that now, Rob. All I know is I found him and now he knows the truth. I did what my mother wanted. And it's thanks to you.'

'Not me. I'm not so sure I earned my fee. The Hamlyn guy handed it to you on a silver platter.'

'But you found *him*.'

'Well, we got a lucky break.' He lit a cigarette. 'So, when do you go home?'

'The day after tomorrow.'

He said, 'I have to fly up to Seattle first thing in the morning and I won't be back till the end of the week. You'll be in England by then.'

'Yes, I will.'

'Well, you're just in time to see a sunset before you go,' he said. 'And it's going to be a helluva one.'

We watched it out on the deck, leaning on the rail as though we were sailing on a luxury liner and gazing out over the ocean. The sun was sinking slowly and the heavens were suffused with pink and tinged with gold. The pink deepened gradually to rose-coloured and then deeper still to a crimson which spread wider and wider like tongues of flame until the whole western sky above the Pacific Ocean was on fire. I'd never seen such a sunset. Ma would have loved it.

'I told you it'd blow your mind,' Rob said. He threw away his cigarette, took me in his arms and kissed me – for a long time. And went on holding me close, his cheek against mine. 'Don't go, Julie. Stay here in California. With me.'

'I have to go back, Rob.'

'Give me one good reason.'

'My daughter, Flavia.'

'That's not a good reason. It's not even a reason. It's another of your lame excuses. She's got somebody of her own – the actor guy who came out here. You told me about him.'

'He might not stay with her – if he gets that Hollywood part.'

'She'll find another guy if he doesn't. It won't wash, Julie. You'll have to think of something else.'

'My work. I have to work to eat. And I can't work here. They won't let me.'

'Sure you can. There's nothing to stop you sending your stuff back to England; you can work from anywhere in the world. So can I. We're both lucky.'

'But they won't let me live here longer than six months.'

'You can apply to become a resident alien.'

'That sounds like something from Mars.'

'It means you can stay as long as you like. You could get to know your father and the rest of the family. And you could marry me while you're at it.'

'Don't be silly, Rob, we don't even know each other. We only met a few days ago.'

'How long does it take? One look – in my book. Why do you think I've been busting my ass for you, right from the start?'

'You mean if you hadn't liked the look of me, you wouldn't have done?'

'I told you I was a selfish sort of guy. Chris tipped me off that you were worth meeting and I found out she was right.'

'So you put your life on hold for me?'

'Well, what the heck, it was the holidays . . . Christmas. And it was a lot more than the look of you, though that's pretty good. So, how about staying?'

I smiled, but I shook my head. 'I'd never fit in here, Rob. This isn't my sort of place.'

'More excuses. You don't know till you try. There are thousands of British living here, did you realize that? Hell, there's even an English pub where they do bangers and mash and steak and kidney pie. I'll take you there.'

'I couldn't eat a thing.'

'Later, I meant. Maybe.'

The beautiful sunset was fading fast, the light beginning to go. I pulled away. 'I really ought to go now, Rob. I've got packing and things to do. And Chris will be wondering what on earth I've been doing.'

'No, she won't. She'll know what you've been doing.'

'Honestly, Rob, I ought to go. Please take me back.'

'*Honestly*, Julie,' he mocked. 'OK, I'll take you. But not yet. Maybe in a couple of hours or so.'

All the neighbourhood Christmas lights had been dismantled and I was sorry to have missed Santa's eventual take-off in his sleigh. I'd enjoyed having him around – dipstick though he undoubtedly was. Chris had unscrewed her instant tree and put it away in storage for another year. I finished packing my suitcase and we drove to the airport in the love-it-to-bits

Chrysler. I'd told Chris about finding my mother's old friend and about who he was. She'd wanted to hear every detail of the Bel Air house and I'd satisfied her curiosity as much as I could.

'I saw it featured in a glossy mag once, Julie. Wow! What a place!'

'Yes, it was amazing.'

'It's supposed to have cost millions of dollars.'

'I should think it probably did.'

'Boy, your mother certainly passed up an opportunity.'

On the dodgem freeway to LAX she said, 'Rob's a really nice guy, isn't he? You know, I hoped you and he would hit it off. That's sort of why I asked him to help. Do you mind?'

'Not in the least. I'm very grateful to him. And to you, Chris.'

'Seems like you've both been getting on rather well . . . will you be seeing him again?'

'He says he'll be coming to London sometime.'

'That's not what I meant.' She switched freeway lanes, terrifyingly. 'I was thinking of you both maybe getting together permanently. How does that grab you as an idea?'

I opened my eyes again. 'I really don't know him well enough.'

She gave me a very old-fashioned look.

LAX was chaotic. We unlocked a luggage cart successfully with a new dollar bill and negotiated a pathway through the crowd to the British Airways check-in. I hugged Chris and thanked her again for everything, still guilty about the tangled web.

'Keep in touch,' she said. 'And come back soon.'

It was night-time when the London flight took off. The jumbo headed west, out over the Pacific ocean, and then turned east towards Europe, crossing directly over the City of Angels. I looked down and marvelled at the millions of lights, at the fantastical Tinseltown in all its extravagant glory. And then, suddenly, we were over desert and the dark, and it was gone.

Sixteen

It was raining in England – a dark, cold and miserable morning. I took the tube from Heathrow into London and the District Line out to Putney. My car was still safely outside the house but there was also a dog's mess by the gate and two empty crisp packets decorating the front garden. Flavia had already gone to work and there was no sign or sound of Callum. He was never an early riser. I found a pile of post for me on the hall table – junk mail, letters, bills, some late Christmas cards, a drinks party invitation, a dentist's appointment reminder. I felt fuzzy-headed from time-travelling and lack of sleep and yet unwilling to give in and go to bed. I made some black coffee, unpacked, had a bath, and phoned Adrian.

'Well, did you run him to earth, darling?'

'As a matter of fact, I did.'

'And?'

'Can we talk about it later?'

'Of course. Meet me at the fish place for lunch.'

He was at his usual corner table, elegant in a charcoal-grey suit and pale silk tie with a yellow rose in his buttonhole. And, as usual, he rose to his feet and kissed my hand, and helped me off with the bargain Balmain.

'I like the blouse, darling. Another of your little finds?'

'Jacques Fath. Oxfam.'

'Ah . . .'

He listened in silence while I told him what had happened – or most of it. Then he said, 'Why exactly don't you want him to tell his family?'

'They'll think I'm a gold-digger. Or some con artist.'

'You wouldn't know where to begin to gold-dig, or how to con, Juliet, darling. As I'm sure he could see perfectly well. And so will they.'

I said, 'In any case, we've missed the boat as father and daughter – you said so yourself.'

'Not completely, from the sound of things. I'd say the outlook was quite promising for you both.' He beckoned to the waiter. 'Now, what are you having to eat? Is it to be the monkfish or the bass? Both are equally delicious.'

At the coffee stage, he said, 'The other American – the journalist who helped you find your father – is he your lover?'

The term sounded daringly romantic. I smiled. 'In a way.'

'There's only one way, generally speaking.'

'Well, then he was.'

'Was?'

'He wanted me to stay in California with him, but I came home instead.'

'May I enquire why?'

'I'd only known him for a few days.'

Adrian sighed. 'You do make such arbitrary decisions, don't you, darling? Stubborn, one might almost say. It was all going swimmingly. Why not carry on?'

'I'm not sure I could live out there. It's so different.'

'Of course it is. It's another country. Another culture. Another people. But it's the man that matters. Nothing else. *He's* the important thing. Do try to remember that. More coffee?'

I went back to the flat and slept like the dead for several hours, not waking until Flavia came upstairs.

'Mum? Are you there?' She appeared at the bedroom door, laden with Safeway carrier bags. 'I'm sorry. I thought you weren't coming back till tomorrow.'

She'd brought bread, milk, butter, cheese, eggs, vegetables, fresh flowers, and a bottle of wine which we opened immediately.

'Did you have a good time?'

'Very good.'

'Callum said you seemed to be enjoying yourself when he saw you.'

'I was. Any news of the screen test?'

'He's still waiting. His agent thinks he'll get the part.'

'I think he will too.'

'So do I. Which means he'll be off to Hollywood.'

'Will you mind?'

'Yes, very much. But only for my sake – not his. It's what he's always wanted. I can't stand in his way, can I?'

'No, I suppose not.'

'Of course, if he goes, I realize he might not come back.'

'You could go there.'

'I don't think that would work, do you? Besides, I do like my job. I wouldn't want to give it up. And I've always known it couldn't last for ever – Callum and me. You've never exactly wanted it to, have you?'

'I want whatever makes you happy, darling.'

She smiled wryly. 'That what all mothers say, all the time. I bet Grandma said the same to you.'

'Well, I do know she always did what she thought was best for me.'

'I miss her very much, don't you?' She poured us some more wine. 'Anyway, tell me more about California?'

'It was amazing. Wonderful sunshine. Palm trees. Blue skies. Blue ocean. Everything so free and easy. You'd have loved the shopping malls.'

'You know, I rather hoped you might meet someone out there.'

'Meet someone?'

'Well, you know . . . some glamorous American who'd sweep you off your feet.'

'That's not what I went for.'

She laughed. 'Don't look like that. I know it wasn't, Mum. I was just hoping, that's all.'

'Actually, I did meet someone rather interesting.'

'Oh?'

'You remember that old black-and-white photo of Grandma's that you were looking at?'

'The hunky Yank bomber crew? Yes, why?'

'Well, I happened to run into one of them in Los Angeles.'

She stared at me. 'Run into one of them? How on earth did you manage that?'

'Well, not run into exactly. Somebody I came across was stationed in England at the same place as Ma and he knew somebody else living in Los Angeles who turned out to be the pilot of that crew.'

'How incredible!'

She was right; it was. I hurried on. 'He remembered Grandma well.'

'Good heavens! Grandma's secret past! What was he like?'

'Very nice indeed. Of course he's quite old now – but you'd still recognize him easily from the photo.'

'They were probably madly in love. A passionate wartime romance. How lovely!'

'As a matter of fact, he's coming to London in the spring. We're supposed to be having lunch. And he'd like to meet you.'

'Would he? That's fine by me. We can talk

about Grandma. He can tell me all about her when she was young, in those days. Do you think he'd mind?'

I said, 'No, I don't think he'd mind at all.'

Drew phoned later that evening and I gave him my news. He seemed hopeful that I'd got the whole thing out of my system and would now settle down as though nothing whatever had happened.

'No need for much further contact, is there, Ju?'

'You mean he and I could exchange Christmas cards and leave it at that?'

'Well, California's pretty far away.'

'Actually, he comes over here several times a year. We're meeting then.'

'But he hasn't told his family. And you haven't told Flavia.'

'No, not yet.'

'Better not, you know. Let sleeping dogs lie.'

'The dogs are already wide awake, Drew. And I'm not sure if they'll go back to sleep again.'

He sighed. 'We should have burned that photo and Ma's letter in the first place. Much the best thing all round.'

'But I'm awfully glad we didn't.'

I phoned Stella Morrison.

She said, 'I'm so glad you found him, Juliet. What was he like?'

'A wonderful man.'

'Even better. No dreadful disappointments or let-downs. How did his wife take it?'

'He's a widower.'

'Any children?'

'Two married sons, six grandchildren. But I asked him not to tell them.'

'Oh, why did you do that?'

Stella and Rob and Adrian would all have got along famously. I said, 'He's got a very great deal of money. They'd think I was after it.

'I've never met you, Juliet, but I'm sure you're wrong. And if he wants to tell them, you should let him. He needs to, as much as you needed to find him. Have you told your daughter?'

'Not yet.'

'Don't worry, the moment will come. Take your time. Everything will work out in the end.'

The alphabet-book illustrations had gone down well and I'd been given another and very different commission to illustrate a book for older children. No bunnies or fairy magic this time. No pretty flowers or spotted toadstools or enchanted woods. The story was bang up to date, about a black foster child growing up in a multiracial city community, and it was a welcome challenge for me. It was also a welcome mind-absorber. While I was concentrating so hard at making a good job of it, I couldn't think too much about anything else. But when I could concentrate no longer, I made some coffee and drank it, staring out of the attic window and thinking about faraway California and two Americans there.

My father had called several times and we had talked without any constraint on either side. We had agreed that I should call him Howard – part of what he had described as 'straightening things out between us'. He was coming over to London in March and we had our lunch date in the diary. I was looking forward to it very much and to us doing some more straightening out. I had heard nothing from Rob, though. I'd read one of his articles in *The Times* – all about the impact of the American way of life on Japan – and he had obviously been spending time there. As Chris had said, he got around. I wondered when he'd get around to London and whether he'd call me when he did. 'I need time, Rob,' I'd told him when I left LA. 'OK,' he'd said. 'I'll give it to you.'

The evening classes started up again and Monica and I resumed our coffee-bar visits afterwards. Naturally, she wanted to know everything about my trip to California, and, naturally, I only told her part of it. Yes, by an amazingly lucky coincidence, I had found my mother's American wartime friend. He was still alive and living in Los Angeles, and, yes, he remembered her very well and we had talked a lot. Monica had listened, her head cocked to one side like an inquisitive parrot, and I knew she was mentally filling in the gaps.

'By the way,' I went on. 'I had two letters from those American veterans' magazines.'

'Oh? What did they say?'

'One chap said he was definitely in the photo – middle of the bottom row – and, anyway, it hadn't been taken at Halfpenny Green but at an air base in Norfolk.'

'And the other?'

'He knew exactly which crew it was and if I cared to send a cheque for a hundred dollars, he would be prepared to give me some more information.'

'Oh, dear.'

'But it was worth a try and it might have worked – and thanks for all your help. Monica.'

She looked at me quizzically and I knew she still suspected the truth, but she could also see that I still wasn't going to share it with her. Not yet. 'Well, that's that, then, Juliet. Mission accomplished.'

'Yes,' I said, guilty but determined. Stubborn, Adrian would probably have said. 'Over and out.'

Callum got the part. There were photos and articles in the newspapers about the exciting new young British actor who was heading for Hollywood stardom, and, inevitably, they'd dug deep into his background. Apparently, he was the illegitimate son of a Welsh miner's daughter, born when she was only fifteen. The parents had kicked her out, the boy father had skipped off and she'd brought Callum up entirely single-handed, working in factories and shops, seeing him through school and, later, drama school where he'd been awarded a grant. Not even Flavia had known the details. It was a very brave story and I wished he'd told us about it before. When he came upstairs to say goodbye, I said so.

'I learned early from Mum to keep my mouth shut,' he said. 'It's been a whole lot better that way.'

I kissed his cheek, rather than air, and wished him luck. I could have told him that I was illegitimate myself.

January had turned to February and one evening towards the middle of the month the phone rang. It was Joyce Atkins, the ex-WAAF who had trained at Morecambe with Ma. She'd been up in her attic, having a tidy-up, she said, and had come across a suitcase full of old papers. 'Roy never found it because of his bad back. He couldn't manage the ladder, you see.'

I remembered the clutter-hating husband and his regular fire-risk clear-outs.

She went on, 'I've had a knee operation and I've been out of action for months, or I might have gone up there a lot sooner. I do hope it wasn't important.'

Apparently, when she'd gone through the suitcase she'd found a letter that my mother had written to her during the war.

'You said you wanted to find out the name of

her station in Suffolk. Well, she put it at the top. It was Halfpenny Green. I knew it was a nice sort of name.'

I thanked her very much.

Then she said, 'I read the letter again, of course. Made me quite nostalgic after all these years . . . they were wonderful times, you know. Everybody pulling together in a common cause, doing their bit without complaining. None of the selfish greed and grab and whining you get nowadays. I was lucky to have been part of it. I expect your mother felt the same.'

'Yes, I'm sure she did.'

'By the way, she mentioned that American you were asking about – the one she fell for. The B-17 pilot.'

'Oh?' I was all ears. 'What did she say about him?'

'Just that they were going to get married as soon as he'd finished his ops. It was all planned. He was a chap called Howard Hamilton – from a place called Pasadena in California. Nice name that, too. Then, of course, he went and got killed. Jolly sad. Would you like me to send you the letter?'

I took out the old record, put it on the gramophone turntable and pressed the start button. Frank Sinatra sang for me, exactly as he had sung for my parents all those years ago, and I listened to him as they had done. And it made me weep. Life is full of all sorts of weird and wonderful happenings, and coincidences, and surprises, and ironies. And of some things that, perhaps, were just meant to be.

Later the same evening, the phone rang again. It was dark outside and raining hard.

'Julie? It's Rob here. How are you doing?'

'Fine, thanks. How are you?' I was very casual. Non-committal. But I was smiling.

'OK.'

'It's a very good line. You sound awfully clear.'

'Could be because I'm in London. I got in this morning.'

'London!'

'That's right. London, England. Not the other one.'

'I didn't know there *was* another one.'

'It's in Ontario.'

'How long are you here for?'

'Several months. A guy I know has lent me his apartment while he's away. In Kensington.'

'Sounds wonderful.'

'Yeah . . . no ocean view though, and lousy sunsets. When can we meet? How about this evening?'

'Isn't it getting a bit late?'

'Hell, it's only one o'clock in the afternoon.'

'That's in California.'

'I haven't gotten around to changing my watch. I'll come by your place in half an hour. OK?'

* * *

I heard a taxi stop outside, the front doorbell ring and Flavia cross the hall to answer it. Then I heard his voice, very American, and Flavia's answering, very English. They were chatting away as I reached the landing – he was joking about the wonderful weather and brushing the wet off his trench coat and the raindrops out of his hair, and she was laughing. I could tell she'd liked him at once.

He saw me standing there – stuck halfway down the stairs, hesitating. We looked at each other for a moment. I noticed that he was wearing a tie.

'Hi there, Julie,' he said.

THE END